13 STEPS FOR CHARLIE BIRGER

A Novel

"If history were taught in the form of stories, it would never be forgotten."
~ Rudyard Kipling

by
Kevin Corley

While this novel is a work of fiction, the author has based the characters, places and incidents on real individuals and actual historic events. Using the historical record, the writer has created a fictional story while trying to remain true to the spirit of the time.

Published by Sixteen Tons Publication, 2019.

ISBN: 978-0-578-56928-4

Front cover art work and book cover design by
Hilary Rea Remm
Back cover illustration courtesy of William Carr
Outlaw Associations: Dancin' and Dates at Shady Rest
https://www.heritech.com/soil/birger/birger.htm
Interior book design by D. Bass

Contact Kevin Corley at charliebirger@yahoo.com

DEDICATION

For
Mark and Lesley
Ronald and Jennifer   Natalie and Emily
& Scarlett

Also, to:
Taylor and Liz Pensoneau

Also special thanks to the following historians without whose research this book would not have been possible:

Angle, Paul M., *Bloody Williamson: A Chapter in American Lawlessness*, Prairie State Books, 1959.

Pensoneau, Taylor. *Brothers Notorious,* Downstate Publications, 1998.

Pensoneau, Taylor. *Dapper and Deadly: The True Story of Black Charlie Harris,* Downstate Publications, 2010.

DeNeal, Gary. *A Knight of Another Sort: Prohibition Days and Charlie Birger* Southern Illinois University Press, 1998.

Johnson, Ralph and Musgrave, Jon. Secrets of the Herrin Gangs, IllinoisHistory.com

Author Unknown. *Life and Exploits of S. Glenn Young: World Famous Law Enforcement Officer*, Forgotten Books, 2008.

Shelton, Ruthie. *Inside the Shelton Gang: One Daughter's Discovery,* Illinois History.com, 2014.

13 STEPS FOR CHARLIE BIRGER

A Novel

Kevin Corley

MAJOR CHARACTERS

BIRGER GANG

Charlie Birger – Legendary leader
Art Newman – Member of both gangs
Connie Ritter
Pat “Max” Pulliam
Steve George
Elmo Thomasson
Harry Thomasson
Rado Millich
Ward “Casey” Jones
Freddie Wooten
“Hogshead” Davis
Noble Weaver
Orb Treadway
Ural Gowen
Bert Owens
Leslie Simpson
Riley “Alabam” Simmons
Ernest Blue
John Renfro

SHELTON GANG

Carl Shelton – Legendary leader
Earl Shelton – Friendly and amiable brother
Bernie Shelton – Ruthless youngest brother
Ora Thomas – Member of both gangs
Harry Walker – Former Herrin policeman
Ray Walker – Carl’s bodyguard
Lyle “Shag” Worsham – Both gangs.
Jack Skelcher
Charlie Briggs
Monroe “Blackie” Armes

continued

KU KLUX KLAN

Glenn Young - Prohibition enforcer
Caesar Cagle - Williamson County leader
D.C. Stephenson – Grand Dragon
John "Smitty" Smith - Herrin garage owner
Arlie Boswell – Williamson County state's attorney
KKK, then gangs

OTHERS

Joe Adams - Mayor of West City
George Galligan – Williamson County Sheriff
John Small – Saline County Sheriff
Jeff Pritchard – Franklin County Sheriff
Lory Price - State policeman
John Rodgers – *St. Louis Post Dispatch* reporter
Phil Hanna –Humane hangman
Harold Williams - evangelist

MOLLS

Helen Holbrook
Blondie- The Blond Bombshell

WIVES – MARRIED TO

Maude Young – Glenn Young
Betty Birger – Charlie's 2nd
Bernice Davis Birger – Charlie's 3rd
Margaret Shelton – Carl
"Blond Bessie" Newman – Art

CONTENTS

Chapter 1	1	Hog heaven
Chapter 2	5	Birth of a Nation
Chapter 3	21	The Herrin Massacre
Chapter 4	47	Country folks and Klansmen
Chapter 5	61	Charlie Birger
Chapter 6	69	Glenn Young's Klan meets the Shelton's
Chapter 7	85	Charlie's new shirts
Chapter 8	93	Charlie Birger meets Carl Shelton
Chapter 9	103	The KKK raids
Chapter 10	115	Moonshiners
Chapter 11	123	The Rome Club shootout
Chapter 12	137	Danville trials and incarcerations
Chapter 13	151	The Shelton's ambush Glenn Young
Chapter 14	161	The Smith garage shootout
Chapter 15	167	The cigar store gunfight
Chapter 16	181	The tri-state tornado
Chapter 17	187	Robin Hood outlaws
Chapter 18	201	Hallelujah and gangsters
Chapter 19	221	The Shady Rest
Chapter 20	231	The election day shootout
Chapter 21	247	Tensions build
Chapter 22	257	The Shady Rest shootout
Chapter 23	269	The gang war begins
Chapter 24	279	Shelton and Birger top hits
Chapter 25	295	The Shelton Tank
Chapter 26	313	The Shelton Air Force
Chapter 27	323	Joe Adams must die!
Chapter 28	331	Shady Rest destroyed
Chapter 29	341	The trial of the Shelton brothers
Chapter 30	355	The trial of Charlie Birger
Chapter 31	363	The thirteen steps

Chronology of Events 375
About the Author 379
About the Franklin County Historic Jail Museum 380
Other books by the Author 381

1

"Bernie, quit hittin' on Clyde. I want him alert for this."

"Ah, heck, Earl, I'm just softin' him up a bit."

Bernie didn't appreciate being reprimanded, even by a brother ten years his senior. To show his independence, he gave one last punch to the naked man draped like a sheet over the wooden fence. Then, he quickly backed away. Being recently widowed, Earl had a tendency to get a bit testy, and given the opportunity, was likely to sucker punch. Such an assault wouldn't be anything the twenty-one-year old Bernie couldn't handle. It was fear of gaining the wrath of their eldest brother, Carl, that should be avoided. Carl's disposition was always hard to judge. Generally quiet and patient, he still had the capability to go into a violent rage, such as they had seen that very evening when he put a bullet in Clyde's stomach. Getting rid of bodies always seemed to bring out the worst in him. Luckily, he knew an old hog farmer who delighted in and had perfected a fool proof disposal system.

"Hittin' him won't make him no softer anyhow," the good-old-boy farmer cackled. He dragged a large silver milk can out of a fire. "But this'll make him sweeter."

Since the dying man was Carl's personal project, he helped the farmer heft the can and pour the scalding milk over Clyde, whose scream was stifled by the gag in his mouth. Over fifty hogs on the other side of the fence grunted, stuck their snouts in the air, and licked at the milk as some of it splashed like rain on top of them.

Bernie pulled out a wad of bills. "Wanna bet on how long it'll take them hogs to make ol' Clyde disappear?"

"I'd hate to take your money, young fella." The farmer clucked. "'Cause I can tell you how long it'll take almost right down to the minute. I been holding back them sows' feed for several days—ever since Carl told me he had another job for me."

"I'll take that bet." Earl produced a wad of bills that were rolled up like a head of cabbage. "I'll bet five dollars it'll take five hours."

"You're crazy." Bernie laughed. "I'll bet ten it'll take at least until midnight."

The farmer shook his head and chuckled again as he pushed Clyde's body into the hog lot. The seven-hundred-pound sows swarmed the screaming man like a school of piranhas, ripping off chunks of flesh and swallowing them whole. The feeding frenzy continued for nearly an hour, until finally the swine spread out and scrounged around for more food.

"I guess that skinny Baptist wasn't enough for 'em." The farmer chuckled. He accepted a handful of bills from Carl. "Come around next time, when more of the sows are lactatin', and it'll cut ten minutes off the entire operation."

"You sure there'll be nothing left of him?" Bernie asked.

"If you want to come back tomorrow, you can sift through the pig shit." The farmer spat out a wad of tobacco. "You might find a tooth or two."

Shaking their heads, the three brothers walked around the barn to their broken-down farm truck.

The farmer placed a new wad between his cheek and toothless gum. He shaded his eyes as the truck puttered down the road.

"Land sakes, Daddy," an old woman said from inside the screen door of the house. "What were those men doing here?"

"Don't be frettin" yourself, Mother. They was just passin' by and was nice enough to help me slop the hogs."

"Well, what are their names? I'll send them a nice mincemeat pie."

"Why, you know them, Doris. They's Agnes and Ben's boys. You know. The Shelton brothers."

"Oh, well, sure. Such a nice, church-going family. Well, come on in for coffee, Daddy."

2

Saturday night in Herrin, Illinois, started pretty normal. Then a trumpet sounded, and a dozen men dressed in white sheets galloped down Main Street. Their mounts were decked out in lily-white saddle blankets that hung down almost to their hooves. Red insignias decorated each side. While the men sported cone-shaped hats, the horses seemed oblivious to the unicorn-like horn emerging between their wideset eyes.

The long line of citizenry in front of the Opera House turned and cheered. The lights on the marquee flashed, causing some folks to look up at the announcement of the evening picture show.

D.W. Griffith
Presents
The Birth of a Nation

Horns blasted from a few of the automobiles parked nearby, encouraging two of the more skittish horses to rear back on their hind legs. When the crowd cheered again, some of the other riders tried to rein their own mounts into the dramatic stance. Most of them being field nags, the animals either didn't understand or were too tired from the day's work to oblige.

One of the horsemen produced a revolver and fired a single shot into the air.

"The Ku Klux Klan to the rescue!" the riders all shouted at once.

With the crowd cheering, they spurred their startled horses into a gallop and headed back out of town.

The dramatic exit lost some of its effect when a young boy on the boardwalk spooked one of the horses by enthusiastically waving an American flag in its face. The nag darted under a lamp post, nearly decapitating its rider and sending him toppling backwards onto the road. This brought more laughter than concern from the men watching. The women reacted with motherly instinct by stepping forward. They quickly stopped when the de-horsed rider sat up and pulled his pointy white hood off, revealing he was uninjured.

"Why, it's only Joe Chesnas," Bernie Shelton shouted, "the village idiot."

"My hood got turned around and I couldn't see that pole," the boy whined.

The Opera House doors opened and the crowd noisily filtered inside. Earl followed Bernie toward the front row near the big organ. The instrument had been placed facing the white wall that the movie would be projected onto.

A moment later, Ora Thomas arrived. He slid into a rickety wooden chair next to Earl. The two were the same age, but Ora was small and frail compared to the big, strapping Shelton brothers. Bernie called him a sissy behind his back, but never to his face. The man was feminine looking, but turned into a fearless, holy terror when riled—that was, if his smarts couldn't set matters straight. He used the latter trait when Bernie started hissing insults at the old school marm who began playing the organ.

"Bernie, you give ol' Miss Gobel a heart attack, and they might cancel the picture show," Ora whispered to tease the younger Shelton into leaving her alone. When not aggravated, he had a sense of righteousness.

"Ah, I hate that old bat." Bernie scowled. "She gave me more beatin's when I was in school than Pappy ever did." He tossed a spit wad at Miss Gobel's head.

Carl reached forward from the row behind and smacked him in the head. Bernie hadn't seen his older brother arrive with his wife, Margaret.

"Confound it!" Bernie muttered, then sat back and looked toward the white wall as if the film had already begun.

Carl was in a foul enough mood even before entering the theater. He hated wasting an evening when there was money to be made. He was there because Margaret had thrown a hissy fit during supper because he had been too occupied with cleaning his guns to eat. It wasn't that he didn't come to the dinner table, but that he brought his pearl-handled, frontier-type revolvers with him—even pushed aside a plate of vegetables so he'd have room to continue the maintenance. Carl finally figured out his wife was angry when she tossed a baked potato at him rather than serving it leisurely. That was when he suggested the picture show. Three hours of a wasted evening would be better than allowing Margaret to silently carry the grudge for days, maybe weeks or even months.

He was hoping that sitting in the row behind his brothers might offer a chance to sneak out with them a time or two and have a smoke. Sleeping would, of course, be out of the question. Carl slept with his mouth open and snored loudly. He had left many a picture show with bruised ribs from his wife's elbowing him awake.

Just when Carl thought the evening couldn't get any worse, a man strutted into the theater. Both Carl and Ora reached inside their jackets to make sure their weapons were untethered.

Glenn Young was accompanied by his pretty young wife and her father, George Simcox, a U.S. Marshal.

Ora started to stand until Carl reached forward and touched his shoulder. The thin, little man's eyes were drawn tight and narrow as he looked at the senior Shelton. Carl just shook his head and motioned him to sit back down, which he did. Ora had good reasons to hate Young, the most powerful being that the lawman had recently shot and killed a friend named Luke Vukovic, a bootlegger in rural Madison County.

Young liked to brag that he had more worldly experience than anyone else in the southern Illinois region known as Little Egypt. Besides having been a Texas Ranger, the former lawman had been hired by the government during the Great War to track down deserters. Now he and his father-in-law were working for the Treasury Department's new Prohibition Unit, chasing down anyone in violation of the Volstead Act—a profession that had brought him in conflict with Ora's friend.

Ora made it well known that he believed the obnoxious Glenn to be nothing but a pompous loudmouth. Carl believed it only a matter of time before the two would have at it.

The lights dimmed. The picture show began with Miss Gobel providing the organ music. The owner of the Opera House stood in the back of the room. In his booming baritone voice, he read the narrations that appeared on screen, and also provided the voices to all the male parts. His wife sat beside him, ready to stand and read the words of the females when they appeared.

Despite the threat of having his ears boxed by his older brother, Bernie couldn't sit quietly. He ducked down low in his seat and provided his own sound effects by meowing for kittens and neighing for horses as they appeared on the screen. Since his efforts drew laughter from the audience, he was encouraged to continue.

The film depicted the South prior to the Civil War as a paradise of elegant sophistication on the part of the White gentry. Even the Negro slaves appreciated the dominant White race—they smiled as they worked in the cotton fields at the pleasure of their benevolent masters. The darkies knew their place, and during their free time, loved entertaining the Whites with their lively music and dance.

"Them actors playin' niggers look like White folks wearing blackface," Bernie whispered to Earl.

"Shut up and watch the picture show," Carl ordered from the row behind. He was busy watching Ora, who hadn't taken his eyes off Glenn Young.

When the heroic Confederate soldiers departed the town to go fight for their state's rights to have slavery, Bernie settled down and paid more attention to the film. Even Carl watched as entire communities—along with Negro slaves—came out to cheer the Rebel soldiers going off to war.

"The Confederates to the rescue!" the Opera House owner enthusiastically bellowed the words that appeared on the screen.

Glenn Young was the first to stand and clap. Never had anyone in the audience seen such realistic action. The film switched constantly from one scene to another, showing simultaneous actions occurring at different places. Miss Gobel's rendition of the battle scenes were authenticated by her striking the ivory with added enthusiasm to represent the booming of the cannons during battle scenes.

Finally, after nearly an hour of drama, the Confederacy succumbed to the overwhelming numbers and resources of the Northern Army. A realistic rendition of Lee surrendering to Grant at Appomattox Courthouse was followed by the reconstruction of the south. White carpetbaggers descended on the defeated southern states, intent on making a profit from the chaos after the war.

Bernie elbowed his brother and pointed to Glenn Young in the row behind them. Glenn scowled and his lips quivered as he watched a scene that depicted evil mulattos convincing southern Negroes to quit bowing down to White men. The words of the President of the United States appeared on the screen.

> **q** *History of the American People*:
> "...the policy of the congressional leaders wrought...a veritable overthrow of civilization in the South...in their determination to 'put the white South

> under the heel of the black South.' In the villages the negroes were the office holders, men who knew none of the uses of authority, except in insolences."
> Woodrow Wilson

"President Wilson loved this picture show," Glenn said loud enough for all those near to hear. "He watched it in the White House and called it, 'history written with lightning.' Now watch how savage these jiggaboos act in the State House."

"How many times you seen this film?" Simcox asked.

"This makes four."

> **q** Election day.
> **q** All blacks are given the ballot, while the leading whites are disenfranchised.

The audience gasped as they watched Blacks lining up to vote, and many voices in the theater shouted "No!" as one Negro snuck an extra vote into the ballot box. Then when White men arrived to vote, they were turned away by colored soldiers.

> **q** The riot in the Master's Hall.
> **q** The negro party in control in the State House of Representatives, 101 blacks against 23 whites, session of 1871.

The South Carolina State Assembly was shown with Negro legislatures drinking alcohol, eating turkey legs, and putting bare feet on their desks.

> **q** The speaker rules that all members must wear shoes.

A Black representative reluctantly dons his old, dirty boots.

> **q** It is moved and carried that all whites must salute negro officers on the streets.

Glenn Young jumped to his feet and screamed, “NO! NEVER!”

> **q** Passage of a bill, providing for the intermarriage of blacks and whites.

Now nearly every man and woman in the theater joined Glenn by standing and shouting, “NO! NEVER!” Ora and the Sheltons remained seated, not because they weren’t appalled by the idea of a White and Black marrying, but because they didn’t want to go along with Young’s antics.

The audience finally returned to their chairs as the film moved to a calm country setting near a river. A saddened White Southern gentleman watched a White boy and girl playing nearby. When several Negro children arrive, the White children scare them away by putting a white sheet over their heads.

The White man rose, his eyes showing brightly as he snaps his fingers.

> **q** The inspiration.
> **q** The Ku Klux Klan. The organization that saved the South from the anarchy of black rule, but not without the shedding of more blood than at Gettysburg.
> **q** "The white men were roused by a mere instinct of self-preservation... until at last there had sprung Into existence a great Ku Klux Klan,
> A veritable empire of the South, to protect the Southern country."
> Woodrow Wilson

White sheets and hoods adorned hundreds of men as well as their horses as they galloped dramatically across the screen; the Silent Empire led by a Grand Titan.

"The Ku Klux Klan to the rescue!" Glenn shouted. The audience cheered.

Ora gave a disgusted cough and tossed a licorice stick over the tops of Earl and Bernie's head. The candy struck Glenn in the face. Never taking his eyes off the screen, Glenn swatted his cheek as if at a fly. He was mesmerized watching hundreds of Ku Klux Klan on galloping horses arriving in town in time to rescue the White citizens from the carpet-baggers and their evil Negro followers. The movie projector was nearly as loud as Betty Gobel's organ playing; her fingers dancing a merry jig across the ivory playing Wagner's *Ride of the Valkyries* above the roar of the audience. Then, she leapt into a lively rendition of *Dixie* as the Klan marched triumphantly through the town to the cheers of the White community they had saved.

The final scenes of the three-hour film showed Satan in Hell striking hundreds of evil Negroes with a sword. Jesus was seen in Heaven watching over peaceful White men and women dancing merrily through eternity.

Ora and the Sheltons remained in their seats while others in the audience noisily left the auditorium.

"That picture show was something, weren't it?" Earl said. "Them Klansmen sure put them niggers in their place."

"We ain't got no problems with niggers in this town," Carl said and shrugged.

"Why do you torture that organ so, Miss Betty?" Bernie asked the schoolmarm when they finally stood to leave.

Miss Gobel's lips puckered and quivered.

“I’ll bet there’s a hundred dogs howlin’ all across town,” Bernie chided.

“That attitude, Bernard Shelton is the reason you never graduated from the fifth grade,” Miss Gobel responded. Tucking her sheet music tight under her armpit, she stiffened her narrow shoulders, and with short, quick steps, departed the room.

Once outside the theater, the Shelton brothers and Margaret hung around on the street corner and had a smoke with Ora—who inconspicuously produced a flask that Bernie quickly intercepted. The boardwalk was filled with men and women doing the same, but it was the Young party that Ora kept his eyes on as he tried to listen to their conversation.

“The Klan’s havin’ a rally Saturday night,” Young said after a long exhale of smoke. “You goin’, George?”

“You sure is a racist, Glenn.” Simcox laughed. “You don’t like colored folk at all, do ya?”

“I ain’t never really knowed a nigger,” Glenn said. “Not personally, anyway. It’s them damned Catholics I hate. They’s the ones that corrupts our country with their liquor and gamblin’. You saw in that movie how the Ku Klux Klan is keepin’ law and order. Why, without the Klan, them darkies would have ruined this whole country.”

“Aren’t we makin’ enough on our legitimate raids to keep my daughter in furs?” George asked.

His daughter, Maude, had gone down the walk to talk to some other ladies.

"Maybe, but why not give her diamonds too?" Glenn asked after a long hesitation. "I'll go to that Klan rally anyway and see what they got to offer. In the meantime, the Herrin Coal Mine is hiring security guards. I believe I'll try my hand at that."

"So," George scoffed, "you'd rather protect a bunch of damned scabies?"

"Just 'cause they ain't United Mine Workers don't make them strikebreakers, George." Glenn shook his head slowly. "Herrin's a strip mine, not an underground mine. They's Steam Shovel Union boys I'd be protectin'."

"The UMW is the only coal miner's union," George grumbled, then added a spit. "Period."

"Unions are anti-American," Glenn argued. "They's just them socialists' excuse to destroy our Constitution and replace it with the type of corrupt foreign governments they came from."

The two turned and walked to where Maude stood with her friends.

"I'll kill that son-of-a-bitch one day," Ora hissed when they were out of earshot.

"I'd 'spect Young'll get his licks in if you try," Bernie said. He had been hitting the flask pretty hard and was swaying a little.

"We got a job to do this weekend, Bernie," Carl reprimanded. "You need to slow down."

"Yeah," Bernie smirked, his eyes half-closed. "We're relievin' a herd of dairy cows from a blind, old farmer—"

Carl quieted his brother with the back of his elbow.

"There's money to be made on the fairer side of the law too." Ora frowned. He worked as an occasional sheriff's deputy, where taking bribes was plenty lucrative.

Bernie smirked when Ora took another pull on the whiskey. Carl waved off the drink when their friend passed it his way.

"Carl's a *tea-toddler*, Ora," Earl said. "He don't indulge."

"Well, that's good," Ora said. "Then he don't mind prohibition."

"Ever time the government tries to legislate morality," Bernie said, sticking out his chest, "it opens the doors for gangsters. I aim to be one of them that gets rich off such nonsense."

"There ain't a little town around here that ain't gonna miss its whiskey." Carl nodded, despite his refusal to drink. "These farmers may vote dry on election day, but they drink wet on Saturday night."

"We figure we can run enough rum here from the Bahamas to flood all of Little Egypt," Earl added. "And if the day *comes* along we can't, we'll hijack a load from the boys across the river in St. Louis. You want in on it, Ora?"

"I'm in," Ora replied eagerly. "My friend Charlie Harris knows some thugs in Detroit might be interested in running some booze down from Canada."

Bernie looked up into the night sky and staggered around in a little circle. Carl and Earl got on either side of their little brother, took him by the arms and half-dragged him toward their farm truck.

3

Glenn Young's biggest fault was his impulsiveness. He remembered with regret the several times he had pulled a trigger without regard for the consequences. In most cases, he was able to explain his actions. Like the time he killed an Indian down in Texas after the redskin fired a shotgun blast into the air. Glenn knew the man's shot had only been meant as a warning, but he unloaded on him anyway. To make matters worse, it was found that the redskin's weapon had been loaded with buckshot—hardly lethal from the distance between them. Glenn's own shotgun, though, had a shell in its chamber. He discharged it without thought or reservation. The Indian had bled to death before they could get him the eighty miles to a doctor. The Ranger committee investigating the incident decided it was the distance from civilization that had killed the man. The necessity of their Ranger returning fire seemed inconsequential.

Now Glenn found himself adjusting the sights on his Enfield carbine while weighing the necessity of returning fire against the six hundred or so United Mine Worker picketers surrounding the Herrin Coal Mine. It was the second day of the siege. Every time one of the miners Glenn's men were guarding tried to cross the mine yard a gunshot would send them scurrying back behind cover. Since keeping the strip mine from working only required a few marksmen the rest of the United Mine Workers were reveling as if on a church picnic just beyond rifle range.

Being a highly accomplished marksman, the distance was not too great for Glenn Young. Any of the picketers would be easy targets for him. Most of his fellow security guards protecting the mine yard were from Chicago, where long distance gunfire wasn't necessary. That gave them a disadvantage against the UMW picketers, who had developed sharpshooting skills as hunters. The strikers had kept the fifty steam shovelers from doing any mining all morning, and with work not getting done, it was possible the coal company would decide to not pay Young and the other security guards. Besides making certain he got his wages, Glenn wanted to show off a little for the Chicago boys. He didn't much appreciate how they considered themselves so much better than the down-state folks they called hillbillies.

"What youse waitin' for, Young?" the gangster known as Little Archie said from just behind Glenn's shoulder.

"I'm waitin for you to quit blowin' your stinkin' breath down my neck," Glenn grumbled. He had Ora Thomas in his rifle sights at that moment and didn't want to take his eye away from his target. Two hundred yards away, Ora was laughing and wrestling with another picketer while several men and women enjoyed the morning distraction. The union leader, Otis Clark, hustled through the crowd, placing bets on the outcome of the wrestling match. It would be a tough shot to hit Ora, since he was moving so much, but no other target would be quite as delicious.

Thomas had been the man who had tried so hard to get Glenn convicted for the killing of the bootlegger, Luke Vukovic. When he had been acquitted of the shooting, Ora confronted Glenn in the courthouse hallway immediately after the trial. There was a small crowd around them at the time, and the lawman wanted to appear reasonable.

"Of course, I regret very much having been forced to shoot Vukovic, but I was only performing my duty," Glenn said, repeating the story he had given the jury. "He tried to shoot me first, but his gun hit on an empty chamber. It was later proven that the next chamber was loaded. Had I waited a second longer, I would have been killed."

"You'll be killed all right!" Ora had shouted. "Luke had six holes in his front and two of 'em was in his head. I promise you'll be gettin' the same."

There were times when he'd been a bachelor that Glenn wouldn't have a second thought about a curse from a man like Ora Thomas. But now he had to think about his wife and children.

Eliminating the enemy on this day in Herrin was made more difficult by the low morning sun behind the target, as well as a slight cross breeze. Luckily, there were plenty of men standing behind the wrestling match, so even if Glenn missed Ora, someone was likely to get blasted.

Glenn liked the prone position for firing. As he waited for Ora to hold still, he checked to make certain his body was straight behind the firearm, his strong-side leg slightly bent. His elbows were grounded firmly with his supporting elbow right beneath the rifle, his head level with the ground. One more time he pulled the butt of the rifle snug into his shoulder.

Finally, Ora intentionally—or unintentionally—kneed the other wrestler in the head. Since kicking might be conceived as a questionable tactic, Ora stepped away and waited for his opponent to recover. That was the split second when Glenn eased the trigger back. It was also the moment the other wrestler chose to surprise Ora by charging him with a head butt to the chest. The thirty-aught-six-caliber bullet that exploded into the wrestler's head had been designed to bring down virtually any big game in North America.

The damage it did to the human's head—as well as the chest of the unfortunate man standing directly behind him—was enormous. Both picketers were killed instantly by the same bullet.

Glenn's triumph was short lived. The dozen Chicago security guards barely had time to cheer and slap the successful marksman on the back before the mine yard was riddled with hundreds of bullets—at least one of which found just the right angle to ricochet off the iron on a steam shovel and drop one of the strikebreaking coal miners.

The revengeful onslaught from picketers lasted the rest of the day. That evening, Little Archie crawled over to where Glenn and his friend Caesar Cagle were hunkered down between the protection of two coal cars.

"I ain't stayin' here to get kilt by no union man," Little Archie said.

"How we gonna get out?" Caesar asked. "The hills all around us is filled with picketers."

"The rest of the Chicago guards don't want to be here neither," Little Archie said.

"I don't give a damn about those thugs," Caesar said. "Let 'em stay."

"We might need 'em if the Mine Workers don't let us pass." Glenn rubbed his chin. "I know Otis Clark and Ora Thomas. They's just on the other side of that southern mound. Tell the Chicago boys to follow me and stay low until I can get to the top of that bluff. If Clark don't let me pass, have the boys come runnin', or that Ora Thomas will skin me alive. He hates my guts."

A quarter of an hour later, Glenn and Caesar crept up on two sitting men with their backs away from a large stack of burning logs. Several other picketers milled around close by.

"Don't look at the fire," Glenn whispered to Caesar. "Your eyes will lose their night vision."

They stopped and squatted behind a bush. Glenn could just make out the drift of their conversation.

"Well, I'd never go against a workin' man to support no rich coal company owner like Glenn Young has done." Ora tossed the rest of his coffee into the fire.

Glenn signaled Caesar to stay put, then set his rifle and pistols down and soundlessly slipped a little closer to the two men. When one of them leaned toward the fire to throw another log on, Glenn walked right up beside them and held his hands out toward the warmth of the fire. Without even looking at him, the two men continued their conversation.

"You really hate that man, don't ya?" Otis asked with a chuckle.

"I'd 'spect if that lily-livered scum ever tries me, I'll kill him."

"I don't rush to a fight," Glenn said, "but you will find me to be a mighty reluctant victim."

Otis and Ora were caught so off-guard when they realized Glenn stood beside them, neither of them showed surprise.

"It would appear somebodies been turnin' over rocks." Ora slowly pulled his revolver from his shoulder holster and halfway aimed it at Glenn.

"I won't be turnin' my back on any dark alleys long as you're alive, Thomas."

"When you meet your demise, you and me will be standin' face to face," Ora replied. "Like we are right now."

"I'm unarmed, Thomas." Glenn held open his coat.

"Yes, but I recall you carry a spare in your boot."

"You'll be gettin' your comeuppance one of these days," Glenn smirked, "but tonight I came here to negotiate."

"I don't see that you got nothing to negotiate with, Mr. Young," Otis said.

"I'll admit this whole business is perplexing." Glenn nodded. "But you may not want to act rash. There are twelve guns on the two of you right at this second. Now, you want to talk?"

"Don't believe him, Otis," Ora said. "He can sure enough lie like a Texacan."

Otis's eyes narrowed as he peered into the woods. "You out there, Caesar?"

"I'm right here, Otis."

"Fancy that," Otis said. "Snakes don't get far away from one another, do they? Put the gun down, Ora. This ain't no time for reckless hate."

"All right, mister." Ora holstered his pistol. "Say your peace."

"Me and the boys want safe passage to the train station."

"You don't like the odds, Glenn?" Otis smiled. "Hired gunfighters against coal miners? I heard it was you who kilt them two boys with one bullet today."

"Unfortunate shot." Glenn looked at Ora. "As for why we want to leave—truth be told, you oughtn't never take an axe to the branch you're sittin' on."

"How we know you won't return with a whole army of Chicago thugs?" Otis asked.

"I swears it on the grave of my sainted mother."

"Your mother was a whore and you know it," Ora said.

"Yes." Glenn grimaced but refused to take the bait. "But she died a Christian."

***

The following morning, Ora sat in front of the campfire with Otis and tried to recall the last time he'd slept. Several men wrapped in thin blankets lay about the camp, though there was no snoring.

"I believe I might have slept a little two nights ago," Ora recalled.

"No, no." Otis shook his head. "That was the night we got the letter from John L. Lewis telling us to give the scabies what fer. Remember? That was also the night we tore up all the stores in town and confiscated weapons."

Sleep would have been easier had it not been for the inebriated picketers who liked to fire off a few shots into the mine yard every time they rose to relieve their bladders or fetch another bottle. Ora's head was spinning from lack of sleep and excessive coffee. Alcohol usually started soon after the morning coffee, then the two fluids took turns as the alternating beverage of choice for the rest of the day. He didn't feel he had the right to complain, though, since most of those gathered around the dozens of picket fires had suffered the same ailments. Food was plentiful, but it didn't sit right on stomachs filled with excessive drink.

"I 'spect things will come to a head in the next few hours." Otis scratched his belly. "Soon as them scabies wake up and find their security guards missing, they'll give up and come running."

"Then what?" Ora had been asking himself that question ever since he'd watched Glenn Young and his security thugs board the northbound train just a few hours before. Being how much he hated Young, it had been a hard compromise for Ora to tolerate their getting away unharmed.

A Negro named Jim Brown slowly raised up from his blanket, tossed it around his shoulders, and joined the two men sitting by the fire. Brown wore overhauls and a partially broken helmet that had received some hard use in the recent war in Europe. He shivered as he pulled a tin cup from his pocket, filled it with coffee from the pot on the fire, and looked up at Ora.

"Then we kill 'em, Mr. Ora," Jim said. He sipped the coffee as other men also slowly rose from their bedrolls and trudged closer to the fire. Jim was a policeman from the nearby town of Dewaine, a colored community near Carterville. He had achieved the respect of the other union members despite his complexion. He knew his place among the Whites, but when he spoke as a member of the United Mine Workers, the anger inside him filled his voice with a sense of righteousness that the White union men couldn't ignore. Jim threw another log on and gave it a stir as the men leaned forward to listen.

"You men may not know this, but my people were brought from Tennessee to Carterville in 1898 to work the mines. They weren't told until they got there that they was to be strikebreakers. My daddy were one of 'em, and he didn't like it one bit. That first night there, he snuck out of the mine yard and went to visit the members of the UMW. At first some of the White union men beat him a might, but their leaders came forward and stopped them. To make the story short, them Tennessee coloreds joined the United Mine Workers of America. In fact, a year later, them same colored union boys stopped a trainload of niggers being brought in from a town up north called Pana. My daddy got kilt that next night in a battle that lasted for two days. It were union coloreds against scab coloreds mostly, but soon after that, the coal company agreed to hire only union miners."

Jim sat quietly for a few minutes as those around him reflected on his story.

"I don't know why it is," Jim continued, his voice growing stronger in conviction with each word, "but sometimes the only way to give folks more freedom and rights is to kill those who stand in their way. Now these scabs at Herrin know they are standing in the way of men who only want fair pay and better working conditions, yet, there they be, taking the food right out of our family's mouths."

The eyes of the men became as inflamed as the fire at which they sat. Teeth gnashed as jaw-lines grew firm. As the sunrise peeked above the tree lines, the men went to retrieve their rifles. Despite the wet dew, some took prone positions. Others sat or kneeled. On the hills around the mine yard appeared the barrels of over one thousand rifles. Another hundred or so men and even women raised their heads to watch, some of whom grabbed young boys and pulled them back behind whatever protection there was.

Not a human was in sight in the mine yard, yet a single gunshot was followed immediately by thousands. Flashes and smoke from the weapons came from every direction. Hundreds of holes shredded the office building walls. The windows were whittled away until they resembled jagged, open doorways.

A few minutes later, someone inside the compound ran a white cook's apron up the flagpole.

Ora felt a great relief. As much as he hated the hardened men who had come down from Chicago to be scabs, he was glad that no more blood would be shed. The vision of Joe Pitkewicius' head exploding just inches from him the day before was still fresh in his mind. A simple wrestling match had turned into tragedy for two men as well as their families, and though his rage centered mostly on Glenn Young, who he now knew fired the shot, he couldn't forgive those scabs who stubbornly remained.

"God damn them," a voice behind them shouted. "They oughta have known better than to come down here. But now that they're here, let them take what's comin' to 'em."

Ora looked over his shoulder to see the UMW official Hugh Willis getting into a car and driving away. His heart seemed to miss a beat. *What was Willis saying?*

"You heard him, men," Otis shouted as he raised his gun. "Let's give 'em what fer."

A strong voice echoed from within the mine yard. "My name's McDowell. I'm the mine superintendent. I want to talk to your leader."

"What do you want?" Otis shouted back.

"The men inside will surrender if they can come out and not be harmed."

"Come on out, and we'll get you out of the county!" Otis said, then added quietly under his breath. "And straight to hell."

In the compound, men slowly emerged from under heavy equipment and from behind buildings. They threw their guns to the ground, then, with hands high in the air, waited. A few of them looked terrified, but most had an arrogant, defiant smirk that brought the blood back to Ora's face. *They know nothing's going to happen to them now while there are over a thousand witnesses,* Ora thought.

"Round 'em up, boys!" Otis shouted.

The strikers slowly and cautiously approached the mine gate before going through. Rumors were the coal company had machine guns, and no one wanted to be the first to find out. Once the picketers had surrounded the fifty strikebreakers and were searching them for weapons, dozens of women and children whooped loudly and ran down from the hills to join their men in screaming curse words at the scabs.

Ora wanted to scream too, but his hatred was still directed toward Glenn Young. To release some of that rage, he shoved to the ground a smirking strikebreaker who carried a piece of luggage.

"You won't need that where you're going," Ora shouted at the fallen scab.

The smug smiles that were on some of the strikebreakers faces quickly disappeared. "But we surrendered!" One of them screamed in a high, almost girlish voice.

Jim Brown, the Negro police officer who had spoken in an angry yet eloquent manner just moments before transformed into a hysterical, out-of-control instigator. "We got the scabs! We got the scabs!" he shouted. He skipped forward and spit in the face of one.

"See these white sons 'a bitches?" Otis asked as he placed a hand on Brown's shoulder. "We don't think as much of them as we do you, colored boy."

Those words inspired Brown to raise the butt of his rifle and strike the scab in the head. As if that were the signal, the fifty strikebreakers were pounced upon by the frenzied mob members who could get close enough to hit or kick. Only when the men on the ground had tucked their heads and curled their arms and legs into protective tight balls did the crowd back off.

A few striking miners mumbled discontent about the brutal treatment. Some even threw their guns over their shoulders and started back toward town. Ora considered being one of them, but then someone shouted a suggestion that sounded reasonable.

"Let's march 'em to Herrin!"

Strikers pulled the bruised and bleeding scabs to their feet and made them stand two abreast in a line. Many women and young children squeezed through the crowd of males and spat on and kicked the scabs.

The union men encouraged them by laughing. Some handed children switches to swat with.

They slowly moved along the railroad track toward town. The huge procession grew even larger as word spread throughout the community that the scabs had surrendered and were being brought in. After about a mile, someone shouted to Otis, "What do we do with 'em now?"

"The only way to free the county of strikebreakers," Otis shouted, "is to kill 'em off and stop the breed."

A few union men lowered their guns and moved back and forth from one foot to another. Many more, though, cocked their pieces and stepped closer.

"Listen, Otis," Ora said quietly, "don't rush things. Don't go too fast. We have them out of the mine now. Let it go at that."

"Hell, you don't know nothin'," Otis said gruffly. "I've lost sleep four or five nights because of these scab sons-of-bitches, and I'm gonna see them taken care of." He pulled one of the strikebreakers out of line. "Here's ol' peg-legged McDowell. How many of you remember what this bastard said when the strike started?"

"I do," Jim said. "He said he was going to work this mine with miner's blood if he had to—union or no union."

"That's right!" Otis grabbed the mine superintendent by the neck. "And he said for all us union men to stay away if we didn't want trouble."

Men, women, and children shouted obscenities.

Jim gave McDowell's wooden leg a brutal kick, and the mine superintendent rolled to the ground. "We oughta hang that peg-legged son-of-a-bitch!" the Negro shouted.

"I can't walk no more!" McDowell cried. He reached for his wooden leg, which had fallen off from the violent kick. One of the young boys ran forward, picked up the souvenir, and raced back to his mother.

"You bastard!" Otis shouted at McDowell. "I'm gonna kill you and use you to teach these dirty scabs a lesson."

The crowd screamed approval.

"Let me do it!" A miner named Oscar Howard yelled.

Otis grabbed McDowell's arms and Oscar took hold of the stump of his amputated leg. They pulled him off into the woods, McDowell screaming and grabbing at grass all the while.

The crowd stood for a moment, unsure as to who to follow since Otis had abandoned them. Finally, some shuffled again along the tracks with the other captives.

The sound of several shots from the woods behind them echoed through the trees.

"There goes your god-damned superintendent!" a heavyset miner named Peter Hiller shouted. "That's what we're gonna do to you fellows, too. We'll take four scabs down the road, kill 'em, and come back. Get four more and kill them, too."

An automobile raced along the dirt road that ran parallel to the railroad tracks. It slid to a dusty stop. Three men jumped out and climbed through the ditch toward the crowd.

"Hugh Willis is back!" Hiller shouted. "Let him through! He's the union president!"

"Listen," Willis said, slightly out of breath, "don't go killin' these fellows on a public highway! There're too many women and children around to do that. Take them over in Harrison's woods and give it to 'em. Kill all you can." Without another word, the three men turned, walked back to their car, and were quickly on their way.

"Here's where you scabies run the gauntlet," Hiller shouted. "Now, damn you, let's see how fast you can run between here and Chicago, you damned gutter-bums!" He pulled his rifle up and shot the nearest strikebreaker straight through the mouth.

The captives turned and ran into the woods as dozens of bullets mowed down the ones closest. Hiller led hundreds of miners chasing after the men, firing at the slowest and those who stumbled.

The man Hiller had shot rolled over on his back and moaned just as Otis and Oscar returned from their execution of McDowell. Ora and several others stood over the dying man, their eyes glazed and mouths open.

"The son-of-a-bitch is still breathin'," Otis said to those few left behind. "Anybody got a shell?"

Jim Brown handed Otis shells, which he quickly loaded. Both the Black man and the White man aimed pistols at the strikebreaker, who raised a hand as if it would block the lead pellets of death. Instead, he lost two fingers—along with the top of his forehead. Without further comment, Otis and Jim moved quickly into the woods, leaving Ora and the other stunned men to stand and look down at the dead strikebreaker.

The pops of sporadic gunfire continued to echo through Harrison's woods. Ora's small group finally moved along the railroad tracks. A hundred yards later, they found a giant of a man leaning against a fence with blood from a bullet hole in his stomach. Three of those who'd previously been in shock took turns beating him.

Peter Hiller reemerged from the woods with his small band. When he saw the wounded and beaten strikebreaker, he drew his gun and aimed it at his face. "You big son-of-a-bitch, we gonna kill you!" Hiller shot him through the forehead. The strikebreaker crumpled to the ground. "By God! Some of 'em are still breathin'!" He spotted another of the wounded a short distance away who crawled on the ground. They unloaded a half dozen shots into his back. "They're hell to kill, ain't they?"

Someone screamed for help. Hiller and his crew rushed back into the wooded area.

"This is crazy!" one of those with Ora said. The union man, a few moments before, had been one of those beating the scab. But now, he dropped his pistol and walked back toward the mine yard. Others followed.

When the remainder of Ora's group strode into the wooded area, a miner named Phillip Fontanetta stood over a wounded strikebreaker. Fontanetta, wearing an army uniform, calmly put his revolver in the man's mouth and blew his jaw away.

"That was the assistant mine superintendent," Fontanetta explained calmly. "The one who fired the machine gun at us from the mine yard." He holstered his weapon and rushed deeper into the woods in search of more game. Those with Ora seemed more alert now and followed.

Moving on alone, Ora came across another man lying nearby. A group of men removed his shoes and then tied a rope around his neck. Despite the man's wounds, they urged him to crawl towards Herrin.

Ora followed along behind the slow-moving group until they came to the town cemetery. Here were gathered hundreds of men, women and even small children who had captured five bloody strikebreakers, whom had been tied together by a single rope around their necks.

The women and children beat the scabs who lay on the ground at the top of a steep ditch. The man Ora's group had brought was quickly tied to the other prisoners.

"God damn you!" Hiller shouted at the prisoners. "If you've never prayed before, you'd better be doin' it now. Nearer my God to thee!"

A miner named Carnaghi pulled his automatic revolver and shot the biggest of the prisoners in the stomach. The heavy man fell into the ditch, dragging the other wounded behind him.

A thin little union man stood above the hole. "Don't kill 'em yet," he shouted. "Place your bullets in places that will make 'em suffer and die slow." With that, he aimed his gun at the shoulder of one of the scabs and pulled the trigger. Without hesitation, he placed shots in the arms and legs of the other victims. When his gun hit on an empty cartridge, he borrowed a gun from another miner and emptied that one too. The crowd cheered.

"The sheriff's in town!" someone shouted. "We need to get this over with!"

Peter Hiller jumped down in the ditch and cut one man's throat. He then calmly went around cutting the throats of two others.

While he was waiting his turn to be killed, one of the strikebreakers moaned. "Please, water, please!"

Don Ewing, a newspaper reporter, jumped down in the ditch and opened a flask.

"Keep away, God damn you!" a miner named Bert Grace shouted as he cocked his rifle and aimed it at Ewing. "I'll see you in hell before he gets any water!"

The scene became even more surreal as a beautiful blonde carrying a baby stepped into the ditch. She put her foot on the dying man's stomach. He screamed. She laughed when blood and clear liquid gushed and then bubbled in the gaping wound.

A young man unbuttoned the fly on his pants and stood over the man who still screamed. "Here's your water," the boy said as he urinated in his face. No one in the crowd protested, although several turned and walked away.

Ora felt emotionally numb. With weak legs, he followed those leaving the cemetery. Many jumped in the back of trucks to ride to the hills beyond the Herrin Mine, where they'd left their automobiles. Some were still excited and talked non-stop about the events of the past hours. Ora, like a few others, moved with the stiff, soullessness of guilt and shock. No one, though, seemed anxious to follow the same path back through the wooded area where so many bodies lay on the ground or hung from trees.

Wanting to be alone, Ora chose the longest route around the horrible scene of carnage. The forest through which he walked seemed as quiet and dead as the bodies of the strikebreakers. His mind's eye still saw their horrified eyes, smelled their sweat, their blood and the inevitable bowel release that came from each body as its soul left them. He still heard their cries for mercy, their moans, and, especially, that final, terrible, death rattle.

And then a loud moan sounded nearby. He wasn't certain if it came from inside his head or out. He stopped walking and listened. There it was again. This time softer, yet more intense. Ora moved toward the whimpering, stopping every few moments to listen for the groan to give him new direction. Then he saw the scab. He'd covered himself with brush to hide, but his wounds were too painful to keep him silent. When Ora pulled away the branches, he recognized him as the man Phillip Fontanetta had shot through the face. How he'd traveled in his condition this far from the site of the massacre seemed beyond belief.

The man was going to die. Of that Ora was certain. Besides the side of his face missing, he was bleeding from nearly every place on his body. His face was ashy grey and his eyes seemed rolled upwards and back into his head. *What was keeping him alive?* He struggled to tell Ora something, but no words could form. *Perhaps he is asking me to put him out of his misery.*

Ora looked into the man's eyes as he drew his gun and held it so the man could see it. The dying man gave a faint nod. Ora pointed it at the man's temple and pulled the trigger six times, feeling no more emotion than if he had been shooting figures of ducks at the Herrin carnival.

The second the final chamber fired, he dropped the gun on the ground and lethargically began walking again. After a few moments, he felt a powerful wave of energy throughout his body. He stopped and looked up into the trees. A small group of birds were singing the most beautiful song he'd ever heard. He laughed when two squirrels playfully jumped from one branch to another and then from tree to tree. A sweet whiff of daffodils from a nearby field sent waves of pleasant memories through his mind. And with it, part of a poem he had learned in school by William Wordsworth.

For oft, when on my couch I lie
In vacant or in pensive mood,
They flash upon that inward eye
Which is the bliss of solitude;
And then my heart with pleasure fills,
And dances with the daffodils.

The nightmare of the past few hours found a quiet place in the back of his mind. The exhaustion he felt moments before was gone. He felt alive as he hadn't in years. The thought of his wife's warm, bare skin made him walk faster and faster until he was at a dead run.

He had just killed a man.

He liked it.

***

The young mother grabbed her four-year old son by the back of his hair and pulled his face away from her skirt. The boy didn't want to look.

"Don't you turn your head away, boy!" the mother shouted. "I want you to look at the dirty bums that tried to take bread outa your mouth."

The youngster's squeal brought no sympathy from his mother or the dozens of men, women and children lined up in the warehouse to look at the nineteen bodies lying on the floor before them. In the hours after the violence, the bodies had been cleaned, but little effort had been made to hide the damage the gunshots had done to their faces or mask the smell that three days in the hot warehouse had brought. Each strikebreaker was covered with yellow and green ooze from hockers and snot that had been shot at them from mouths and noses. The decaying body odor was nearly masked by the urine that many boys and men had left on the corpses on the occasions when no women were in the building. Still, people had come by the thousands from as far away as St. Louis and Chicago to catch a glimpse of the dead. To the citizens of Williamson County, the killings had been justifiable homicide, not a massacre, as many newspapers called it.

"I leave you boys alone for one week, and you get the whole town to become murderers," Carl said to Ora and Otis as they watched the scene from a corner of the room. "Christ, all the newspapers in the country are callin' us Bloody Williamson County. And can't you get rid of them bodies? You got the whole of Main Street stinkin'."

"We do gotta bury them bodies sometime, Otis." Ora nodded.

"They's getting buried tonight," Otis grumbled. "I guess."

4

“We ain’t blood,” Carl’s wife Margaret said. “Only blood relatives sit at the kitchen table in Ma Shelton’s house.”

Earl’s latest girlfriend pouted and pushed her plate across the coffee table. “Well, I don’t like it.” Known as *Blondie* to her friends and *the Blond Bombshell* on the marquees that announced her performances, she was accustomed to being the center of attention. At Ma Shelton’s house, though, she wouldn’t be asked to sing or dance or even receive more than a nod from the matriarch of the family.

“It could be worse,” Margaret said. “You could be put in charge of Ma Shelton’s grandkids, like Dalta’s wife. Then you’d be eatin’ in the smokehouse.”

Blondie hadn’t taken her eyes away from the open archway into the kitchen since Ma Shelton exiled her and her in-laws into the living room to eat. The four brothers and two sisters sat dining with Ma and Pa, who sat at opposite ends of the long table. Bernie told the joke she’d taught him that morning.

"So, the little cannibal boy threw his fork down on the dinner table and said, 'Mama, I don't like grandma.' And his cannibal mama said, 'Well, just pass her on and eat your spinach.'"

"Well, that's just fine, Bernie," Pa said. "You can tell those sick jokes after you and your friends didn't even give them strikebreakers a fair chance. Shot most of 'em in the back."

"Fair is a fantasy created by the weak," Bernie said. He enjoyed sharing the advice he so often received. "Besides, I told you I had nothin' to do with them killin's in Herrin, Pa."

"Of course, he didn't, Ben." Ma Shelton nodded. "Our boys ain't criminals like them newspapers is makin' 'em out to be."

"They stole that vehicle!" Pa almost shouted.

"We didn't steal it, Pa." Earl scowled. "We just borried it a little."

"All that matters is what God knows," Ma said, "not what a bunch of gossipy old ladies think they know."

"You've spoilt our boys with your lax parentin', Agnes." Pa glared at his wife.

"I cuffed 'em a time or two when they was kids." Ma looked at her youngest son. "Bernie, why don't you comb your hair before you come to the dinner table?"

"I never comb my hair. I just let the wind do it," Bernie replied, then added, "Unless I be goin' callin'."

"Why don't you never give Bernie credit for the good things he's done, Pa?" Lula asked. "Remember the day he brought home a whole bushel basket of morel mushrooms?"

"Even a blind squirrel finds a nut now and then," Pa said. "Besides, he was just tryin' to curry favor with his ma."

"I wish I'd been there in Herrin, Bernie." Lula leaned toward her brother. "I'd like to have seen them scabies gettin' what fer."

"That's just great!" Pa threw down his spoon. "Now Bernie's corrupted his sister."

"That ain't fair, Pa," Hazel said. "Brother Roy corrupted Lula long before he went to prison."

"There ain't nothin' like good whiskey and bad women," Bernie whispered to Earl for no reason at all. They both snickered.

"When is Roy getting out this time, Ma?" Dalta asked. Being the more respectful and reliable of the five brothers, he liked to stay informed.

Ma shrugged, then pulled out the kerchief sticking out the top of her dress. She wiped her eyes.

"Good God, Dalta," Earl whispered, giving his brother a hard punch on the arm. "Now you got Ma weepin'."

"You got more sweet taters, Ma?" Carl asked, apparently oblivious to the entire conversation.

"We got a good plenty," Ma said. She rose to fetch them, but stopped and blew her nose on her apron first.

"Why'd you bring up Roy anyway, Hazel?" Dalta whispered with an elbow to his sister's ribs.

"I didn't mean nothin' by it," Hazel said, scooting away and rubbing her side. "I was just defendin' Bernie. My intentions were good."

"The road to Hell is paved with good intentions." Dalta leaned back and crossed his arms.

"You're full of good intentions, ain't ya, Dalta?" Bernie asked. "Is that why you won't join the gang?"

"Why did you tell Ma you didn't have nothin' to do with them scabies dyin'?" Dalta asked.

"I didn't lie," Bernie said. "I just borried from the truth a bit."

"You and Earl is always borrowin', ain't ya?" Dalta muttered.

"Bernie's worse than a pet racoon," Pa grumbled. "What he doesn't tear up, he shits on."

"Don't be a hedgin' on your opinionatin', Ben," Ma said as she returned to the table with a big bowl in her hands. "Speak open."

"Bernie's been stubborn," Pa continued loudly, "since the day the doctor turned him over and slapped him on the back."

"How would you know?" Ma asked. "You was out drinkin' ever time one of your young'uns were birthed."

"I can't blame Pa for that," Earl said. "If I had my druthers, I'd just as soon wake up next to a bottle—or, at least in church hearing the preacher's voice."

That brought a chuckle from the usually quiet Carl.

"Well, would you look at that?" Lula said. "I declare, Carl's smiles are as rare as a cold wind in August."

"Just hand me some more vittles, sister," Carl growled. "My belly ain't gonna get filled by joinin' in on all this yapperin'."

***

When the Methodist Church near Fairfield was built, the Shelton family purchased room for three rows of pews, which Ma Shelton insisted be installed at the very back of the rectory. Almost all the pews in the church were the same, but the three Ma had her son's build had slots on the back for Bibles and hymnals. It wasn't that she scorned sitting near the front where the most socially prominent members of the congregation strutted their affluence and virtuousness—Ma just didn't want to draw any more attention to her son's attendance as was necessary. She believed with all her heart that Carl, Earl and Bernie were spiritual beings. But it didn't matter that Carl taught Sunday School and played the organ when called upon. If somebody got killed in Little Egypt on a Sunday, one of her boys was always the first to be suspected.

Her protective instinct was even more powerful now that the trial of the eight men accused of the Herrin killings was over and had been found innocent. Few in the community feared for those charged, though everyone acknowledged they had been the ones to send the scabs to hell where they belonged. Had it not been for the national attention the murders had brought, there never would've been a trial—nor the need for dozens of local citizens to perjure themselves so as to alibi for the eight.

"The prosecution is reluctantly obliged to admit that justice cannot be obtained in Williamson County," State's Attorney Delos Duty said after the trial.

It seemed that most everyone outside of southern Illinois, from the newspapers to President Warren G. Harding, publicly vilified the good citizens of Williamson County. The community reeled from the national scorn they received. That, plus the lack of respect so many of the citizens had for Prohibition laws meant no one was overly surprised when the Reverend's sermon was interrupted and a dozen fully costumed Ku Klux Klan members entered the church. They marched two abreast to the pulpit.

It also didn't surprise anyone when several members of the congregation, including the Shelton brothers as well as a dozen bootleggers and tavern owners, put their hands inside their suit jackets and untethered their weapons.

"I wondered when they'd hit this joint," Bernie whispered. "They invaded all the Baptist churches last Sunday."

"This ain't a joint, Bernie," Carl said quietly. "It's a church, and these scumbags is gonna mean trouble for our roadhouses."

"I heard they initiated over two hundred new members last week," Earl added. "They claim to have over two thousand Klansmen just from Williamson County alone."

The men in masks and white robes walked like silent ghosts. They lined up on either side of the aisle and stood at attention while their leader handed the minister an envelope, bowed his head and then walked back down the aisle to the door. His Klansmen followed.

As soon as the door was closed behind them, the preacher opened the envelope and read the letter aloud:

> *Please accept this token of our appreciation of your efforts and great work you are doing for this community. The Knights of the Ku Klux Klan are behind this kind of work to a man and stand for the highest ideals of the native-born white Gentile American citizenship which are:*

The tenets of the Christian religion; protection of pure womanhood, just laws and liberty; absolute upholding of the Constitution of the United States; free public schools; free speech; free press; and law and order.

Yours for a better and greater community,

Exalted Cyclops.

The Reverend then held up the three ten-dollar bills that were also in the envelope.

***

Maude Young agreed to go watch the Klan initiation ceremony with Glenn, but she didn't promise to join. After parking their Lincoln on the side of a dirt road, they followed others who walked up a nearby hill. Had it been daytime, the clearing with its plentiful trees and a rocky little creek would've been a fine site for a church picnic. The half moon in the sky and the hundreds of torches carried by men and women in white sheets and hoods made the setting seem more appropriate for Halloween than a warm summer evening.

Maude firmly grasped her husband's arm as a Kleagle handed him a thick torch and then lighted it with his own. "Are you here to be initiated?"

"We were invited to observe so we can decide." Glenn produced from his jacket a letter of introduction.

"A rare privilege," the Klansman said, carefully inspecting the paper. When he was satisfied of its authenticity, he handed it back. "We ask that you remain in the area below the creek bed so as not to disturb the proceedings. I am certain that after you behold our sincerity, you will feel honored to join us."

After walking to the designated area, they found a tree stump. Removing his jacket, Glenn draped it for Maude to sit upon.

"This is so spooky, Glenn. Why must there be an organization like this?"

"The Klan is trying to get folks to see they are here to protect the American way," Glenn said. Because of his law enforcement background, he was being heavily recruited. He hadn't told Maude he had already agreed to join. "We need to remind everyone of the American way in our homes, church, school, and in every tradition, including weddings and holidays."

"Well," Maude said and hesitated. Then, developing more conviction with each word, she continued, "I'm just not sure I want to be celebrating Christmas by having our child sit on the lap of jolly old Kris Kleagle of the local Klan, and singing Christmas carols next to a tree lighted by a burning cross."

"They do not call it a burning cross, Maude. The lighting of a cross represents the light of Christ," Glenn argued. "You believe in that, don't you? God brings light to darkness, just as the Klan does."

"It's your decision, my husband." Maude smiled. "If you do join, though, I hope you'll get me the contract for sewing together these outfits. Somebody's making a lot of money doing it."

Every Klansman was dressed in the official white robe with the KKK mioak sewn over the heart, the red teardrop on its cross. The slow beat of a single drum announced the ceremony was about to begin. Klansmen who had not already done so, pulled their masks over their faces.

David Curtis Stephenson, the Grand Dragon of the Indiana chapter, stepped forward. The round-faced man was also the head of Klan recruiting for seven states including Illinois. He preferred to be hailed by his initials, D.C. After some preliminary meeting procedures, he began his oratory.

"I hold no grudges against the Jew," Stephenson told those standing before him. The acoustics in the wooded area were good and his voice traveled well throughout the glen. "They are a wonderful people and should have the same basic rights as anyone who lives in America. The fact is, though, that they are not willing to assimilate into American life. All the Ku Klux Klan demands whether it be Jew, Chinese or Jap, is that they shall be true to the Constitution of the United States of America.

We must secure the existence of our people and a future for white children.

"As for the Negro, we do not secretly or openly hate them. In fact, we hold sympathy for them. They did not ask to come to this continent, but once they were here, were they not better off than they had been in Africa where slavery and poverty have remained to this day?

"The assimilation of the Negro race into the White culture is unthinkable and entirely outside the divine destiny of our Lord. Social equality would never be possible for the Black man, who lacks the responsible nature as well as the desire to self-govern. The true Klansman says, 'promote the health and happiness of the Negro, but the reins of government must be kept in the hands of the White race.' To do otherwise would be suicidal to the life of the American Republic." He paused, looking over those gathered. "We will now have our Kleagle's organize our initiates for the swearing in ceremony."

Since there were cameramen present, the leaders spent several minutes getting the large number of initiates lined up.

"I just don't understand why they think that just because other folks are different, they must be against the American way," Maude said. "Maybe the good Lord didn't mean for us to all be alike."

"Would you want our children marryin' outside our race?" Glenn asked. "Why, they wouldn't know if they was Black or White."

Maude didn't have an answer for that. It was true she couldn't imagine what life would be like for a mixed baby. She had once had a friend who was half Indian, and she had a rough enough time adjusting in the two separate cultures. Still, she sometimes wondered if all this hullabaloo might be overblown.

When they were ready for the swearing-in ceremony, even Maude had to agree that it was an impressive spectacle. Though they weren't too close to the ritual, she and Glenn felt obliged to stand, despite the fact that the over two hundred initiates were told to kneel.

A Kladd officiated the procedure by having a single representative for the two hundred approach a great alter stone and kneel before it.

"We, the Knights of the Ku Klux Klan, magnify the Bible as a basis for our constitution, the foundation of our government, the source of our laws, the sheet anchor of our liberties, the most particular guide of right living, and the source of all true wisdom. We honor the Christ as the Klansman's only criterion of character, and we seek at His hands that cleansing from sin and impurity which only He can give."

"Maude," Glenn whispered in her ear, "tell me now. Is that not Christian? Won't those principles make for a stronger, better, richer America?"

"Furthermore," the Kladd continued, "in the presence of God and man, I solemnly pledge, promise and swear that I will, at all times, in all places, and in all ways, help, aid and assist the constituted authorities of the law in the proper performance of their legal duties, so help me God. Amen."

Glenn's chest puffed with those words. He was looking forward to telling Maude the Klan had already asked him to lead their law enforcement agency to stop the bootlegging businesses in Little Egypt.

"I swear," the Kladd finished, "to never recommend for membership any person whose mind is unsound, whose reputation is bad, whose character is doubtful, or whose loyalty to the United States of America is in any way questionable.

"Therefore, I sacredly swear unqualified allegiance, pledging our property, our votes, our honor and our lives. Free education, free speech, free press, separation of church and state, White supremacy, just laws, the pursuit of happiness—all these each Klansman swears to seal with his blood; be Thou my witness, Almighty God."

The Kladd produced a huge sword and placed it on the shoulder of the initiate kneeling before him in behalf of all the rest. "I hereby declare you Knights of the Ku Klux Klan."

5

Charlie Birger was content to be a highly respected criminal. He liked to carry an article with him in which a writer named Paul Angle described meeting him.

> *Visitors meeting Birger for the first time are invariably impressed by his attractive appearance and pleasant greeting. Dark skin, prominent cheekbones, and heavy black hair suggest his Russian parentage, but he speaks with no trace of accent. His handshake is hearty, his smile quick. The riding-breeches, puttees, and leather jacket that he customarily wears are neat and clean. Just under six feet tall, he carries himself with military erectness, and looks younger than his forty-four years. He usually wears two guns in holsters, and often cradled a sub-machine gun as he sat and talked to me.*

Further, Charlie had a beautiful young wife who didn't need even an occasional beating—and now she was pregnant again. He had pledged to himself that if Betty had a son, he would only go drinking and whoring on weekends. His girlfriend Helen Holbrook had tried to veto that idea.

"Why, Charlie, you couldn't stay away from these bazonkas for a whole week," Helen snapped. They were lying in bed nude at the moment he informed her of his semi-abstinence plan. The real reason for her anger was that he hadn't bothered to share the information *before* enjoying her pleasures. "Besides, why would you do that?"

"'Cause I want to make you happy," he replied.

"How would that make me happy?" She kicked his naked leg off her naked leg.

"I wanted to give you something to bitch about," Charlie replied coldly. He rolled out of the bed and started dressing. "You ain't happy unless you have something to bitch about. Now you can be happy for a while."

It wasn't that Helen was jealous of Betty. After all, Charlie's wife wasn't nearly as beautiful as was she, nor, she was certain, did the little housewife have bedroom abilities—skills that Helen had been perfecting since she was thirteen. Betty was necessary to take care of Charlie's two young daughters and to give the gangster an air of respectability.

"Besides," Charlie continued while fumbling with his tie, "you said there couldn't be nothing between us as long as you're still young and beautiful."

"Yes, but that don't mean I didn't think we had an understanding, that someday we'll reach an understanding."

"What?" Charlie asked. Giving up on the tie, he stuffed it in his pocket. "Never mind explainin'. There ain't nothin' worse than a woman havin' a word fit."

"Oh, hell, you're getting too old to satisfy a beautiful young thing like me anyway." Helen flopped to her stomach to show Charlie her disgust—as well as to give him a parting look at her well-defined derriere. "What are you, fifty years old?"

"Getting close, but I've got a lot more years to be old than you've got to be beautiful, and that there's a fact."

Charlie didn't want to push his thoughts hard enough that he had to make a choice between his wife and Helen.

***

When he got home that night, the Saline County sheriff, John Small, was waiting for him on the porch.

"What the hell are you doing here, John?" Charlie asked. His face grew red when he saw his garage door was up and three deputies stood around the big safe in the back.

"We have a search warrant, Charlie." Sheriff Small held up a paper. "Betty let us in to search your house, and you'll be happy to know we found nothing there or in your garage. If you'll just open that safe, and if there's nothing in it, we'll be on our way."

"I ain't openin' that damned safe," Charlie said.

"Well, then, Charlie," Small said, "we're gonna have to drag it out of there and blow it open."

Charlie stared at the sheriff.

"One of you boys, you." Small pointed at a deputy. "Run on over to Mitchell's machine shop and see if you can't borrow a little dynamite."

Betty was walking down the stairs from the bedroom when the explosion shook the entire house. The expectant mother fell the last few steps. She rolled protectively onto her side.

Outside, her husband juggled excuses and options in his head as the deputies waited for the smoke to clear. By the time they looked in the now doorless safe, he had decided on a plan. The cops quickly retrieved several bottles of whiskey as well as uncut liquor. Charlie wasn't too worried about those items. He was certain the constabularies would be reporting to work the next day with massive hangovers. Then they found a box full of counterfeit federal liquor stamps and handed them to Sheriff Small.

"Looks like hard time, Charlie," Small said, shuffling through the papers.

"I'd 'spect so, John. But I've got some pretty good lawyers and a few boys that can handle things while I'm up the river. I'd 'spect I'll be back pretty quick, and you and me will just continue right from where we're leavin' off."

Small gave the gangster a knowing look. "I think a suggestion is coming, Charlie. I hope it won't be a bribe."

"Then, how 'bout a promise, John? What if I give you my word that my days in Saline County is over? What if you become the only sheriff in Little Egypt that don't have to worry about Charlie Birger Enterprises?"

"Why would you do that?"

"Just call it being a good neighbor, John. Harrisburg is my home, and I want residents to know I will defend it from bad influences."

"You still handin' out those groceries, Charlie?" Small asked. The rumor around town was that Charlie liked to load up his car with sacks of groceries and drop them off in the middle of the night on the porches of folks who were having a rough time. Whether Charlie was the one doing it or not, the appearance of groceries was a fact. The gangster getting the credit made him a Robin Hood among the citizens of Harrisburg.

"You know I can't answer that, John. Don't you know, we can't have folks thinking there's a free meal at my doorstep?"

"I figure you for a lot of things, Charlie, but a welcher ain't one of 'em." He pulled off his glove to shake hands. "If you abide by your promise and stay out of Saline County, you and I will get along right fine, I'd 'spect." The honest sheriff tucked the box of liquor licenses in through the window of his police car, got in, and drove away.

***

Betty didn't tell Charlie that she had fallen when the dynamite blew the safe open. He told her of the deal he'd made with the sheriff. She was afraid that if he knew the cause of her losing the baby, he might renege and possibly even take revenge. She so desperately wanted a normal family life. When they married, she fell in love with her husband's four-year-old daughter, Little Minnie, immediately. In fact, she even liked the girl's mother, whom Charlie had never married. So much so, she allowed Winnie to come visit Little Minnie when she thought Charlie wouldn't be home. Betty's benevolence got Winnie a severe beating one day when Charlie came home unexpectantly and caught his wife, ex-girlfriend and their daughters sitting around the kitchen table talking and laughing.

"You ever let that woman in this house again, and it will be you takin' the beatin', you hear?" Charlie screamed after kicking Winnie through the back door.

When the miscarriage came, Betty was so afraid of her husband's wrath, she exaggerated her illness and hid in bed for three days. She had little need to worry, though, because when the doctor told Charlie the stillborn had been a boy, he went on a bender and didn't come home for two weeks. When he finally did, he was minus a finger.

The loss of his appendage was indirectly the result of Charlie wanting a son. In fact, he wanted a boy so bad he had already made arrangements with a rabbi to do the circumcision. So, when a young street shave tail named Earl Estes made the mistake of teasing an inebriated Charlie about being a Jew, Earl got a mouthful of fist and Charlie got an infection in a knuckle that lead to an amputation.

Since it was a warm day in August when Charlie finally came home, Betty took note of the gray suede gloves he wore—and so did Little Minnie.

"Why are you wearing gloves, Daddy?"

"Well, that's an interestin' story, darlin'." Charlie held both girls on his lap. Being only a year and a half old, Charlene, his daughter with Betty, was more interested in the peppermint stick her father had brought. "You see, I was visiting a nice, old man the other day, and he didn't have even one finger on either hand. The nice, old man told me he would give anything to have just one finger so he could get down in fruit jars and reach what was at the bottom. So, I let him chose one of my fingers, and we had the doctor sew it on his hand. Now when he sits around every day, he can enjoy pullin' jelly and such out of jars. In fact, Mother," Charlie looked at his wife for the first time since being home, "would you send the nice, old man some of your good, blackberry jam? I sure do think he'd enjoy that."

"Let me see your hand, Daddy." Little Minnie squealed happily. "Which finger did you give the nice, old man?"

Charlie removed his right glove, and Little Minnie counted aloud all five fingers. "Oh, Daddy, you gave him one on the other hand."

Charlie removed his left glove and held up four fingers; the ring finger missing. He and Little Minnie sat together and counted fingers until dinnertime.

6

The wooden cross was a good twenty-five-foot tall, so when it was set afire on top of the one-hundred-foot-high Monks Mound in Cahokia, it could be seen ten miles away in St. Louis. Glenn Young was among the twenty dignitaries sitting in the semi-circle of chairs on a wooden platform. He surveyed the twenty thousand men and women dressed in white Ku Klux Klan outfits. Many of them carried torches, swords and shields; others crosses; and still others, either American or Confederate flags. He was certain they all toted lethal firearms beneath their robes.

"I guess this'll teach them damned Catholics we mean business," Caesar Cagle said to Glenn while citizens continued to gather. "They'd better start payin' attention to the Eighteenth Amendment—or we'll be givin' 'em what fer."

"This ain't just about Prohibition, Caesar," Glenn explained, as he did so often to his wife. "It's about stopping them damned Bolshevik Unions from interferin' with the American way."

"Not to mention them foreigner's propensity for gambling, prostitution and destroyin' the purity of the White race," added D.C. Stephenson, who sat nearby. "In order to get our brothers to join, we must convince them the Klan is not an organization that takes Negroes out, cuts off their noses, and throws them into a fire. The Klan is a strictly patriotic organization."

"Maybe," Caesar whispered to Glenn, "but I still wouldn't mind cuttin' the noses off a few of them niggers."

Stephenson's attention was suddenly drawn to a female Klanswoman in a white robe that couldn't adequately hide her figure. She took a seat next to a less attractive lady whose face could only enhance those around her.

"I'll have to let my erection digress before I stand," Stephenson snickered. "Next time, I'll bring a podium to lecture behind. Maybe I can get that gal to kneel down inside it while I talk."

Glenn didn't appreciate the Grand Dragon speaking in such a way about the pretty young woman. Both he and Maude had developed great respect for Madge Oberholtzer in the past several weeks. In fact, after his promotion today, his wife suggested they try and coax her into working in his office.

Stephenson finally rose from his seat and held his hands high over his head. It took several moments for the large crowd to quiet.

"My worthy subjects, citizens of the Invisible Empire, Klansmen all. Greetings. God help the man who issues a proclamation of war against the Klan. We are going to Klux Illinois as she has never been Kluxed before."

The cheering seemed muffled by the vastness of the empty acreage around the mound. The area was so large, in fact, that twenty thousand people seemed insignificant—if not for the bright white of their outfits and the hundreds of torches glowing throughout the hill.

"We must appeal to the ministers of Illinois to do the praying for the Ku Klux Klan and let them know that we will do the scrapping for it. And if we do the bidding of God, the fiery cross is going to burn at every crossroad in Illinois—as long as there is a White man left in the state."

For a second time, the crowd cheered until Stephenson again held his hands high into the air. He then spoke for nearly an hour about the Klan's goals for the state and the nation. Finally, he got to the point of the gathering. "I come here today to present to you, the law-abiding citizens of the Law and Order League under the direction of The Exalted Cyclops," his voice suddenly grew louder as he shouted, "your new leader—the greatest law enforcement officer in America, S. Glenn Young."

Glenn rose and strutted to the platform. The applause went on for several more minutes.

Finally, Stephenson raised both hands to silence the audience. "I might add," he said, "that Kleagle Young is a dead shot and lightning fast on the draw. He is so accurate when he cuts loose that the figger on the ace of spades would cover his cluster of bullet holes."

The crowd laughed. Instead of returning to the seat he had just vacated, Stephenson took one next to Madge, causing the other Klan leaders to shuffle over one seat.

"Yes, but you need to mention that I never pulled a gun first," Glenn said with a smile. Then he grew serious as he raised a wooden cross above his head. "Here, tonight, I raise the ancient symbol of an unconquered race of men, the fiery cross of old Scotland hills. I am a man of action, and we ain't waitin' for no mansy pansy governor to do something about these bootlegging sinners. Tonight, the holy order of the Ku Klux Klan is gonna raid East St. Louis and shut down every house of sin in the Valley."

The crowd on the hill applauded and sang, "America the Beautiful" while Glenn and the other leaders began the tedious trek down the long hill. At first the crowd cheered him as he and the other dignitaries walked the gauntlet of saluting followers, but by the time they finally reached the bottom, many of the twenty thousand who had come in horse drawn carriages headed home. Still,

Glenn was able to stand on the running board of his own vehicle and direct hundreds of motor cars as they filled with Klansmen.

His powerful feeling of being part of the righteous cause of the Klan went a little sour when he saw Stephenson getting into the back of a four-door sedan with Madge. She gushed shyly at the gentlemanly attention the Grand Dragon gave her. Stephenson shut the door quickly behind him, preventing a Klan officer from joining them in the back. For just a moment, Glenn wished that his wife was there to ride with Madge. The caravan of cars was ready, though, and began the short drive to the infamous Valley of East St. Louis.

Caesar Cagle sat in the front seat between Glenn and the Herrin Kleagle John Smith while four burly Klansman squeezed into the backseat.

"Now we'll give them Sheltons what fer." Caesar checked his revolver.

Twenty minutes later, the caravan entered the streets of the Valley. It wasn't until then that Glenn realized he hadn't thought through the invasion of East St. Louis very well. Once, when he had been in Texas, he led a band of Rangers through a narrow canyon in pursuit of desperados. When the ambush came, they had been able to dismount and seek shelter in the rocks. But today, with most of his Klan members stretched out behind him for several blocks, seeking cover in The Valley of East St. Louis wouldn't be as easy.

Taverns and brothels emptied quickly when the large number of cars and trucks appeared so late at night. The curious partiers stood on the boardwalks staring at the vehicles. Draped from each of the driver's side windows was a single white cloth with red crosses. Many cars had nooses hanging ominously from the sides.

Unexpectantly, a loud clap of thunder announced a sudden downpour of heavy but cool summer rain.

"Jesus, Mary, and Joseph!" Caesar swore a few moments later when they rounded a corner.

Glenn saw it too—but all he could do was keep driving slowly forward in the rain and mud toward the strangest sight he'd ever seen.

***

The events that led up to Glenn and Caesar's shock had begun a few hours earlier that night. When Carl entered the Arlington Hotel lobby after dinner, Bernie and Earl watched him for clues as to what type of evening it would be. If Carl went upstairs, it probably meant that his visit to Fairfield to see his wife Margaret had not gone well. In that case, one or more of the prostitutes would undoubtably profit from the gangster's marital problems. Afterwards, though, the evening might get bloody if Big Carl didn't get proper satisfaction.

Lucky for everyone's sake, Carl ushered Art Newman out of the only comfortable reading chair in the lobby by giving him a friendly smile along with a jerk of his head. Breathing easier, Bernie resigned himself to sprawling across a love seat and cleaning his favorite shotgun.

Earl, being half-stewed from excessive drink, slapped Art on the back. "Introduce me to that Shawneetown dame you've been braggin' about, Art," Earl slurred. "I wanna see if her gazongas are as fine as you say."

"Oh, yes," Art stammered. "They are fine, indeed. And maybe we could shoot some craps later. I always was a good hand at the dice, just like any of the boys can tell you. I learned most about shooting them in the Army, and I can bean any old game. I think. Leastways, I don't remember ever losing a gamble at dice."

The hotel business had picked up when the Shelton gang began to frequent it, but so too had the violence. Since the brothers usually paid for damages, Art, the owner, was learning to tolerate the gangsters—and the St. Louis area had plenty of gangs. The membership of most kept along ethnic lines, Irish and Italian being the most vicious. Others like the Shelton and Birger gangs had only one criterion for membership—the ability to kill. In fact, Art had also become drinking chums with the notorious Harrisburg gangster Charlie Birger, though Charlie spent most of his time running Canadian booze across the border and down from Detroit, which was where he was on this night.

Carl enjoyed reading about his gangs exploits in the *St. Louis Post Dispatch*. *Gang battles in southern Illinois and St. Louis have reached a peak in bloodiness unparalleled in United States crime history*. He smiled as he read. It was quite a statement for them to consider that the Sheltons and others had *out-bloodied* the Chicago and New York bootleggers. Part of the reason he outmaneuvered other gangs in the East St. Louis area had been his success in either charming or paying off politicians and law enforcement. When the dollars were produced, the public officials were easily convinced to ignore the brothers' shady business dealings. If that didn't work, Bernie used muscle and his own form of persuasion.

From the top of the stairwell, one of the prostitutes screamed and then shouted, "Don't point that weapon at me!" She ran back into her room, slamming the door behind her.

Bernie laughed and pulled the trigger on the unloaded shotgun. Carl returned to reading his paper just as Earl reemerged at the top of the stairs, a buxom blonde on either arm.

"Honey, mine is the best bordello in the Valley," Art's wife said from Earl's right arm. Blond Bessie Newman was the madam of the house.

"Why Carl Shelton," the blonde on Earl's other arm said as they descended the steps. "You're even handsomer in real life than you are in the newspaper pictures."

"I ain't in the market for a gal today," Carl said without looking up from the front page. "Try Bernie. He's younger and more amorous."

"Why, honey," the blonde said in a voice full of sarcasm, "I could buy you three times over. I ain't no sportin' gal."

"This here is Helen Holbrook, Carl." Blond Bessie said. "She wanted to meet you."

Carl glanced up. He stifled a breath. This woman did not have the platinum blond curls and milky white skin of so many working girls. Her hair was naturally blond and cut short like a school marm's. What little skin showed was smoothed a golden brown from hours spent in the sun. Her white blouse was long sleeved, lacey across the chest, and would have been fitting to wear in church. The word that immediately came to Carl to describe her look was *wholesome*. Helen's voice had fooled him. It had been feminine yet a little raspy. He didn't want to take his eyes off her, but he did. Helen Holbrook was one of Charlie Birger's girls. Though Carl had never met Birger, he respected the rival gangster's property rights.

"What's wrong, Big Carl?" Helen asked. "You boys church goers?"

"Ever Sunday," Bernie replied.

"Bernie?" Carl asked like a parent correcting a child.

"Well, ever Sunday." Bernie hesitated, then added, "unless somebody needs kilt." With that, Bernie jumped to his feet, pulled a .45 caliber pistol from beneath his belt, and started firing into the ceiling. "Whoopee!" he shouted. "All broads to the street for a mating dance. Come on, Blond Bessie, roust them whores away from their fornicatin'. I'll pay five dollars to each gal that'll dance naked in the street."

Bessie ran up the stairs two steps at a time and started pounding on doors.

"Bernie wants a Valley shake!" she shouted.

Squealing, naked and half-naked prostitutes emerged from their rooms and ran down the stairs chanting, "Boobiebash! Boobiebash!"

Angry or, more often, confused men followed as they hastily pulled on trousers and came out into the hall. At the outside doorway, Bernie smacked each lady on the buttocks as she passed and Earl helped some strip down to their birthday suits. When they were all in the street, Bernie grabbed Helen's arm.

"Get your hands off me, you big oaf!"

"Leave that one be, Bernie," Carl warned.

Bernie released her and followed the other men outside just as a loud clap of thunder shook the glass in the windows. Helen rubbed her arm. Without any prompting from Carl, she walked over, sat on his lap and rested her head on his shoulder. The feel of her curvaceous body inspired him to make a snap decision.

"I reckon them rooms upstairs is goin' to waste," the crime boss said. He lifted and carried the Shawneetown dame as easily as he would a small child.

On the street, the ladies danced while the heavy summer rain pounded their flesh. Men came out of buildings to watch and shout their encouragement. Across the street, a half dozen Negro prostitutes joined the spectators on a covered boardwalk and waved bottles of liquor as their clients whooped while palming the women's breasts. The impromptu performance became even more erotic when the dirt road turned sloppy from the rain. Some of the more inebriated Valley shakers slipped, then came up laughing. They smeared the mud across their bodies and glared seductively at the watching men.

Two policemen dressed in raincoats walked around the corner, but when they saw the frolicking, they stopped, and laughing, stepped backwards into the darkness of an alley to watch.

Carl and Helen appeared on a second-floor balcony as men joined the naked women on the streets, rubbing mud on them, kissing them, and, in some cases, slipping and sliding as they tried to engage in standing coitus.

From down the street came the honking of horns, then lights from a long row of automobiles approaching the Valley. The dancing women screamed and waded through the mud back into the brothel. Members of the Shelton gang hurried into the building, retrieved their weapons, and remerged, brandishing them toward the approaching vehicles.

***

"Jesus, Mary, and Joseph!" Caesar repeated.

Glenn had seen many strange things in his life, but naked, muddy women dancing in the middle of the road made his mouth drop.

By the time he stopped his vehicle, the ladies were already inside and the boardwalks filled with armed men from the Shelton gang. Glenn didn't like the odds. Many a Tommy gun was pointed in his direction, and not enough vehicles carrying Klansmen could pull up close enough to be of help in the event of a shootout.

It was almost a relief to see two policemen approach his automobile. The officers drew their service revolvers from beneath their raincoats. Behind Glenn's car, a few of the Klansmen vehicles turned off the street, hastily exiting the scene.

"Top of the mornin' to ye fine gentlemen," the older of the officers said to Glenn when he opened his window. "Now, reckless drivin' ain't a neighborly thing this time o' night, is it?"

"Why'd you stop us," Glenn asked, "when there's a hundred other cars doing the same behind us?"

"Well, now, ya didn't expect us good sons of the ol' sod to arrest 'em all, did ya, lad?"

Glenn looked around. Carl stood on the balcony in the rain, wearing only trousers, his suspenders, and a shoulder holster crossing his bare chest. The beautiful woman beside him appeared to be half clothed herself and shared a wry smile similar to that of the eldest Shelton brother.

"Them boys is drinkin' alcohol!" Glenn shouted, pointing directly at Earl and Bernie, who sported a bottle in one hand and a Tommy gun in the other.

"Now we won't be deprivin' our good Catholic friends of a wee nip durin' communion," the officer said.

"They ain't holdin' no Mass!" Glenn shouted, bringing laughter from the gangsters lining the boardwalk. "Besides, them Sheltons is Methodists."

"Now we don't want to go tellin' no parishioner how to show his respect to the Lord" the officer spoke calmly. "And if them lovely white sheets is your way of bein' angels, you might wanna keep 'em in the countryside where dey won't be getting' spoilt with dis city wickedness." He opened the car door and pointed his revolver at Glenn. "Now, come along to the hoosegow with ya, lads. The good magistrate would like a word with ya."

***

"That Klan caravan last night got me spooked," Art said to Carl during noon breakfast. "It's getting mighty crowded on the east side. What with the dagoes and niggers cuttin' into our business, and now Glenn Young's Klan army?"

"I'll take care of the east side," Carl said. "Them Sunday blue laws in Missouri drives thirsty men to the Valley in droves. We open our speakeasies in southern Illinois on Sundays, and we'll make a mint."

"What are Sunday blue laws?" Helen asked. She refilled Carl's coffee without being asked, but ignored Bernie, who held his empty cup out to her.

"Laws that restrict folks from doing much of anything on Sundays except go to church and shit," Art answered.

"That's fine for your liquor sales," Bessie said, taking up the carafe and filling her own cup. "But how you gonna help my sportin' gals, Carl?"

"Bernie," Carl said slowly as he chewed on crackling, "why don't you fetch up a parcel of schoolboys ever Sunday for Bessie? Tell 'em the first trick is on the house, as it's a rite of passage into manhood."

“We ain’t givin’ no freebees to no children, Carl!” Bessie shouted. “These thighs don’t spread for free for nobody.”

“Why, Bessie,” Carl said with a smile, “you think them boys will stop with one little jaunt? I’ll wager they’ll be so thirsty they’ll be buckin’ bales all week for another Sunday delight with your gals.”

“Good thing you never went honest, Carl.” Art grinned. “Why, you’d be a regular Rockefeller, you would.”

“How low a grade in school you figure I oughta make the invites, Big Carl?”

“Well, Bernie,” Carl said, “you was almost fourteen when you almost gradeated from fifth grade. If they’s got peach fuzz on their lip, then I’d ‘spect they’s old enough to appreciate good tail.”

***

Glenn had only been back in Herrin for a day after his brief arrest in East St. Louis when he received a surprise visitor to his new office.

Madge Oberholtzer was shaking as she related to Glenn her ride in the back seat of the car with Grand Dragon Stephenson. “I’m telling you, he would’ve raped me if he’d had five more minutes.”

“Now, Miss Oberholtzer,” Glenn reassured calmly. “That’s our Klan leader you’re talking about. You sure he weren’t just funnin’ ya a little?”

"Do these bite marks look like he was funning me?" Madge pulled the lace down from her neck. "I could show you the bruises he left on my arms and legs if you want."

"Why are you tellin' me this?" Glenn asked. Not sure where to put his eyes, he tried to focus on her high-laced shoes. "Shouldn't you be tellin' your pa?"

"Pa has consumption. I can't be troubling him with this." Madge struggled to keep her voice from shaking. "You and Maude have always been nice to me. I just thought you were the one person I could trust."

As usually happened when Glenn was at a loss for a rational thought, he blurted out the first thing that came into his mind. "I reckon he'd leave you alone if you didn't try to look so pretty."

"What?" Madge said with a sarcastic laugh. "Would you let Stephenson do this to your wife? She's pretty."

"Well, my Maude wouldn't put herself in a position to have that happen to her," Glenn said, his eyes still on her shoes. The left foot took a step back.

"You call yourself an honorable gentleman." Madge abruptly pivoted and left the room.

7

Being a gambler and from Alabama, Cecil Knighton liked to dress in expensive, light-colored suits. Harrisburg's finest haberdashery, Rathbone and Brown, welcomed his patronage.

"Wouldn't you like a little darker suit?" Mr. Rathbone inquired one day in early November. "Winters in Illinois are not like in the South."

"No, sir," Cecil said as he felt the material in a folded silk shirt. "I believe I'll stick to my customary color. Do you have these in my size?"

"No, Mr. Knighton, but we could order some and have them for you in about a week."

"That would be fine, Mr. Rathbone. I'll take six. And would you have the letter C embroidered on the pockets?"

"Of course, sir."

Cecil was feeling cocky and lucky. He had won four thousand dollars in a card game the night before. He was scheduled to bartend that night at Charlie Birger's Halfway Roadhouse, but he was feeling too pretty to get dirty. The Boss insisted all his gang members take a turn at barkeep each week or so. He liked to use that time to visit with them and get a sense if they were being disloyal or holding out on him from the loot they collected. Everyone knew that was why they had to work the bar, but the gangster's likeability usually made the conversations pretty amicable.

The past few months, though, Charlie's moods ranged from extremely happy to melancholy and often violent. Cecil had seen the Boss slap plenty of prostitutes around, and once in a while, he'd punch one of the young want-to-be gangsters. Youth and inexperience didn't seem to be a good trait when dealing with hardened men like Charlie and his boys.

"Evenin', Blondie," Cecil said when he saw the Blond Bombshell covering his shift at the bar.

"Where the hell have you been?" Blondie responded.

The dapperly dressed gambler pulled up a stool and sat down. "I'm taking the night off. I didn't have any other clothes to change into and I'm not about to get my new suit dirty."

"Well, I ain't working the night shift unless you make it worth my while."

"I'll tell you what I'll do." Cecil put his mouth as close to Blondie's neck as he thought she would allow. "You go in the back with me and let me hit that tail, and I'll pay you enough to make it worth your while. How much you want?"

"For you, it'll cost three Cs."

"Three hundred dollars? I'm not wantin' to buy it. I'm just wantin' to rent it."

Charlie approached the bar. "What's goin' on here?" the crime boss asked.

"Oh," Cecil's face reddened, "this whore said she'd work my shift tonight if I'd take her in the back and give her what for."

"You filthy, little dirt bag!" Blondie grabbed a knife and came around the bar after him.

"Yeah, well." Cecil stepped behind Charlie. "I'm a big man around these parts, sister, and a slut like you ain't gonna get the better of me."

"You gonna let him talk to me that way, Charlie?" Blondie held the knife low, palm up, like she knew how to drive it under a man's rib cage and through his heart.

"I'm not feelin' particularly bloody tonight." Charlie smiled through sleepy eyes. "You go ahead and work Cecil's shift, and I'll make it worth your while. I'm going outside for some air."

Charlie turned and walked out the door. Cecil and Blondie watched him through the open window. Standing on the semi-circular porch, he pulled a cigar from his shirt pocket, lit it, and stood staring out into the starry night sky.

"He's ten times the man you are," Blondie hissed. She picked up a few dirty shot glasses from the bar and began washing them.

"Oh yeah?" Cecil patted his chest. "Well, I'll show you. I'm gonna get that Jew son-of-a-bitch and run him out of Illinois."

Blondie flicked water off her hands and followed Cecil out onto the porch. She moved off to the side and stood next to Rado Millich, who, with shotgun in hand, stood guard. Rado was a dark-skinned eastern European with almost black eyes. His long nose and the almost cone-shaped top of his head gave him a cartoonish appearance.

"Charlie!" Cecil stepped off the porch and stood in the grass a few yards in front of the Boss. "I don't like you tryin' to make a fool of me in front of the lady."

Cecil reached in his coat for his revolver. Charlie turned toward Rado, who tossed him his shotgun. Cecil fired first, whizzing a bullet past Charlie's ear and causing him to drop to a knee. From that position, the Boss pulled both triggers at once. Cecil saw the flash from the big gun.

Charlie tossed the shotgun back to Rado, turned, and went back into the bar to get another drink.

"What suppose ol' Cecil thinkin' as head get blowed off?" Rado asked in broken and halting English.

"Well," Blondie said, "maybe he was thinkin', I won't need such a long coffin after all."

***

As Charlie expected would happen, liquor sells slowed for a while after Cecil's decapitation. He used the recession as an excuse to recruit new gang members. Unlike the Sheltons, who kept their numbers small, Charlie liked to have lots of associates around him. He knew better than to let his boys get outnumbered, so each night he invited small groups to Halfway for drinking, gambling and whoring. The third evening, four men arrived with Whitey Doering, a member of the Egan Rats Gang out of St. Louis. They and an Irish gang with the unlikely name Hogan's Jellyrolls, had ran all of the St. Louis area until the Shelton boys took over the Valley in East St. Louis. A gang war was likely, especially since the Birger Gang also had several interests in the Gateway city.

"Whitey is getting sent up for thirty years for that robbery in St. Louis," Charlie told Rado and Hogshead Davis as they stood at the bar watching Whitey and his boys getting to know some of the molls.

"Is that the robbery that netted him over two and a half mil'?" Blondie asked as she wiped the bar.

"That's right," Charlie answered, "and if he hadn't been dumb enough to keep it in his house, he would've got away with it."

"Doesn't sound like we need him, even if he gets out early for good behavior," Hogshead added. Hogshead liked to belittle anyone he could, since his own huge head was usually the source of teasing even by his younger brother whose head was just enough smaller to earn him the nickname *Little Big Head*.

"What about that little guy with him?" Blondie's voice turned raspy as she took in a slender man with dark eyes and hair. "He's cute!"

"I tink I see him with Otis Clark at Herrin massacre," Rado said.

"He serves as a deputy for Sheriff Galligan sometimes, doesn't he?" Blondie remembered.

"That's right." Hogshead snapped his fingers. "I remember him now. Ora Thomas. He's little, but they say he's fearless. But I ain't sure he's ever done anything outside the law."

"If he works for Galligan, he'll step outside the law," Charlie said, "if it profits him enough."

Just then Whitey approached the bar, a girl on each arm.

"Gee, Whitey," Hogshead said, "you're lookin' bad. I bet you've lost thirty pounds since you've been in court."

Whitey's face lost color, giving added relevance to his nickname. "Why you fat-headed ghoul. Don't you talk to me like that."

The two stepped toward each other. Charlie quickly and firmly grasped Hogshead by the shoulder, and Ora Thomas rushed onto the scene and did the same to Whitey.

"Hogshead," Charlie said, "this man is our guest." He then stared hard at Whitey. "And as a guest, I expect you to also show civility."

Hogshead immediately nodded, but Whitey skulked back to the far end of the room with his men. Ora looked at Charlie, gave him a shrug, but instead of joining the men he had arrived with, took a bottle to a table and sat down by himself.

"Whitey's stewing, Boss," Blondie said.

"I know." Charlie said, then whispered to Rado and Hogshead. "If there's trouble, I'll handle Whitey. You fellas keep his friends from back-shootin' me."

"You got it, Boss," both men said as one.

After fifteen minutes, Whitey turned back toward Charlie, who stood with his back to the angry man, but was watching in the long mirror above the bar.

"Kill Birger! Make a good job of it!" Whitey shouted.

Guns blazed for ten seconds from several directions, but only Whitey and Charlie went to the ground. As the smoke cleared, three of Whitey's friends ran out the door, nearly knocking it off its hinges. All the prostitutes followed. Rado and Hogshead quickly carried the Boss out to his car and rushed him to the Herrin hospital.

Ora Thomas hadn't moved. He struggled to steady his shaking hand as he poured himself another drink. Visions of the Herrin massacre had filled his head with each gunshot. It wasn't just the shooting and the blood that frightened him. It was his desire to be the one doing the killing.

Blondie stepped over Whitey as he lay moaning and brought an empty glass over to Ora's table. He poured her a stiff one and struggled to smile. His left eye twitched—something that had never happened before.

"So, tell me, handsome," Blondie said. "Should we have ourselves some fun before we phone the sheriff?"

"Either way is fine with me," Ora said. For a moment, he wondered if he'd be able to perform with the Blond Bombshell. Then he glanced over her shoulder and saw the pool of blood around Whitey still spreading out across the floor. A wave of excitement came over his entire body. "It will take the law thirty minutes to get here anyhow."

Blondie put a long kiss on his mouth. "A gal like me will need a lot longer than thirty minutes."

8

The next day, Ora felt a different kind of doubt. He wasn't quite sure he knew Charlie Birger well enough to make introductions, but when Carl Shelton made requests, it was hard to say no. The two men arrived at the hospital just as Helen Holbrook walked out. Ora couldn't miss the frown she gave the Shelton boss, but since they remained silent, so did he. Charlie's boys were stationed at every turn of the hallways, making no attempt to hide their weaponry. Nurses and orderlies moved nervously about the hospital. He and Carl were searched twice before they arrived in front of the Boss's room. The eldest Shelton had come unarmed, but Hogshead Davis confiscated Ora's revolver.

Rado Millich was the only goon in Charlie's room. He stood in a corner to the left so when the door was opened, he wasn't immediately visible. The window's curtain was pulled shut and a big oak dresser had been moved in front of it. The only light in the room came from a reading lamp placed behind Charlie, who sat up in the bed, a pack of cigarettes and bottle of whiskey on the tray next to him. Ora didn't need to make introductions.

"Carl Shelton," Charlie said.

"Evenin', Charlie. How you feelin'?"

"Better than Whitey Doering. Does that disappoint you, Carl?"

"Doesn't bother me." Carl took a seat in the only chair in the room. With no other choice than to remain standing, Ora turned so he could watch Rado from the corner of his eye.

"The Egan Rats aren't real happy," Carl continued. "That's why I wanted to talk to you."

"So, talk."

"You and me got a good thing goin' in Little Egypt and in East St. Louis."

"Cut to the chase, Carl. I ain't got all day to listen to you tell me stuff I already know."

"The Egan Rats and the Hoganites are sending an army of their best gunmen to take you out."

If the news surprised Charlie, he didn't show it.

"And you care...why?"

"Because if you go down, I'm next."

"So, what do you propose?"

"You got a lot more men than me. I propose we team up and meet them outside of town."

"Ambush?"

"Not if we can help it. I think if they see you and me workin' together, along with a show of force—"

"Friendly persuasion." Charlie smiled. "I heard you was a politician."

"You know I've got the entire East St. Louis police force and most of the politicians on my pay-roll. That's why I don't need a lot of men."

"Until now." Charlie sounded doubtful. "So why do I need you? I've got the Williamson County sheriff if I need him."

"We both have Sheriff Galligan," Carl said. "I got somethin' else that can double both of our takes with no more effort than good bookkeeping."

"What's that?"

"Slot machines."

***

Bernie's job was to prepare for a possible ambush if Carl's reasoning didn't work. He had twenty men with machine guns strung out along both sides of the road leading into Herrin. Since Earl was the sociable Shelton who knew everyone in the area by sight, he was down the road with a pair of binoculars.

"When a local yokel approaches, I'll wave a white flag," Earl told Bernie. "A red flag means cock your guns, here they come."

Carl remained in his car with Art Newman, filling him in on the situation.

"The chief of police in St. Louis recently called the leaders of the two north end gangs together to negotiate a truce," Carl said. "The Egan and

Hogan gangs had been fighting a bloody war of attrition the past few months. No one really cared when bad guys killed each other, but then a few innocent civilians started g'tting' caught in the crossfire. The gangs agreed to the treaty mainly because a large contingent of Mafia members from Sicily has been movin' in to take over the city. They called themselves the Green Dagoes and don't have much respect for the American-born Italians, much less Irish gangsters. I predict a showdown is comin', and I don't think neither the Egans or the Hoganites will be interested in a prolonged fight with the combined Shelton and Birger Gangs."

"Sounds pretty smart, Big Carl," Art said. "I just hope this kid in the backseat don't shit his pants and shoot me by mistake."

"I won't, Mr. Newman," a voice said from behind them. "I'm pretty handy with weaponry."

In the backseat was a scared young St. Louis thug named Frank Wortman. What Carl hadn't told Charlie was that he had also enlisted the help of a group of hired assassins from southern St. Louis called the Cuckoo Gang. These musclemen were always available to the highest bidder and served as guards for the Sheltons' stills and the trucks that hauled bootleg liquor. Frank was a fledgling member of that gang, so Carl gave him an easy assignment. When the cars approached, they would block the road with his car and raise the hood. Frank would slouch down in the back and only raise up with his shotgun if shooting started.

The plan seemed flawless until they saw Earl a half mile down the road frantically waving both the white and the red flags.

"What the hell does that mean?" Bernie shouted to Carl.

"It's better to be ready than to not." Carl shouted. "Get your men hidden."

Carl pulled his Ford into position, blocking the road. He got out and popped the hood. When the cars came up over the hill, he saw Earl's dilemma. An old farmer wearing a straw hat was on a Fordson Model F tractor pulling a wide load of hay stacked up four high on a trailer. Behind it followed a caravan of cars, each full of men in suits. The moment the tractor puffed up and stopped, the old farmer appeared to be as formidable a foe as the assassins behind him.

"Get that damned motor car out of my way," the farmer shouted. He leapt down from the tractor with more agility than it appeared a man his age should have. "If I shut off my machine, I'll never get it started again."

Carl ignored the old timer and walked around the hay wagon to where the driver of the first car was getting out to see what the holdup was. No one in the vehicles behind him seemed interested and stayed in the cars.

"Need a hand pushin' your motor car to the side of the road?" the man asked. If he recognized it was a Shelton he addressed, he hid it well.

The old farmer grabbed a hay hook that had been embedded in a bale and started beating at a snake that had poked its head out of the stack. The man's erratic behavior seemed to have drawn the interest of the men in the cars, and several began emerging with drawn weapons.

The tractor backfired. Loudly.

The explosive sound would have triggered a response from less seasoned men, but the gunfighters present didn't recognize the explosion as coming from any artillery they had ever heard.

Frank Wortman, though, was not seasoned. Wanting to please his colleagues, he raised up from the backseat of the car and promptly emptied his weapon into the old farmer's tractor. The machine gave one final loud puff before sputtering to its demise.

While the assassination of the tractor didn't bring about any other gunfire, it did cause Bernie's men to step out from behind trees to see what was going on. Their emergence, in turn, caused the St. Louis thugs to jump back in their vehicles and prepare to do battle.

"What is this, an ambush?" the thug standing before Carl asked. He was an able man with quick, crafty eyes.

"Doesn't have to be," Carl said calmly. To deescalate the tension, he calmly lit a cigar and handed another to the mob leader. The two stood smoking while their respective armies aimed weapons at one another from cover.

"Your boys are pretty disciplined," Carl told the man.

"So are yours. Except that young fella that kilt that tractor."

"He's a city boy. Probably thought he was shooting at an army tank."

"So, what do we do now?"

"Well, since my boys seem to have your boys surrounded—and, it would seem, better armed, why don't you fellas just get on back to the city and deal with them wops from Sicily?"

"You heard about that, huh?"

"Yes, I'd imagine that after you get done dealin' with the Green Dagoes, and after the Shelton and Birger Gangs finish off them Klan fellas in white nightshirts, why, I suppose then we could continue this conversation, if you're so willing."

"Which gang you with, Shelton or Birger?"

Carl extended his hand. "Carl Shelton, at your service."

***

Killing two men in a three-day period made Charlie feel like he was entitled to treat himself to new clothes. The minute he got out of the hospital, he headed for Rathbone and Brown's haberdashery. After picking out a new suit to replace the one Whitey had put a hole in, he inquired about shirts to go with it.

"As a matter of fact, Mr. Birger," Mr. Rathbone said with a wry smile, "we just got these shirts in this morning. And they just happen to be in your size."

Charlie stood admiring the fine silk shirts with the letter C embroidered on the pockets. "How many of these you got?" He asked.

"Six, sir."

"I'll take the lot. Have them delivered to my home in Harrisburg."

After Charlie left the store, the haberdasher owners smiled at each other.

"Do you suppose it occurred strange to him that the pockets were already monogrammed with the letter C?" Mr. Brown asked his partner. "Or that he had just purchased the shirts that were ordered by Cecil Knighton, the very man he so recently killed?"

"From what I know of Mr. Birger," Mr. Rathbone replied. "I believe he would have been all the more intrigued to wear them. Of course, I was not about to share with him that hypothesis."

***

Charlie made one more stop on his way home. He purchased one of the brand-new washing machines that had just come out. He paid extra to have the machine delivered and set up ahead of his arrival. It wasn't that he was trying to please Betty, but rather that her dinner preparation had been lacking due to all the clothes that he and the girls went through each day. One of Charlie's requirements of his wife was that when he came home, he wanted her and his daughters looking like princesses. Since Betty never knew when her husband might arrive, she spent all day long putting new clothes on the girls every time they got dirty. She blamed the Montgomery Ward catalogue for giving Charlie the idea that a family should look well-groomed at all times.

When he finally got home that evening, Betty had her third load in the washing machine, but in her excitement had forgotten to take the roast out of the oven. Charlie was in too good a mood to be angry, so he took his women out to eat.

A week later, his new friends, Earl and Bernie Shelton, stopped by, and he proudly showed them the washing machine.

"By God, Charlie," Earl exclaimed. "Do you know what you got here?"

"Sure, I do, Earl. I got more time for my wife to cook, and she ain't so tired when I need pleasured."

"Bernie," Earl said to his brother, "fetch some of the distilled water and alcohol out of the motor car. Charlie, you burn me some brown sugar in your fireplace."

"What are you up to, Earl?" Charlie asked as he took the last of his wife's brown sugar from the cupboard.

"I'm fixin' to make us a few hundred dollars—the easy way."

All that night, while her husband and his friends drank and played cards at the dinner table, Betty fumed in her bedroom while listening to her brand-new washing machine mixing distilled water and one-hundred-ninety proof alcohol. Come morning, the gangsters decided that the machine did its job cutting the liquor as efficiently as it had cleaned clothes. Within a week, a dozen washing machines were purchased by bootleggers throughout Little Egypt. Betty's cooking suffered again, but now Charlie didn't seem to mind.

9

In the days leading up to Christmas, Glenn was still torturing himself over his conversation with Madge. Sharing the discussion with anyone—including his wife—seemed out of the question. He wasn't certain he had acted honorably by not sticking up for the pretty young lady. What could he have done anyway? Madge was a beautiful woman, and even he had struggled to not stare at her comely shape. He had left the office door open during her visit so anyone passing through the hall would not think ill of the man and woman alone in a closed room.

Glenn loved his wife Maude with all his heart. The recent birth of their first child had made his life complete, especially now that his first wife had agreed to allow their twin daughters to stay with him for part of the year. His future was just beginning to resemble the stable environment his own father had provided him during his childhood in Western Kansas. Now, this woman, Madge Oberholtzer, who in truth might be jaded herself, had brought him a trouble that was not his nor was a type for which he was accustomed.

Glenn, Maude and baby Bobbie had just finished dinner that night. A hard knock pounded at the front entrance.

Glenn knew the knock, so he rose from the table, walked past the elaborately decorated Christmas tree, and opened the door.

"The raiding party is ready, brother Kleagle," Caesar Cagle said.

Glenn glanced back to the kitchen. Maude was cleaning up. Her eyes were watery, but since they appeared sorrowful and not angry, he picked up his boots and retrieved his hat, jacket and gloves from the closet.

"I'll be back before dawn," he reassured her.

Maude watched her husband leave, then went back to her chores. Having grown up with a father who was a U.S. Marshal, she was accustomed to the man of the house taking off on dangerous missions at all hours of the night. Still, Glenn was her whole life, and she couldn't imagine what she would do without him. She had heard stories that he beat his first wife, which was why she divorced him. Maude couldn't imagine that was true. Her husband treated her better than she deserved. She wasn't a great cook. On the several occasions she ruined a meal, Glenn simply laughed and told her it was still better than the hard tack and dried biscuits he ate when he was chasing down draft dodgers in the mountains out East during the war.

When she couldn't get young Bobbie to quit crying when he had croup, Glenn gently took him from her and walked back and forth across the room while encouraging her to go back to sleep.

The only fault she had yet to see in her husband was the fact that he liked to tell of his numerous adventures as a Texas Ranger and then later as a government man with the Treasury Department. His stories always began with a quiet modesty that escalated quickly into incredibly exciting tales of bloody gunfights with desperadoes. Those bravado stories were reserved, though, for his fellow crimefighters. When Glenn and Maude were alone and cuddling in bed or in front of a fireplace, he would proudly relate to her the times he had reformed incorrigible criminals, sometimes through conversion to Jesus Christ, and other times, as in the case of draft dodgers, by simply sharing with them the importance of America's fight for freedom overseas.

Now, due largely to his previous successes, Glenn was asked to lead a group of men in an endeavor that he felt passionately about. His own mother had been a prohibitionist long before it became law. She and his father had raised their son to believe that the law, even if they didn't always agree with it, was better than no law at all.

Glenn was not totally against the consumption of alcohol. He and Maude imbibed in an occasional glass of spirits. What he was against was the open defiance of the laws of the America he so loved. He had also seen far too many men—and even some women—whose excessive use of alcohol made them abusive and sometimes violent.

After the fiasco in East St. Louis, Glenn realized his next excursion needed to be well planned. Christmas time was a time of good tidings, and holiday cheers would not be complete to lovers of alcohol, especially Catholics, if it didn't involve spirits.

***

Five hundred men were crowded into the grand ballroom at Odd Fellows Hall in Carbondale when Glenn arrived. He moved quickly to the stage that had been set up in the front of the room and stood beside three other federal agents brought in from Chicago and Pittsburgh. The crowd grew quiet, and he got right to the point.

"Some of you may be sent home to your wives as a Christmas present, in a box!" Glenn shouted. "Are you ready?"

A tremendous cheer went up.

The district federal officer stepped to the front of the stage. The crowd instantly became quiet. When the officer raised his right hand, every man in the room did the same. The swearing in ceremony to be temporary federal agents ended with a solemn "I do" that echoed through the room.

As the men broke into groups of five and picked up their search warrants, Glenn stood at the door to give them last-minute reminders as they parted.

"Park down the road from the target, approach with stealth, cover all doors and windows, and then, with guns drawn, demand entrance in the name of the federal government."

He was worried. Though he had been in on the interviews these past months, he could not conceive that five hundred men could go for several weeks without leaking word of the raid.

"These are honorable men, Glenn," Caesar Cagle said as if reading his mind.

"I'm just more comfortable doing for myself." Glenn was still troubled by Maude's sorrow-filled eyes and Madge's condemnation of his gallantry.

"Bet you wish you had ol' Pal with you," Caesar said. He'd heard plenty of stories about the Russian Wolf Hound that Glenn had grown so fond of during his days chasing draft dodgers in the mountains. The animal had survived German mustard gas during the Great War and lived long enough to help Glenn roust many a lawbreaker.

"Did I ever tell you the time I put a circle in the dirt around eight prisoners and told Pal to keep them there until I returned?" Glenn smiled every time he repeated the story. "When I came back twenty minutes later, all eight men were just sitting in that circle with Pal watching over 'em."

"These men won't let you down tonight either, Glenn." Caesar said. "They are all God-fearing Protestants—farmers, store keeps and many of America's best Klansmen. I would bet my life not a one of them leaked a word of tonight's raid."

***

Dalta Shelton refused to run with his brothers when it came to gang activities—but that didn't mean he objected to bartending for Earl. To Dalta, Earl was just about the right mix between Carl's business head and Bernie's cold-blooded brutality. "If Earl threw a nickel into the air, it would come down a quarter," Dalta always told customers as he wiped the bar. "And he wouldn't have to kill nobody to do it, neither."

Earl's roadhouse was an environment Dalta could enjoy. The spacious two-story building provided room upstairs for whoring, as well as private gambling. The downstairs had a nice little bandstand in the corner where musicians performed Earl's favorite bluegrass numbers without fear of being knocked into by the many drunks that stumbled around the dancefloor. If things got hot, Dalta just backed into the kitchen and barred the door with a two by four—where he could watch the shenanigans through a little peephole in the wall.

That's exactly what he did on the night of December 22 when Glenn Young and a large group of armed men burst through the front door. Dalta had the door barred and arrived at his peephole just in time to see Caesar Cagle backhand Earl with a hog leg.

"This here's a raid!" Glenn shouted. "You're all under arrest for gamblin' and violation of the Volstead Act." He grabbed Earl by the front of his jacket. "Who are you Sheltons paying off so you can run these joints? Is it Galligan?"

"I'll give you to the count of three to tell us," Caesar shouted at Earl. "Then I'm gonna put your lights out. One, two—" Caesar pistol-whipped Earl's head. He never got to three.

Caesar kicked Earl. Dalta was tempted to run to his brother's defense, but Glenn intervened first by firing two shots into the ceiling.

"You ain't got no authority to do this," Dalta's sister Lula shouted from somewhere in the room. "You ain't no duly-appointed lawman."

"I'm acting on the authority of a vigilante committee that demands law and order in Little Egypt," Glenn said. "Now, hand over all your weapons and money, and get in the paddy wagon outside. Anyone trying to flee will be shot dead on the spot."

Klansmen used their rifles to push patrons out the front door. Then they turned back into the saloon area and helped themselves to any money or liquor they could find. Others smashed roulette and dice tables, as well as barrels of liquor that were too big to confiscate.

One Klansman grabbed Lula by the arm and pulled her back into the corner where the band had been playing. Dalta again was inspired to rush to the rescue of a sibling, but it was Caesar Cagle who intervened this time. With a sickening crack of his rifle on the back of the head, he dropped the would-be molester.

"Don't forget to tell Earl it was me that saved you, Lulabelle," Caesar said.

"So, you just figured out that Earl survived your beatin' and is fixin' to kill ya, didn't ya, Cagle?" Lula laughed. Dalta had always hated his sister's loud, witch-like laugh, but on this occasion, he appreciated it.

"Et tu, Caesar, you son-of-a-bitch," Lula added. She gave her witchy laugh as she slung a feathery scarf over her shoulder and walked through the doorway.

***

An hour later, Glenn and Caesar knocked at the door to an old farmhouse. They had left most of their fellow vigilantes to take the prisoners to Benton in the paddy wagon.

"Could we trouble you for a drink, my friend?" Glenn asked, then added the password he had been given by an informant at the Shelton Roadhouse. "We come in peace."

"Aw, come in, lads," the farmer said. "Never be it said an Irishman was inhospitable." The accommodating host poured the strangers a tall glass of whiskey. "Dis' wee drink will make a mouse feel big enough to take on an elephant. Now drink hearty. There's many a slip twixt the cup and the lip."

"That's enough. Stick 'em up," Glenn ordered.

Caesar rushed to the door and swung it open. A half dozen hooded Klansmen entered and, using sledgehammers, smashed everything in sight.

"Ah, the ingratitude of me fellow man," the farmer said as he watched his still being destroyed. "Love's labor's lost."

Caesar smashed his fist into the Irish farmer's face.

***

The wide, snow-covered streets of Benton had bright lights of red, green, and gold, and Christmas trees at every corner. Holly with big wooden candy canes through them adorned the sidewalks. Despite the lateness of the hour, the stores were open for last-minute shoppers. Children freshly emancipated from school joined their parents in search of perfect Christmas gifts, their faces aglow with the love of the season.

Then came a sight never before seen on the streets of Benton, Illinois. Over one hundred prisoners shuffled along, many of their faces swollen and bleeding. To make the scene even more bizarre, several of the duly sworn deputies carried machine guns.

Glenn was so proud of the evening raid, he took the procession twice around the town square before stopping at an entrance and allowing the prisoners to be escorted into the courthouse for arraignment. This provided time for nearly everyone in town to line the streets to watch the spectacle.

Since Earl Shelton was the first prisoner to enter the courthouse to be arraigned, he was also the first one to post bail and walk back through the crowd. Lula and Hazel waited for him in an automobile. They quickly returned him to their parents' home in Fairfield, where Carl was anxious to get a report of the raid.

"The Klan stole about seven hundred dollars," Earl testified while holding a beefsteak to his swollen eye, "and smashed some of the liquor barrels."

"Some of it?" Carl asked.

"They didn't turn in about twenty gallons of the whiskey to the state's attorney," Earl answered, then added, "And so far as I know, none of the money."

"They did a pretty good job smashin' your mug, too," Bernie joked.

"Caesar Cagle will pay for this," Earl said, rubbing his swollen jaw. "You can take that to the bank."

***

Three days later, Earl, the old Irishman, and several other plaintiffs were in the Williamson County Courtroom, many of their faces still an ugly mess. The trial had been swift and one sided. The Klan attorneys barely offered a defense.

The closing arguments were made and the jury instructions given. Glenn Young and Caesar Cagle were among those who rose from the defendants' chairs. Several Klansmen noisily entered through the double doorway and stood in back of the room, carrying a big machine gun used in raids. They stared coldly at the jury.

The faces of all twelve men turned pale at the same time, as did that of the judge. The last of the jurymen had no sooner entered the deliberation room and shut the door than it opened again and the twelve men filed out. The foreman struggled to keep his hands from shaking as he read, "On the charge of assault, we find the defendants not guilty!"

10

The howling of the stray dog next to the pigpen was almost as loud as the squealing of the young shoats. Earl found castrating hogs no more vexing than any other farm work. Bernie would grab a piglet by the hind legs while Earl sliced, squeezed the testicles out, snipped them, and threw the Rocky Mountain oysters in a water bucket for Ma Shelton to sell. No one in their family particularly enjoyed eating hog nuts, but they had plenty of neighbors who considered them a delicacy when properly pan fried. Even though her sons were bringing in more money than she and Ben had ever imagined, Ma was never above making an extra buck.

The boys hadn't told their ma where they got the cash they so boldly flaunted, and she never asked. Pa and others tried to inform on her sons, but Ma would have nothing to do with such talk. She believed in her boys despite the fact that her Carl was paying a barber to shave him twice a day while pretty manicurists filed his fingernails. She would never believe that her young'uns were anything but the good Methodist boys she had raised.

Carl enjoyed being the big man in Fairfield and dressed to impress. When he got to his farm, though, he was not above donning a pair of bib overhauls and jumping right into most any farm work that needed done—all the while knowing the manicurist could clean the mud or pig shit out of his nails the next day. He'd have looked like any other sod buster, except that he also favored carrying pearl handled, frontier model revolvers on his hips.

The howling of the dog was getting on his nerves, so he pulled one of his sidearms and aimed it at the noisy mutt.

"Carl!" Earl yelled when he spotted his big brother about to commit the execution. "Leave that critter alone. He ain't hurtin' nobody."

"Aw, I ain't got the heart to really shoot him." Carl laughed.

Earl fancied a .48 caliber revolver, but he was not one to take on airs other than with his weaponry. He also was an animal lover, taking his dog Duke everywhere he went. While he loved his expensive motor cars, he was never against transporting goats or calves in the backseat. Practically a veterinarian, Earl could do everything from vaccines to handling an animal's breach birth—or, when necessary, even a caesarian.

Bernie unloaded a castrated piglet into a separate holding pen where the little patient immediately slid its crotch along the ground in an attempt to remove the sting. Carl holstered his pistol and made for the horse barn. He, like Bernie, preferred horses to what they considered the lesser livestock, the most objectionable being pigs.

Earl, though, was able to coax his youngest brother into the tasks Carl was a little squeamish about. In fact, Bernie loved watching Carl flinch when it came time for killing and dressing chickens. The elder brother always turned his back when Ma hooked a yard rake over a hen's neck, then with a quick twist removed the poultry's head. It seemed funny to his siblings that Carl could emotionlessly order the assassination of a man, but get queasy at the preparation for his own supper.

Sister Hazel also was squeamish—she was a reluctant farmer's daughter who preferred fussing over her hair and makeup to butchering a hog alongside Ma and Lula. The latter had a vicious streak nearly as bad as Bernie's—a point Lula emphasized at that very moment by exiting the kitchen door with a shotgun in hand and blasting the barking dog into a hundred pieces.

Not even animal-loving Earl said a word as his little sister marched right back into the house to finish baking bread and pie for dinner.

***

After a hard day's work with the livestock, the brothers retreated to the Shelton Farmer's Clubhouse, a roadhouse on the edge of Herrin. Fear of another raid kept many drinking men at home, so the establishment was void of customers that evening.

"You know," Ora said, "Glenn Young's gonna be feelin' pretty uppity since he got off on that assault charge."

"You want I should kill him, Big Carl?" Bernie asked.

"Not yet," Carl said. "Let's see if Young has the guts to make another move now that Sheriff Galligan is onto him. Ora, there's plenty of Catholics around here who don't like the Klan tellin' 'em they can't gamble or booze. Why don't you get a bunch of 'em together and form an anti-Klan organization?"

"Why, sure. I've been thinkin' about that same thing," Ora said. "When the KKK raid a place, our boys will carry torches and surround then in a big circle, then move in. Them nightshirts will run like the cowards they are. How 'bout callin' our anti-Klan rangers the Knights of the Flaming Circle? We'll be like the minutemen ever time the Klan makes a move."

For the next few days, Ora's minutemen outmaneuvered the Klan at every opportunity. Carl placed spies inside the KKK organization to keep the Knights of the Flaming Circle informed. Bernie found a new use for a set of brass knuckles that he had a blacksmith specially modify for him. He spent a half hour each evening cleaning blood off of and sharpening the little spikes that protruded above the middle fingers.

Then, just after the New Year, word came that the Klan had switched tactics, and for a while would be raiding the hills for moonshiners. Roadhouse traffic immediately picked up.

***

Little George Gregory had always wanted to follow in his father, Big George's, footsteps—first as a coal miner, now as a bootlegger. From the rolling hillocks of Pope County, they could look out over the wide, winding Ohio Valley into Kentucky. The river here hurried to its destination in joining the great Mississippi waters, making even a sturdy rowboat hazardous in the spring. Young George loved his life of hunting, fishing, and especially gathering morel mushrooms in the spring. Evenings were spent sipping the "white mule" liquor that had made the family more money than laboring in the dusty, dangerous coal mines.

The day his father gave him permission to hit his mother seemed to be Little George's right-of-passage into manhood.

"Now, George, do what you said you'd do too her," the father shouted one day when the two arrived at their shanty house in an extreme condition of inebriation.

"You oughtn't to have informed on us to them revenuers, Ma," Little George growled. He grabbed his mother's neck with his left hand.

"I thought he was just a painter!" Mrs. Gregory said. "I didn't know he was no revenuer!"

Her son's first blow shattered an eardrum. When she protected her head by grasping her hair, Little George attacked her exposed areas by pistol whipping her with his .45 caliber revolver. Since his father was busy laughing and guzzling from a brown jug, the beating continued until the young man's arms tired.

In the woods behind the house, Glenn Young and three law enforcement officers hid in waiting. Glenn was tempted to rush in to save the woman, but one of his deputies steadied him with a hand to his shoulder. The guilt of doing nothing about D.C. Stephenson harassing Madge Oberholtzer still haunted him. A father inspiring such brutality toward his son's own mother incensed him.

The two men finally stepped out on the back porch, and were so heavily armed, Glenn was thankful his colleague had restrained him. He signaled for two of his men to circle around and enter the house from the front.

No sooner were they in position than a pickup entered the lane and drove up to where the father and son unloaded barrels from a wagon. A scruffily dressed but attractive young woman stepped out of the truck, approached Little George, and tried to put her arms around him. When the young man pushed her to the ground, she shook her fist at him and went into the house. Her muffled cries from inside were heard throughout the area. Glenn's men had taken her prisoner. He was suddenly overcome with impulsiveness.

"Stick 'em up, boys!" Glenn shouted as he stepped out from behind the tree. "You're under arrest."

George Sr. turned and fired, the bullet splintering bark on the tree beside him.

"Don't try it!" Glenn warned, but when the father fired another shot that buzzed by his ear, he drew both pistols and put two shots through his heart.

George Jr. had ducked behind the girl's truck. The young man fired two rounds through the windows at the lawmen, breaking glass with each shot. Glenn used the windows as his target, emptying both weapons. With a shrill cry of anguish, the boy dropped to the ground.

A loud scream came from the shanty house doorway. A bloody Mrs. Gregory crawled out of the house toward her son.

Glenn rushed to her and helped her get to the dying youngster.

"Ma," Little George gasped as blood squirted between his lips. "Pa told me to beat you, don't you know?"

"I know, son. But you gave me a towel when you was through, so I knew you still loved me."

Little George smiled at his mother. The death rattle came and then gurgled slowly into nothingness.

11

It seemed every day Ora's eyes grew darker from worry and lack of rest. His mind constantly raced with thoughts, especially at night. It became so bad he tried to sleep in his favorite cushioned chair and with all the lights on. It wasn't just the Herrin massacre that haunted him, although that was a big part of it. He had been friends with the Shelton brothers for quite some time. He was glad they were getting along with Charlie Birger, because he also felt an attraction to him. Then there was Sheriff Galligan who, though shady himself, represented respectability and stability. Ora liked being his part time deputy, even though it sometimes required him to turn his head to the goings-on of his Shelton and Birger friends. He also hoped that wearing a badge would somehow stifle the urge he had to kill again—an urge that was most prevalent when he thought about Glenn Young. That hate was intensified by Young's leadership of the Ku Klux Klan movement, especially since Ora had been one of those arrested in a raid. He thought he would never forget the humiliation of being pulled out of a roadhouse and paraded down Benton's Main Street to be charged like a common thief. Since that day, he wore his deputy sheriff badge everywhere he went. That was why he was proud to be part of the anti-Klan, Knights of the Flaming Circle.

The anti-Klan rally at the Rome Club Hall in Herrin on February eighth was supposed to just be a meeting to plan how to stifle the Kluxer raids, which had recently started up again. Ora sensed trouble when more than eighty well-armed men crowded into the hall.

"Go tell Sheriff Galligan he'd better get down here, quick," Ora told another deputy named John Layman.

"What can Galligan do?" Layman asked. Being one of the most extreme Klan haters in the county, he was hoping for trouble.

"Just having the presence of the law may help keep these folks from acting stupid," Ora said sternly. "Now go!"

Layman wasn't normally a man who could be told what to do, but Ora's dark eyes and angry glare sent him rushing out the door. In the meantime, Bernie Shelton stirred up the anti-Klansmen into a mob mentality. Jack Skelcher and Charlie Briggs, senior members of the Shelton gang, spread out in the room, pouring drinks and encouraging discontent. The Rome Club Hall was nearly at a lynch-mob point-of-no-return when Sheriff Galligan and Deputy Laymen entered through the doorway. The crowd slowly regained a little sense of civility. Men stopped shouting and looked toward the man with the badge. For a moment, Ora thought a repeat of the Herrin killing had been averted.

"You fellas better calm down a little," Galligan said, "or you'll have Police Chief Ford to deal with instead of me."

"John Ford is too clever by half," Layman added. "He's even one of the Klan's high priests."

"Speak of the devil!" Carl shouted, pointing out the window. "Here comes Police Chief Ford now. And he's got his idiot, Deputy Crain, with him."

Ora's heart beat wildly again. Ford and Crain strutted into the room like they owned it. He tried to blink away the struggle his mind fought between lawfulness and homicide.

"You boys hunting elephants tonight?" Ford asked, his lip not hiding a sneer. "Ya got enough weaponry to kill a whole herd."

"Why, Chief," Bernie said, "that ain't none of your damned business."

Carl gave Bernie a nod. Instantly, the youngest Shelton grabbed Ford's arms from behind, and Ora, in an attempt to stop a slaughter, disarmed him. Earl and Layman did the same with Harold Crain.

"No need for that, Carl," Galligan said.

The room became chaotic—men pushing and yelling angry epitaphs. Ora's eyes scanned the room, recognizing facial expressions that brought back horrible memories.

"Get your hand away from that side arm, Layman!" Crain shouted.

"What?" Layman asked, his eyebrows wrinkled with confusion.

Like lions to the slaughter, anti-Klansmen shouted and leapt at Ford and Crain, dozens pushing toward them in an attempt to deliver blows to the policemen's heads.

A single gunshot exploded.

Deputy John Layman dropped like a wet cloth to the ground. Instantly, everyone stopped moving and the room turned eerily quiet.

"That damned Ford shot me," Layman gasped from where he lay on the floor.

"But," Ora held up a revolver, "I got his weapon here."

Before anyone could say anything more, Sheriff Galligan raised his badge in one hand and his revolver in the other. "I'm arresting Police Chief Ford and Deputy Crain," he announced. "You men step aside so I can take them outa here."

The anti-Klansmen grumbled but gave the sheriff and his prisoners room to exit.

"You can't arrest me in my own town," Ford protested when they reached the doorway.

"Would you rather be lynched?" Galligan asked in his ear.

When they were gone, Carl Shelton stood on the second step of the stairway. "Take John to the hospital before he bleeds to death."

Two men helped Layman out of the building.

Ora felt himself losing control, his mind going dark and squeezing all rational thoughts from his brain. The gunshot and the blood at his feet had triggered something that at the moment he couldn't—nor did he want to—explain or even understand. Only one thing could relieve the pressure he felt.

"I'm gonna go kill Glenn Young," Ora announced, his left eye twitching uncontrollably. "Who's with me?"

Shouting their approval, eighty men followed Ora and the Shelton brothers out of the building. On the street, citizens rushed to get away from the angry hoard. Children filled with the invincibleness of youth were roughly grabbed by their collars and dragged into the safety of buildings. Automobiles hastily spun into turnabouts in the middle of the streets.

The three Shelton brothers stepped in front of Ora and assumed command of the mob. Familiar with his role as a lieutenant, he automatically fell in line. That was when he recognized that it was all happening again. Gloom overwhelmed him. *It's going to be another massacre.* His eye twitched. His right hand shook so badly, he stuck it in his pocket. The coat pocket felt so big and empty, he pulled his hand back out, drew his revolver from the shoulder holster, and stuffed the weapon in his pocket. Now, with his fingers embracing the gun, his hand quit shaking.

The mob marched several blocks away from the business district. It was a dark, moonless night, making even trees and bushes mere shadows on those roads without streetlamps. Ora feared ambush, but wasn't certain which side of an ambush his anti-Klansmen would be on. The dark silhouette of a lone man approaching them half a block away materialized.

"Here's Caesar Cagle!" Bernie shouted.

Some of the youngest and fastest members of their group quickly intercepted the Klan leader. Cagle seemed remarkably composed, considering he was surrounded by a throng of men who hated him.

"We have a thousand Klansmen coming," Cagle gloated. "My son told me you low-life scumbags were marching. Let's see if you have the guts to stick around when Glenn Young gets here."

"Stick 'em up, you dirty louse," Earl ordered.

Cagle immediately raised his hands high above his head.

"Oops, too late." Earl put his pistol in Cagle's chest and pulled the trigger.

Before the echoes from the blast had subsided, the eighty men fled in every direction. Cagle lay bleeding on the dark and empty sidewalk.

Ora felt cheated. He should've been the one to kill Cagle, but he had hesitated, while Earl hadn't. Now, it was guilt that sent him running in the direction of the Herrin Hospital, where John Laymen fought for his life. It had been he who had sent Layman to get Galligan. When he got to Main Street, he found that the sound of Earl's gunshot had emptied the streets, so he had time to think as he ran. *No more hesitation! Next time, draw and fire! Don't pass the responsibility to anyone else! If anyone is going to die, let it be me.*

***

Twenty minutes later, one thousand Klansmen shouted and waved weapons as they gathered around Glenn Young on Herrin's Main Street. He raised his Enfield rifle to obtain quiet.

"They just killed Caesar Cagle," Glenn announced. "Block the roads into town. Don't let nobody in unless they know the password."

Several Klansmen scattered. Glenn smiled at the efficiency. It had been Caesar who had organized their militia to react to just such an emergency. That realization caused his smile to turn to an angry sneer.

"Chief Ford had to shoot John Layman when the Shelton gang attacked him," Glenn shouted in a slightly broken voice to those who remained. "Layman's in the hospital with several gang members protecting him. We need to arrest them before they kill someone else."

The crowd shouted approval. Glenn led his army toward the hospital.

***

Ora Thomas and the Shelton brothers stood at the examination table in the emergency room. A bespectacled Dr. J.T. Black leaned over Layman, and, with shaky hands, dressed his wound. When he finally straightened up, his face was as white as that of his patient and his glasses almost fogged over. He removed them and wiped them on a bloody piece of gauze. When he returned them to his face, he was too tense to notice the red tint of the room around him. The fact that he had done the bullet extraction while his patient garnished an automatic revolver in his right hand had made the entire operation one to tell his grandchildren. That is, if he survived the night.

"The Klan has taken over the whole town," Carl announced after conferring with a hospital employee. "They've set up roadblocks and won't let anyone into Herrin unless they know the Klan password. Galligan asked the governor to send the state militia. Even if they do come, it won't be until morning."

"Earl, why'd you have to go and shoot Cagle?" Layman asked. He tried to raise his head, but immediately fell back.

"I didn't mean to," Earl declared. "I was just funnin' him, and the gun went off, I guess."

"Earl was just a bit touched, I'd 'spect." Carl said. "Havin' his head kicked in by Cagle musta left him wobbly."

"Once a bullet is fired, you can't never bring it back," Bernie said. He'd been anxious to share that bit of advice since it had been told to him so many times in the past.

The shouting of over a thousand Klan members approaching the hospital gave Layman the adrenalin to sit up from the examination table and raise his service revolver.

The old doctor took short, shuffling steps over to the doorway, cracked it open, and feebly shouted to the men gathered outside, "A hospital is not the place for these goin' ons."

"Send the Shelton gang out!" Glenn shouted back. "We are arresting them for the murder of Caesar Cagle!"

Bernie put the barrel of a shotgun to the doctor's head.

"You can't come in without a warrant," The doctor squawked. His effort at a stronger voice nearly caused him to collapse, but Ora quickly wrapped one arm around the doctor's waist and dragged him away from the door.

"Here's my warrant." Glenn raised his gun and fired into the glass window of the entry. Bullets from hundreds of Klansmen immediately followed.

Nurses, doctors and patients dove for cover. The Shelton gang returned fire.

The Klan scattered through the street, seeking protection. Neither side seemed anxious to take a bullet. For the next two hours, they fired blindly from behind protection rather than expose a vital body part.

A young boy on the second floor had just had his appendix removed earlier that day. His mother threw her body across her son to protect him from the flying glass.

Finally, around dawn, the state militia marched onto the scene, only to find the Klan had exited the battlefield, leaving hundreds of bullet holes in their wake. Though there were many wounded, the youngster on the second floor was the only casualty. Whether it had been because of the operation or from fear during the battle, his heart had simply stopped beating.

***

"Franklin Cagle may be the youngest member of the Ku Klux Klan in all the United States," Glenn

Young whispered proudly to his wife, Maude. They had just taken their seats in the crowded First Baptist church of Herrin. Thousands of Protestant citizens lined the streets outside, waiting for the procession to the Oakwood Cemetery in Carterville six miles away.

Maude didn't add her thoughts. Seeing the large blanket of white flowers with a KKK inscription in green and a fiery cross of red roses adorning Caesar Cagle's casket worried her. Having grown up with a law enforcement father, she had learned to overcome the fear of his not coming home. Now she had to learn to cope with a similar dread concerning her husband. Little Franklin Cagle standing bravely at attention beside his father's casket brought on a nightmarish premonition of her own little Bobbie doing the same for Glenn.

"I'm glad the Klan didn't wear their regalia," Maude said for lack of any other relevant words.

"No sense inciting confrontation," Glenn said. "Caesar's family deserves a few days mournin' before we cut loose again. We are fixin' to bury his Klan robe and hood alongside him, though."

Following the service, Glenn and Maude walked to their Lincoln.

Major General Millard Freeman of the state militia approached him. "I've got seventeen hundred militia under my command," Freeman warned without even a how-do-you-do. "I'm in charge of this town, Young."

"And I've got five thousand Klansmen," Glenn said, opening the car door for Maude. "The coroner's jury says that Cagle was killed by either Carl or Earl Shelton. There will be no peace until the Sheltons are tried and hanged."

"Where are these notorious Sheltons?" Freeman asked.

"Them cowards ain't been seen since the murder," Glenn said. "I'd 'spect we'll find 'em in a snake hole someplace."

***

"Stick 'em up," Carl shouted while brandishing his Tommy gun. "We're the Shelton Gang, and this is a holdup."

Despite it being early evening, the northern Florida juke joint was hopping. Dozens of Negroes dressed in their best Saturday night apparel filled the room.

Carl turned toward the band leader. "Fellas, play *That Old Gang of Mine* while we relieve this establishment of some of its ill-begotten gains."

The Black musicians nervously struck up a ragtag version of the song, but immediately improved when Carl handed the band leader a generous tip.

The Sheltons, along with Ora Thomas, quickly confiscated loot from the proprietor then tied him to a chair. Sitting down beside him, they ordered drinks all around and enjoyed a barbeque chicken dinner while joking and laughing with the Black band and customers. Bernie and Earl took time to journey to a backroom and partake in a frolic with a few of the dark-skinned ladies before Carl announced it was time for them to take their leave.

Ora came up with the idea to pull the ignition wires on all the vehicles, which he and Bernie quickly accomplished. Many of the patrons of the juke joint, thankful they had been allowed to keep their own money, came outside to help prop the hoods open, then stood out in the roadway waving at the Shelton gang as they sped off in their shiny blue Dodge.

12

Ora was only back in Illinois a day before two state troopers stopped him on a Danville, Illinois, street and arrested him for bootlegging. Since he had already made his delivery of the Jamaican rum he had brought back from Florida, he knew he had been ratted out. In the hoosegow, he learned he wasn't the only one who thought he'd been snitched on.

"They caught me red-handed," Charlie Birger said that night as they lay smoking on hard cots in the Danville jailhouse cell. "That there's a fact. I had about twenty cases in my truck when I came up on the roadblock. I figured that since they was local yokels, they'd let me pass."

"I know," Ora complained. "What's this world comin' to when even a lawman begrudges a man a drink?"

"What I can't figure is that nobody knew I was bringing that hooch down them country roads." Charlie blew a magnificent smoke ring that floated softly all the way to the ceiling.

Ora always envied Charlie's ability to make smoke look like white-walled tires. He took a deep puff and tried to exhale so it would be released all around his tongue at the same time. His cell-mate snickered when a bluish-gray mist rose from Ora's mouth in the shape of nothing. Charlie wore a tight BVD shirt. The gangster's dark muscles on his arms and his flat stomach made it difficult for Ora to concentrate on the topic at hand, much less how to blow fancy smoke rings. He looked down at his own arms that seemed like nothing more than skin on bone.

"Why, who would snitch on you, Charlie?" Ora asked, looking back at the ceiling.

"Probably Carl Shelton so he could crawfish around with my gal, I'd suspect."

"You mean Helen Holbrook?" Ora sat up and leaned on an elbow facing Charlie. His eyes were again drawn enviously to the man's arms. "Why, that gal's been with every gangster from Cairo to Chicago and then some. She's just naturally attracted to bad boys, Charlie. You know that."

"That don't matter. Shelton's got no right to move in on my territory. I don't mess with Fairfield, and he needs to stay away from Harrisburg. That goes for broads, too."

"Helen's a she-devil!" Ora laughed. "She may be warm enough to live, but she's sure cold enough to kill a man."

"She sure enough likes dead men." Charlie laughed. "I took her to see those fellas laid out in the warehouse after the Herrin massacre. She musta stood there and stared at them corpses for an hour."

"You think she'd kill a man?" Ora asked. He shivered when he thought about the many times he'd been alone in a room with the Shawneetown dame.

"Nah," Charlie said after several moments of contemplation. "She'd just make him wish he was dead."

***

No woman tried harder to please Carl than Helen Holbrook, both in bed and elsewhere. The trouble was, Carl really didn't care what happened elsewhere, and Helen never seemed to understand that. When he was done with her, he preferred to go home to his wife and children. It wasn't that he loved his wife, but he did like her cooking—as well as the fact that she left him alone when he asked her to. Margaret liked to garden and even sew, especially when the other ladies put on a quilting bee.

Helen, though, was a clinger. She wanted to be on Carl's arm when he was out in public as well as beside him when he was doing his plotting of auto thefts and bootleg smuggling. He tried to get Helen to take a trip with Bernie down to the Bahamas to buy bootleg liquor, but she didn't like the idea of being alone with the youngest Shelton. Bernie was a masher—and not a quiet one like Carl.

"Why don't you divorce Margaret and marry Helen, Carl?" Bernie asked when his big brother suggested he take Helen on the Bahamas trip. "She's got more money than any of us."

"The only good thing about being married to a rich gal," Carl answered, "is you eat steak and lobster while they make you miserable. Kind a like a last meal before they hang you."

That was why Carl arranged with Sheriff Galligan to have Charlie Birger caught with the goods near Danville. Carl needed more time to dump Helen on another gangster, since gangsters were the only ones she seemed enamored by. He had even introduced her to some thugs from Chicago.

"Those boys from Chicago are small time," Helen said. "And ain't none of them going to amount to a hill of beans."

"What about that fella in the white straw hat?" Carl asked her. "He seemed mighty ambitious."

"That fat little Italian?" Helen pouted. "Why would I want a runt like Scarface Capone when I can have a tall drink of water like Carl Shelton?"

Since Carl had just returned from several days supervising a backwoods still operation, he wasn't feeling very tolerant. Helen sensed he needed some coaxing.

"I think I got somethin'." Helen moved closer.

"Well, don't give it to me," Carl said.

"I'm wantin' to bargain." Helen's voice was now low and breathy.

"From here," Carl said, taking a step backwards, "your bargaining position don't look real good."

"Well, then let's get to bargaining." Helen reached behind her back. Her dress fell to the floor.

The sight of the Shawneetown dame's flesh helped Carl remember there hadn't been any women near those backwoods stills either.

"I guess I'll call your bluff." Carl moaned as he ran his hands along her slim waist.

***

Ora's hands shook during his trial. Charlie, on the other hand, was supremely confident he could charm his way out of any trouble that came his way. His businessman-like dress and smug smile were on clear display to the throng of newspaper reporters who lined the Vermillion County Court House. While Ora had remained in jail until the trial, Charlie had been out on bail and enjoying a hotel room with his wife and daughters.

"Mr. Birger, look this way," a photographer shouted. After the camera bulb flashed, he added, "Anyone ever tell you that you look like the actor, Tom Mix?"

"He looks like a piece-of-shit sheep-humper to me," Glenn Young said, stepping in front of Charlie.

Charlie pushed Glenn, and the entire hallway erupted in shouts and more shoving. A dozen tall and husky U.S. Marshals swarmed in from every direction.

"I'm going back to my hotel room," Charlie announced, glaring at Young over the broad shoulders of two marshals. "I left my thirty-eight on my bed."

"You won't be needin' it, Charlie," one of the marshals said. "No weapons are allowed in the courthouse."

"No weapons?" Charlie looked stunned. "How d'you expect a fella to protect hisself?"

Twenty minutes later Glenn Young's father-in-law, George Simcox, testified from the witness stand. "Operating undercover, I was served alcohol by Charlie Birger at Halfway Roadhouse on November seventh, eighth, and fourteenth."

"You stated earlier that you and Mr. Birger have been acquaintances for eight years" the state's attorney asked. "Why didn't he recognize you?"

"I was considerably lighter in weight and didn't have my teeth in."

"Would you object to taking your teeth out, Mr. Simcox, so the jury can see how you look without them?"

"It's rather embarrassing, but I'll do it."

"Objection, your honor," the defense attorney shouted.

"I sincerely hope your objection may be sustained," Simcox said.

"Objection sustained," Judge Lindley said. "I see no good in Mr. Simcox taking out his teeth."

"Thank you, Judge," Simcox wheezed.

Even Charlie joined the rest of the courtroom in the laugh.

***

Judge Walter C. Lindley had sentenced nearly two hundred bootleggers in the first three months of 1924, but when he was ready to pronounce sentence on Charlie Birger and Ora Thomas, he allowed the jury twenty-four hours to get out of town—the reason being that several of Charlie's friends were giving jurors hard looks during the proceedings.

Lindley gave the defendants similar hard looks on their judgment day. Both were exceedingly handsome young men. In fact, the judge's own granddaughter and several of her young friends had attended the proceedings throughout the two-day trial. Lindley himself was getting to old to notice the girls were dressed in their Sunday best, with hair that spent many hours in curlers.

Their stylish hats were tilted low so when they caught the eye of one of the gangsters, they could demurely bat their eyelids.

"I don't know what to do with so-called citizens like you," Judge Lindley said as Charlie took the first turn standing before his bench. "You have money to hire lawyers. You have been defended as ably as any man could be. You've taken the witness stand and perjured yourself. Maybe I can't stop you people from doing these things. I don't know. I am going to give you the limit. I will fine you five hundred dollars on the possession count. Two thousand dollars on the sale count, and send you to jail for one year on the nuisance count." The judge glared at Charlie.

"You are going to jail right now, Mr. Birger. I will give your attorney sixty days to file a bill of exceptions, but you cannot have one minute of delay in starting your sentence."

The judge leaned forward and rested his hands on the bench. "If anything in the world should wake a man up, it should be the possession of the wife and children you have. It is hard for me to deprive wives and children of the support to which they are entitled, but the law is supreme in these matters."

Ignoring—or possibly not hearing the moans from the area of the gallery where his granddaughter and her friends set—the judge continued, "I hereby sentence Ora Thomas to serve four months plus pay five hundred dollars in fines."

Ora saw Glenn Young smirk. The Klan leader placed his hat on his head and gave it a flamboyant tip toward him before he left the courtroom.

***

The following week, back in Herrin, Illinois, a nervous grand jury foreman read their decision to indict. "A reign of terror on February 8, 1924, and succeeding days emulated from actions of oppression and persecution from the so-called Ku Klux Klan. The attack on the hospital was unlawful and without any justification whatsoever, a most amazing display of mob violence. Therefore, we believe there to be sufficient evidence to indict all ninety-nine members of the Ku Klux Klan for the attack on the hospital."

The shouts of disapproval from the gallery nearly resulted in the judge clearing the courtroom. Only a wave of Glenn Young's hand from the defendant's table brought control back.

"Further," the foreman continued, "we, the grand jury, find enough evidence to indict Glenn Young for false imprisonment, kidnapping, assault with attempt to murder, falsely assuming an office, malicious mischief, and parading with arms. He was a usurper, plain and simple, an individual intending along with his cohorts to overthrow the civil authority in Herrin and in Williamson County, seize and imprison the sheriff and mayor, and take upon themselves the task of government without any legal authority whatsoever."

Chaos returned to the courtroom as reporters ran from the room to find telephones so they could be the first to report the story. Glenn stood and turned to Maude, who sat crying in the front row.

The following afternoon, the same jury foreman was just as nervous, but he bravely stood in the same spot and announced, "Caesar Cagle came to his death by gunshot wounds at the hands of one Shelton described as tall and slim, and one Shelton described as heavy-set and sleepy-eyed."

The judge set a trial date for August.

***

Ora's time in the jail in Danville was shorter than Charlie's, but not as comfortable. The Birger money and reputation seemed to have quite a bit of influence with the Vermillion County sheriff. So much so that when Charlie complained the cell was too cold and damp, he was moved to a place in the jailer's quarters. The gangster so charmed the officers, he wasn't even locked up and had the run of the house. When his wife, Betty, and their two young girls came to visit, they stayed with Charlie, even playing games with the deputies who would get down on their knees to give the girls horseback rides.

Despite the homelike setting, things grew sour between the Birger couple. He visited Ora one morning in his cell so he'd have a friend to talk to.

"Betty caught Helen leaving the jailhouse last night," Charlie admitted.

"They let you have your girlfriend in there with you?"

"Why, Ora, truth be told, if I lose enough money playing poker with 'em, them deputies will bring me a gal most every night." Ora's downturned eye lids made Charlie sympathetically add, "I could ask the sheriff to let one of the whores stay a night with you, if you'd like."

"That's not the type of comfort I'm needin' right now, Charlie." Ora averted his eye's when Charlie gave him a perplexed look. Being in jail alongside hardened criminals made him feel insignificant. He was hoping his fellow inmates would treat him with more respect after having the famous Charlie Birger visit him.

"Anyhow, Bea's parents never did approve of me," Charlie continued his lament. "Her ma saw me in a car with a gal once, and she followed me and threw a brick through my windshield. I tried to tell her I was just driving the whore to work at my roadhouse, but she wouldn't hear it. Another time, I said hello to her when I passed her on the street, and she hit me over the head with a brand new clock she had just bought. Yes, sir, I'd sure admire that lady's spunk—if she wasn't so hostile towards me."

Ora still hung his head.

"Say, Ora, I got something else that'll perk you up." Charlie reached in his jacket and pulled out a small case. He opened it to show his friend the hypothermic needle and a small vile. "Morphine," Charlie said. "One of the whores the deputies brought me thought it might help pass the time. She was right."

Ora politely declined the invitation. He only had a week left on his four-month sentence. Besides, he had never cottoned to needles.

***

Betty was scared for her life. She could tolerate her husband's whoring, but she had seen him beat up plenty of people when he got angry. Once he had nearly pistol whipped a young boy to death for a minor mishap. The poor boy was just learning to drive and accidently ran Charlie's car off the road. There was no damage, but her husband was in a foul mood that day already, so he beat the young man until his face looked like mashed potatoes. On another occasion, one of Charlie's prostitutes had brought a message to Betty that her husband wanted her to stop by an old shack where the gangsters played cards. When she knocked on the door, Charlie answered, and grew angry when his wife described the woman who had summoned her. He went back into the building, dragged the prostitute out by her hair, then beat the daylights out of her until some of his friends dragged him off her.

Betty knew that Charlie loved his daughters and would never hurt them. Because of his involvement in the rackets, he would also never be around them much anyway. If their mother disappeared, they would be safe and well taken care of. She knew her husband was having her carefully watched while he was in jail, so she began sneaking clothes out of the house a little at a time, and leaving them in a trunk at her parent's house. Then one moonless night she took what money she could find, then snuck out the backdoor and down the street to where her father awaited in a furniture truck. He drove her to a train station in Eldorado, Illinois. She kissed him on the cheek and boarded the passenger car, content to know that only he knew where she was going.

When Charlie got word that his wife had disappeared, he asked for and was surprised to get permission from Judge Lindley to go home for a week and check on his daughters. The letter he received from Betty said she was going to another country so he wouldn't be able to find her. He doubted she would go that far, but just in case, he brought his daughters back to Danville to stay until his sentence was up.

13

Glenn knew when he married Maude that D.C. Stephenson was jealous. He also knew it wasn't that D.C. wanted to marry Maude himself, but that he didn't get a chance to have a taste of her. It was becoming commonly known throughout the Klan's leadership that Grand Dragon Stephenson's thirst for young women—especially very young girls—was becoming a liability. Many were willing to overlook his quirks as long as they also had a pretty young Klanswoman to disrobe. This was frowned upon by men like Glenn, who were still in the honeymoon of his marriage—even if it was his second.

Glenn had twin daughters that he adored from that previous marriage. Now that he and Maude had added a little boy to the family, he was as content in his homelife as he had been in quite some time. In fact, he hadn't even strayed during the several long months when Maude insisted that they abstain from copulation until after the baby was born.

Stephenson's fixations on the women he considered part of his personal harem was the cause of Glenn's apprehension when the Grand Dragon summoned him to attend the special Klan meeting. He was used to attending regular gatherings, but being summoned to a special one so soon after being indicted by the grand jury had him bristling. Did Stephenson believe he could use that against him when his own life was so full of hypocrisy?

"You fellas think that with Cagle dead you can take charge?" Glenn's voice was lower than he intended in his effort to hide his anger.

"You've been indicted by a grand jury," Stephenson said. "Your strong-arm tactics are making the Klan look bad."

Glenn wanted to tell Stephenson that his own antics with the ladies wasn't doing the Klan reputation much good, either, but he kept his mouth shut.

"We're just askin' you to back off for a while," Klansman John Smith said less harshly. "Lay low."

"I'm not gonna have you fellas making me look bad," Glenn said.

"We'll say we're sending you to St. Louis to clean up the bootleg joints there," Smitty said.

"Pack up my family and leave?" Glenn stiffened.

"You could always leave Maude and the children here," Stephenson suggested. "You know they will be safe with us."

"Would they?" Glenn stared hard at the Grand Dragon. "I think I'll leave the kids here, but I'll take my wife with me—for her protection."

"If you can shut down those speakeasies in East St. Louis," Smitty added encouragingly, "they may elect you governor."

"Sure," Glenn said. "Big Carl thinks he runs the Valley. I'll clean those bastards out over there like I did here, then that'll be the end of the notorious Shelton gang."

***

The Youngs were not at the front of the procession, but they were still the center of attention as Glenn drove his shiny new Lincoln sedan through a gauntlet of applauding well-wishers. The elaborately costumed Ku Klux Klansmen parading through the streets of Herrin, Illinois, was becoming routine. While it always brought out the youngsters, many of the businessmen found it to be a burden for regular shoppers. At the town hall, Glenn stopped the car, stepped out, and held up the bail bond that had been signed by every Klansman in Little Egypt. The two thousand onlookers cheered. Maude sat quietly in the car, smiling at her husband, who stepped up on the running board of their sedan so he could be better seen. She was so proud of her man. To her he was the sweetest, kindest, most loving human on earth.

"It is with a great deal of pride and pleasure that I bid an affectionate farewell to a county that is now free of the dastardly crime and corruption of bootlegging gangsters. I'm off to clean up East Saint Louis like I cleaned up Williamson County."

Glenn waved his hat one more time before settling into the driver's seat. The crowd parted. Many patted the side of the vehicle as Glenn piloted it slowly through the widening wake of humanity.

"If those anti-Klansmen could only recognize these are good God-fearing folks," Glenn said while he steered and waved. "Farmers, bankers, coal miners and just plain old day-laborers—they are the heart of this great country and only want to see the laws enforced."

They finally made it through the crowd and picked up speed as they hit the hard road. With a hint of irritation, Maude moved her husband's weapons from the front seat so she could snuggle next to him.

"Here now, woman," Glenn reprimanded as he allowed her to tuck her head under his arm. "We get attacked by a bear, and we'll be needin' those instruments."

Maude smiled. She ran her hand between his shirt buttons and caressed his hairy chest. The windows were down. The air smelled fresh and clean with just the slightest hint that a spring rain was on its way.

Glenn smelled good too. She wondered why her man always smelled so good while others were so rank. D.C. Stephenson was one of those—always smelling of sweat and stale tobacco. Glenn had saved her from men like that. Now she had a beautiful two-year old son and twin step-daughters she also loved dearly. The girls were ornery as could be—except when around her. Then they were mannerly and helpful, even to the point of assisting her with house duties.

Maude wasn't a talker, a trait that she could tell her husband, like most men, appreciated. After her mother died, she had developed the ability to anticipate her father's needs by his behavior. Since he was a U.S. Marshal, he often set silently in their home solving crimes in his head. Glenn was the same, his mind on outmaneuvering bands of bootleggers, gamblers and racketeers.

Today, though, her husband's mind was on her, and she relished his attention. Contentment covered his handsome face. As it had been with her father, the young couple felt no need for idle conversation. A beautiful spring day lay before them with trees full of life all along the Atlantic-Pacific highway they traveled. When they finally left the blacktop, a wake of dust kicked up behind them from the dirt road, blocking out all the horribleness of bloody Little Egypt.

Glenn's smile told her he also looked forward to a bright future. Then she felt his body tense. The last thing Maude Young ever saw was her husband looking in the rear mirror.

***

"Glenn, Glenn, do you remember what happened?"

Glenn's head hurt. Opening his eyes, everything in the room moved from right to left and downward. He cocked his head the opposite way to get the room to quit spinning. It was like his brain was floating around inside his head. When he recognized a ceiling lamp above him, he forced himself to focus on it. Slowly, everything around the lamp seemed to right itself and finally quit moving.

"What happened?" the voice asked again.

"I had no chance to get my two forty-five caliber automatics or my submachine gun," Glenn muttered. "Maude had set them in the backseat. She was cuddled under my arm. My God, we were so happy. Then, I saw in the mirror, something—coming out of the dust—behind my car. I swerved my machine to the right—nearly drove down the embankment into the river. Maude screamed! I finally reached my machine gun and threw a few blasts at them. A blue Dodge sedan."

Nauseousness overwhelmed Glenn. The room spun again. It seemed only a few moments, but when he opened his eyes again, daylight filtered through the window. A nun passed his doorway.

"What the hell am I doin' in a Catholic hospital?" Glenn shouted. Raising his head, he looked at his bandaged right leg that was suspended from ropes.

"Ah, yes," a doctor smirked. "Ironic that the high cock-o-lorum of the Ku Klux Klan be here, their duly canonized patron saint."

"Get me out of this God-forsaken hell-hole!" Glenn shouted.

"That, sir, would be to our pleasure," the doctor grumbled. "I myself am a Catholic and the son of a saloon keeper."

"Where's my wife?" Glenn asked. "I want to see Maude."

"You may see her, but she won't see you," the doctor said coldly. "Your wife took a full face of buckshot. She will be blind for the rest of her life."

"Ora Thomas fired the shotgun!" Glenn shouted. "I'll kill that bastard!"

"Well, you better hope he comes to you, because you won't be chasing him down. A bullet shattered your leg bone. You'll most likely be limping the rest of your life."

***

Glenn remained a holy terror to the hospital staff the entire day. He was on a different floor from Maude and not allowed to see her because his leg was in traction. His head injury from impact with the windshield made breathing through his nose difficult. He took his frustration out on everyone who came in his room, especially the nurses who were nuns. The worse he treated them, the worse they treated him. He was sound asleep that night when a nurse entered his room.

"I'm Sister Margarete here to take your temperature. Roll over, please."

"Damned Catholics!" Glenn said as he rolled as far over on his side as his suspended leg would allow. He felt a slender prick in his anus and tried to go back to sleep.

"I'll return in just a moment," the nurse said softly. "Don't move, please."

She exited the room, leaving the door open. Glenn fell into a deep sleep, dreaming of burning the Catholic hospital to the ground with Ora Thomas and the Shelton gang inside.

Sometime later, he was awakened by laughter coming from the hallway. Feeling a cold breeze on his rear, he realized his gown was open in the back. When he reached behind him to close it, an object was lodged between the crack of his butt cheeks. Pulling it around in front of his face, he saw it was a short-stemmed rose.

***

Shelton gang members Charlie Briggs and Jack Skelcher had a quiet friendship. They could hunt and fish together all day with barely a word between them. If they were driving down the road, one of them might say, "Let's holdup that fillin' station." Then, other than, "Stick 'em up," and, "Give us your money!" no more words were spoken for another day or so.

They were partners, so when Carl Shelton told them to dispose of the blue Dodge Touring car they had used to ambush Glenn Young, they both knew how they would do it—sell it. The bullet holes in the vehicle would make them conspicuous, so Briggs drove the car that night toward Herrin. They had a friend who owned a garage and would give them a few dollars for it.

When they passed through Carterville around midnight, many armed men lined the streets. About halfway to Herrin, a roadblock waited ahead of them. Several headlights pointed in their direction, and the silhouettes of a dozen men stood facing them.

Skelcher stuck his shotgun out the window on his side and let loose both barrels as his partner tried to steer around the vehicles. The squealing of tires on the hard road was followed by dozens of gunshots and the sound of bullets ricocheting off the front hood or making spider-web looking holes in the windows. Briggs lost control of the car when he bumped it hard into the side of a parked vehicle, and then into a farm truck. The runaway Dodge skidded up the truck's low back end and did a complete rollover into a freshly planted field of corn.

With blood dripping down their faces, both men opened their car doors, staggered away from the vehicle a few steps, and then broke into a run. Briggs was a step behind Skelcher when the top of his friend's head came off in an explosion of blood. A moment later, Briggs' right leg was shot out from under him. He lay on his side looking at Skelcher's dead face while Klan members rushed forward and surrounded him.

14

Maude had never seen the ocean and never would, but she smelled it, and she heard its waves breaking softly on the beach. And the Florida sunshine warmed her face. From the chair close by, her husband's hand extended to hers, gently caressing her fingers as he had each moment they'd been together since the ambush—day and night. The doctors in Atlanta pronounced her blind with no hopes of restoring her sight. Somehow, that didn't matter. Her husband was alive, and though she could hear his shuffling limp and the click of his cane, they were lucky to still have each other and the love of their children.

Sometimes, when Glenn wasn't near, she ran her fingers over her face, feeling the scars left by the shotgun blast. When she asked her husband if they were ugly, he laughed and said they were just adorable dimples that made her all the more beautiful. Their lovemaking had not suffered. He was more tender than ever; each touch of his body on hers brought sensations of love and pleasure as she had never before felt.

Her hearing was so much more acute as she used it to accommodate for her lack of sight. The phone call at noon had not been meant for her ears, but even with the bedroom door closed, she understood the one-sided conversation. It helped, too, that Glenn's anger prevented him from being able to contain the volume of his whispers. The Caesar Cagle murder case against the Shelton brothers had been dropped because witnesses had failed to show up at the trial.

"You can thank Ora Thomas for that," Glenn hissed into the telephone mouthpiece. "He took the only eyewitness out target shooting and threatened him. I'll kill that bastard next time I see him."

It took her husband twenty minutes after the phone call before he returned to the bedroom. When he did, he took her in his arms and kissed her scarred face several times.

"I'd 'spect we'd best be headin' north in the morning," he said. "How about one more visit to the beach before we go?"

***

At the same time Maude and Glenn headed to the beach, the courthouse in Herrin emptied of spectators from the dismissed Cagle murder trial.

"We might as well go get the Dodge," Sheriff Galligan told his deputy, "since they won't need it anymore for evidence."

Deputy Bud Allison felt cautious. He was friends with John Layman, and he didn't want to also wind up with a hole in his stomach. Things got a little better when they ran into Ora Thomas in the hallway and the sheriff invited him to join them. Then about a block from the garage, the Shelton brothers were enlisted. They were well armed. Now Allison felt like he was part of an invincible army. He stepped in formation next to Bernie, who wielded not only an angry scowl, but also a sawed-off shotgun. The youngest Shelton acted cocky, as usual. When they walked into the garage, he waved his shotgun at the six Klansmen hanging out with John Smith. Knowing the spread pattern of a scattergun fired from the distance across a room, the Klansmen, their faces full of anger and hatred, moved away from one another.

"You boys here to fish or cut bait?" The tallest of the Klansmen said with a challenging grin as he wiped grease from his hands. "Make your move if you're man enough."

"We came to get the Dodge," Bud Allison announced.

When Smitty waved a disgusted hand at the men, Bernie slammed the butt of the shotgun into the stomach of the Klansmen unfortunate enough to be nearest. The Shelton brothers had a lifetime of fistfights under their belts. The trio fought back to back. When one brother knocked an adversary to the ground, the Shelton next to him kicked the downed man in the head. Just as Smitty and his friends appeared whipped, the garage door flew up, and the silhouettes of a dozen Klansmen appeared, a bright morning sun to their backs.

Carl, Earl and Ora spun toward the new arrivals, pulling guns from their shoulder harnesses. Without hesitation, they blasted away. Bernie discharged a single explosion from his shotgun that lifted the nearest Klansman completely off the ground and flung his dead body into a shelf full of tools. His second round just missed Smitty, but blew a hole through the wall behind him.

The chaos the shotgun caused gave time for his brothers and Ora to take aim. Carl and Earl both fired several shots at the same Klansman, causing his body to compulse like a fish on a hook. At the same time, Ora dropped another who mistakenly thought an empty crate would stop a bullet.

Deputy Allison was caught standing flat-footed with a blank look on his face. He took that expression to his grave when a bullet passed through one side of his head and out the opposite ear.

“Get in the car!” Carl shouted. He jumped into the front passenger seat, alongside the sheriff, who had already assumed the driver’s position.

With bullets whizzing, Ora leapt through the open car window and into the backseat. His hands came up, both packing a pistol as he fired blindly toward where he recalled the Klansmen had been standing. With Bernie and Earl firing while standing on the running boards on either side of the car, Galligan drove out of the garage, and with squealing tires, careened down the street. The four dead in the garage were joined moments later by two men walking on the boardwalk. Like many others, the bystanders had mistaken the pops from the guns for early Independence Day fireworks.

"We're gonna need to get out of Little Egypt for a while," Carl said when they were outside the city limits. He looked back at Ora, who was reloading his revolver. "You said something about a bank in Christian County that would be easy."

"I learned about it from an inmate when I was in jail," Ora said, glancing out the back window. "The coal company payrolls come in at the end of every month. There are several small-town banks that'd be easy pickin's. Those hicks would shit their pants if the Shelton Gang drove into town."

Carl reached under the car seat and pulled out a weathered paper magazine. He liked to consult the Farmer's Almanac before each job. Besides the weather and the amount of moonlight, it gave him an idea of what the harvest would be like this time of year in central Illinois. Unharvested corn meant plenty of country roads with limited visibility, making it easier to hide from the law—should the occasion require. September twenty seventh offered just such an occasion.

***

A month later, it was Ora driving the getaway car that banked on two wheels around the country roads of southern Christian County.

"Earl got shot by a broad!" Bernie laughed.

"No, I didn't." Earl held a handkerchief against his bleeding leg. "That fella came out of the grocery store and shot me. And he shot Carl in the hand, too. Ain't that right, Carl?"

"Where's my shotgun, Ora?" Carl shouted.

"I dropped it when that gal started shootin' at me," Ora said as he drove.

"That's just *fine!*" Carl said. "You drop my favorite sawed-off shotgun and Earl gets shot and drops the loot. Fine bunch of gangsters you guys are." He glared at Ora. "You said this was a hick town and an easy take! Hell, was there anybody in Kincaid that wasn't shootin' at us?"

"Well," Ora said as he gunned the engine, "at least Bernie didn't kill nobody this time."

15

"Glenn Young is fixin' to kill you," Sheriff Galligan told Ora a few days after Christmas. "You blinded his wife, and she can't cook or clean no more. That buckshot in the face didn't do nothin' for her looks, neither."

"It was unfortunate for her, all right," Ora said, "but that dirt road was bumpy and jarred me just as I was pullin' the trigger."

"Well, I'm makin' you a full-time deputy. That way when Young kills you, he'll be breakin' the law extra. Now, raise your right hand."

Grumbling, Ora raised his hand. "I'm ready to go if those other fellows are willing to swap."

When Ora exited the courthouse, Charlie Birger sat in a sedan, smoking. Without being asked, Ora opened the passenger door and got in beside him. The gang boss hadn't been out of the Danville jail long, so he was still trying to lie low and stay out of trouble.

"You gonna use that badge as an excuse to kill Glenn Young, ain't you?" Charlie asked, then offered a cigar. When Ora lit up without answering, Charlie continued, "You know that's gonna piss off the Klan. They'll most likely start up their raids again."

Ora puffed slowly on the cigar, thinking. He'd been obsessed with hate for five years—since Young killed his friend Luke Vukovic. But that wasn't the only reason for his loathing. It was also Glenn's wicked tenacious wit that riled him. The man never seemed to lack an insult that didn't strike right to the core of a man's pride. To make it worse, he always did it in public, and then, just as a person would finally think of a return insult, Glenn would turn his back and arrogantly walk away.

There was something else though. Something he had never revealed to anyone, even his wife—especially his wife. He glanced at the handsome man sitting next to him. Charlie was everything Ora had always wanted to be. Ora had been tiny and frail-looking his entire life. Bullies had always taken advantage, leaving him beaten and humiliated each time. The day he met the Shelton brothers and learned to fire a weapon, Ora felt like he had grown six inches. Still, being around those big, strong, scrapping men always made him feel like the runt of the litter. Here was Charlie—a man close to his own size—who walked with the confidence and swagger of a giant. Ora wanted to be like him. The thought of killing again, especially a man like Glenn Young whom he hated, once again brought a fire inside him that he could not comprehend. It was a tremendous sense of power and invincibility. Without thinking, he tilted back his head, puckered his tongue to his lips, and blew a perfect smoke ring.

"You did it!" Charlie shouted. Then his face turned grim again. "Ora, if you're goin' after Glenn, let's do it my way. The Klan is providing him with bodyguards everywhere he goes. You'll need backup."

Ora smiled. A flood of adrenalin coursed through his veins. Adrenalin along with the euphoria that came only when a gun was in his hand and the fate of a human life in his power. Moments like this were the closest he may ever get to what he desired most.

***

Folks had been talking about the Herrin Massacre for three years. It seemed to Glenn every discussion led to a different conclusion as to whose idea it had been to kill the scabs. But when he and two of his bodyguards walked into the European Hotel's Canary Cigar Store in Herrin on Saturday night, a brash, young coal miner named Elias Green had the audacity to boldly claim that the whole thing had been Glenn's fault.

"You were the one protectin' them scabs until it got too hot for you," Green shouted at him. "Then you and them Chicago thugs high-tailed it outa there in the middle of the night. You left them fifty scabies high and dry, so's we could butcher them the next day."

"I ain't never protected no scabies," Glenn lied. "And I weren't never at that Herrin mine."

"Hell, yes, you were there, Glenn," Ora Thomas said as he entered the store and stood with both hands in his overcoat pockets. "I seen you kill two of our union boys that day, before you ran yellow for the hills later that night."

"Don't pull that gun, Ora!" Glenn shouted as he reached for his own firearms.

The two bullets from Ora's pocket-shots ended up a few inches below Glenn's neck. As he was being blasted backwards, the former Texas Ranger only had time to tilt his side holsters up and fire through them. It was a technique he'd used in previous gunfights. One of his bullets drilled the Shelton brother's best friend through the face. Gunshots from the street immediately poured through the windows, shattering the glass and sending Glenn's two bodyguards flying backwards into the big glass cigar humidor.

Elias Green made it out the back door and into the hotel lobby, but Glenn, seeing he was the only one not quite dead, crawled slowly toward the open archway into the barber shop. When he tried to push with his knees, they kept slipping in the trail of blood gushing from the holes in his chest. He was just able to round the corner when he bumped heads with the pretty manicure girl who was trying to squeeze under a table next to the shoeshine boy.

"Sorry" the girl whispered.

"That's okay," Glenn gasped. Then he lost consciousness.

***

Maude set in darkness at her husband's bedside, listening to his gargled inhales and raspy exhales. Footsteps sounded in the hallway. Another gargled breath. A bird chirped outside the window. A gargled breath. The smell of antiseptic. Far away voices. A gargled breath. A door opened, steps, then rustling of sheets. A gargled breath. Steps again and the door closing. An interrupted inhale. Silence. Silence. One, long, slow rattle of air.

Maude held her husband's hand, her fingers on his wrist, feeling the last beats, each growing weaker than the last, until, finally, no more. She had no idea how much longer she sat beside him. At some point, someone touched her shoulders. She heard the sheet being raised over her husband's head. Glenn's hand was cold, but his grip on hers was still firm. When her hand came away from his, she laid her head on his chest, feeling a sticky wetness.

Hands on either side of her gently lifted her to her feet. Someone rinsed her face and hand with a warm, wet towel. She wasn't certain why. Tears had not yet come. Her legs moved along in a slow march, aided by those beside her. To a bed. She lay on her side and pulled her knees to her chest. Her mind remembered a bright warm day and the feel of her husband's beating heart against her ear—as he drove their Lincoln through a beautiful valley of grass and trees. One of the happiest and saddest days of her life.

***

Dr. C.E. Black turned around in the hallway. Half a dozen Klansmen approached Ora Thomas' room. The first exit door he came to led to the roof—a less dangerous alternative than facing vengeful robed crusaders. Dr. Black had removed far too many bullets from Shelton and Birger allies to be considered a neutral by Glenn Young's friends.

Ora was half asleep when he heard the door open. His left eye was swollen shut from the bullet that had entered just below it. The doctor had told him there was little hope of stopping the hemorrhaging into his brain. Somehow, seeing the Klansmen had gone to the trouble to don what Ora called their spook outfits made him kind of proud.

"Did I get Young?" Ora asked.

"Yes, you killed him."

"Well, I'm willing to die, then."

Mercifully, the first of many blows granted his wish.

***

Ora Thomas' funeral had several hundred mourners in attendance, as well as dozens of well-armed state troopers and militia. The snow on the cemetery ground was well muddied, so most of those standing near the internment wore rubbers over their shoes.

"I can't believe they buried our Ora that close to where Glenn Young will lie." Ma Shelton said to no one in particular. "And look at that mausoleum they are building for that thug."

"They says they's building him an even better one next summer," Hazel told her mother.

"Good," Lula said with a smirk. "It'll give me somethin' to shoot at when I come visit Ora."

"Look, Mama." Hazel pointed. "Ora's gonna rest right close to those union boys who were kilt at the Herrin doin's."

"Why, ain't that sweet?" Ma said. "Oh, look. There's Charlie Birger and some of his boys."

"I heard 'twas Charlie hisself who dropped Ora off at the cigar store," Lula said. "Then after the shooting, folks saw several men with smoking guns jump into Charlie's car and get away."

"Well, anyway," Ma said. "I'm so glad he came."

"Why ain't your boys here for Ora's buryin'?" an old lady with a bent cane asked. She had the front row pew at the Methodist church and constantly reminded everyone she was the congregation's largest contributor.

"My boys is doing church work down in Collinsville. The work of the Lord!" Ma Shelton's shouting causing the preacher to stop right in the middle of his prayer.

"Let's go, young'uns," Ma said, leading her clan away from the service. "I got soap to make. Goodbye, Ora."

***

At the very moment Ora was lowered into the grave, Earl shouted instructions to a Collinsville mail truck driver. "Put your hands up and your head down."

The driver immediately did as he was told, but it took him a moment to realize the truck had been moving at nearly fifteen miles an hour when the two gunmen jumped on either running board and stuck the revolver in his ear. Since the bandit had not told him what he was to do with his feet, the driver slammed his foot on the brake.

The sudden stop caused Earl to roll forward off the side of the truck. He was brushing himself off when the driver opened the door and leapt from the vehicle. Earl had dropped his revolver when he fell.

"Here's your gun, Mr. Shelton," the driver said, holding the .44 out to him.

"Thanks, Joe," Earl said. "Now get back in that truck and put your head down so you won't see me."

"Yes, sir, Mr. Shelton." Shaking, the driver hurried back into the truck and did as he was told.

By then Bernie had ransacked the mail and exited the passenger side.

"Here it is, Carl!" Bernie shouted.

"Don't say my name during a robbery, Bernie!" Carl shouted from the getaway car. "How many times I got to tell you that?"

Earl and Bernie rushed to the blue Buick with side curtains and jumped in.

"You know any poems, Joe?" Carl shouted at the driver.

"I know the Gettysburg address," Joe said, his shaking hands up and head still down.

"Well, say it ten times, then you can go!"

"Yes, sir, Mr. Shelton, sir. Four scores and seven months ago..."

***

S. Glenn Young's body lay in state at the Herrin Baptist Church. Two robed Klansmen stood as guards of honor while Maude sat next to the casket, wearing black sunglasses over her blind eyes. Few people did more than touch her shoulder and say, "Sorry for your loss." Each evening, Glenn's twin daughters guided Maude to the Layman Hotel, where her two-year-old son ran into his mother's arms. Weeping reporters from all around the country struggled to keep tears off their camera lens as they attempted to capture the heartbreaking scene.

Maude made it through three long days of this vigil, but on the morning of the funeral, she felt dizzy as she listened to the voice of Rev. Lee giving the eulogy. Lee had performed her wedding ceremony to Glenn. Hearing his voice brought back the anger she felt at the Klan's intrusion into their matrimony. Though she couldn't see it, she knew the church was decorated with an American Flag—and maybe even a Confederate one. The thought of white robed men and women with their hateful red and white mioaks embroidered on their silly costumes made her sick at her stomach.

Maude's father was a virulent Klan supporter and probably would've been disappointed in her. But George Simcox was not there. He was lying in a Patoka, Illinois, tuberculosis hospital with only a short time to live. The only family she had to support her now were her children.

Following the sermon, several Klan leaders gave their own testimonials they called Klantauguses, in which they told those in attendance exactly who were the true enemies of the American way. During these speeches, Maude almost wished the Sheltons' gunshots would've left her deaf as well as blind. Then she could just ignore all the hate and brutality of the world and just hold her children close.

When the patriotic music began, Maude finally told Rev. Lee she was about to be sick. She asked if he and his wife would escort her back to her hotel to rest before the burial.

"Eighty thousand people have been counted paying their last respects to your husband," Mrs. Lee said as they walked across the street. "Our murdered Kleagle Young had Klaverns from all over Missouri, Indiana and Arkansas represented here today. Four truckloads of flowers, wreaths, bouquets and floral designs from nineteen different states have been taken to the cemetery."

"Two of the floral wreaths were even sent by nigger organizations," Rev. Lee added.

"Why? Why would *they* send wreaths?" Maude asked.

"Because the smarter niggers know they don't belong living alongside decent White folks," Rev. Lee said.

Maude sat down in the lobby and enjoyed a few sips of coffee. One of the Klan leaders said it was time to get into the automobiles for the procession to the cemetery.

Rev. and Mrs. Lee walked on either arm. A moment later, Maude felt herself being tucked into the front seat of a vehicle. There was something strangely familiar about the smell in the car. She felt with her hand along the door where her finger found a small, jagged hole.

"Whose car is this?" Maude asked. "Is this the Lincoln?"

"Yes, Maude," Rev. Lee said as he took the driver's seat. "We felt the community should be reminded of what evil besmirched our benevolent dry crusader. This battle-scarred sedan will chill the hearts of those who fail to see the war being waged against our American dream."

Maude felt for the doorknob. She wanted to get out—she had to get out. She had to escape this metal cage and go back to her room in the hotel and cuddle beneath several layers of quilts. She couldn't find the latch. Panicked, she sobbed.

"That poor, poor woman," someone on the boardwalk said.

The funeral procession was more than a mile long behind the Lincoln. Countless cars moved slowly across town, led by snow-white horses ridden by fully outfitted Klansmen. The cars in the parade were big machines, many of them enclosed, denoting the wealth of the mourners.

The procession passed buildings and grounds decorated with hundreds of American flags. When they reached the outskirts of town, the road was covered with a soft cushion of wind-swept snow until, at last, they arrived at the village cemetery. Maude remained in the warmth of the Lincoln for nearly an hour until mourners had time to gather around the burial site. When she was finally escorted from the car, warmth reached her face. And the smell of burning oil. *A burning cross. They ruined my marriage, now their sanctimonious hate is ruining my husband's funeral.*

Maude felt faint as the Lees helped her sit in a wicker chair. She sensed the coffin in front of her and buried her head in her arms on top of it. Cameras clicked. The Klan burial ritual was read. Maude was too exhausted to protest.

16

Charlie was shocked to get thrown into the Harrisburg jail so soon after his release from Danville. He suspected it was because of the many rumors stating that he had arranged the Thomas-Young gunfight. As he had predicted, the Klan was riled to the point of violence. Raids on bootlegging joints intensified. In fact, the other boys incarcerated with Charlie were mostly small-time hill folk who hadn't even heard about the gunfight until the Klan raided their stills. The body odor and uncleanliness of the overcrowded cells made Charlie wistful for his Danville apartment-like incarceration. Sheriff John Small's pudgy wife Cora was one of the only highlights of the entire experience. Cora struggled to keep the prisoners well fed. She also scolded them like school children when they misbehaved.

One of the rednecks in a cell near Charlie's was an idle-brained young man named Leroy. The other prisoners liked to tease Leroy because he collected bed bugs, cockroaches, flies, and spiders, and struggled to keep them corralled in a half-filled matchbox that he kept under his mattress. He claimed he was protecting the little critters from the bug oil that was sprayed on the mattresses and around the cells every few days. At first, it was funny to watch the boy's face light up when someone brought him an insect for his collection. It seemed harmless entertainment—until the day one of the more hardened criminals smashed the matchbox with his foot.

Leroy went into a wild rampage and beat the bigger man senseless. Cora came in and threw a bucket of dishwater on the boy to calm him down. The bug murderer was unconscious, so Leroy just crawled onto his mattress and started crying. One of the other inmates felt sorry for the boy, so he scooped up the matchbox and gently put it in its place under the mattress.

Everyone was asleep when the unconscious man woke up, shook his head and saw the matchbox sticking out below Leroy's mattress. He took a safety match and lit Leroy's little bug mosque. The unlit matches in the box exploded, and the mattress went up in flames. Leroy leapt to his feet, took off his shirt, and fanned the flames. A horrible gas developed from the bug oil drenched mattress. Screaming men, including Charlie, dropped to the floor to seek fresher air.

When Cora ran into the lockup, the men jumped to their feet and begged her to let them out to escape the fumes.

"But I'm alone in the jailhouse!" Cora shouted. "My husband and his deputies are out birddogging bootleggers."

"Cora," Charlie pleaded. "If you let us out, I will personally assure you that no man will escape. You have my word."

Cora fumbled with the keys. She unlocked Charlie's cell door, then ran back into the sheriff's residence. Charlie unlocked the other cells.

"If any of you tries to escape," Charlie shouted. "I will have my boys hunt you down and kill you."

Later that night when Sheriff Small returned, every prisoner was accounted for and sitting on the lawn. Cora and Leroy walked around, serving coffee.

***

The little roadhouse northeast of Murphysboro had been unoccupied since a raid by Glenn Young's boys the week after his gunfight with Ora. It had been so torn up during the raid, even hoboes avoided the structure. When he entered the establishment, Charlie Birger quickly knew why. Hundreds of fat rats scurried across the floor, tables and chairs. And the sweet smell of corn liquor told him why the roadhouse had become a rodent rendezvous. The Kluxers had apparently decided there were too many barrels of the good stuff to hide away until their next Klan meeting, so they had busted up a dozen or so kegs. The liquid courage seemed to have as much effect on this kind of rat as the human kind. Subsequently, several of the critters chose not to give up their treasure so easily. They turned toward Charlie, arched their backs, and gave the human a cold, hard stare.

Charlie dealt with this insubordination by pulling his revolver and emptying shells into as many rodents as he could before the last of them fled the battlefield.

An automobile noisily approached. Charlie listened, then reloaded, just in case Carl had double-crossed him and brought a few of his thugs along. But Carl exited the vehicle alone.

Charlie found a chair that wasn't bloody from his ratslaughter, set it upright, and tried to look casual by putting his booted feet up on the table.

When Carl entered, he beheld the massacre site with contempt. "Damn, Charlie, if I'd knowed you had such hate for rodents, I'd have picked a more hospitable climate for us to meet. You suppose there's a chair that ain't covered with blood or brains?"

"You think this room looks like that cigar store did after Glenn and Ora had it out?" Charlie asked.

"I think Ora might have won the war against the Klan for us by killin' Glenn Young," Carl said as he found a suitable chair and straddled it backwards in such a way that his hand resting on the back was close to the pistol in his shoulder harness.

"Ora was a good man." Charlie lazily brought his feet off the table and leaned forward so his own holstered weapon was more easily assessible. "If the Klan don't win elections next November, they'll be through."

"I'm glad they let you out of the Harrisburg jail so fast. I heard you was a hero for getting them prisoners out and keepin' them from escapin'."

"But you didn't call me in here to pin no medal on me, did ya, Carl?"

"Charlie, I'm no gangster." As if to emphasize his words, Carl held up the thumb and forefinger of his right hand and slowly extracted his gun from beneath his overcoat. He placed it on the table and backed away from it. "I'm a businessman. Your job was to collect money from our slot machines, bring it to me, and we divvy it up equal like. Why couldn't you just ask me if you needed some extra cash?"

"You sayin' I'm embezzlin'?" Charlie didn't try to hide his anger. "What about that diamond ring your boys stole from me? It wouldn't have bothered me so, but they did it in my hometown. We had agreed that Harrisburg and Fairfield would be off limits."

"Come on, Charlie. You know the real problem is that Helen prefers me over you. You have blood in your eyes, and it's mine!"

"Huh!" Charlie scoffed. "That Shawneetown dame don't mean nothin' to me."

"We need to work together, Charlie. Now that the Klan's about gone, there ain't nothin' but an act of God—"

Charlie suddenly held up a hand. "You hear a train?"

"There ain't no train tracks around here." Carl tilted his head and listened. "What the hell?"

The two men rushed to the door. When Charlie turned the knob, a gust of wind nearly took it off its hinges.

"Holy shit!" Charlie and Carl shouted at the same time.

Less than a mile away, a dark cloud of dust and debris stretching a mile on either side swirled toward a two-story farmhouse and a large red barn. The sky was black and dark blue on either side of the storm.

"Dust storm!" Charlie screamed.

"Dust storm, my ass!" Carl shouted.

The entire house, barn and all the large trees around it came off the ground and flew into the heavens.

"That's the finger of God!" Carl's mouth remained open.

The tornado moving toward them was nearly two miles wide.

17

Carl and Charlie ran from the doorway and toward a protruding mound of earth. Powerful winds nearly blew the men off their feet. It took all his strength for Carl to pull open the heavy storm shelter door. He fell across it so it wouldn't blow back shut. Then he reached inside the little room and took a firm grip on a pipe that ran underground from the windmill. With his other hand, he reached out to Charlie, who, being much lighter in weight, crawled toward him. Once their hands met in a tight grip, Carl pulled with all his might.

For just a moment, Charlie's entire body seemed to float off the ground. Then a brief lull in the wind allowed him to get a grip on the ground, and he dove into the little shelter. Carl fell in next to him. Jars of preserves were sucked off the shelves and into the sky until the storm door blew shut with a loud bang.

Both men grabbed a long two by four at the same time and bolted the opening as best they could from the inside. The bouncing of the door as it fought to remain on its hinges lasted only about a minute, but to the men inside it seemed much longer.

The storm passed as quickly as it had come. Breathing heavy, Charlie immediately unbolted the door and threw himself out of the small room with as much violence as when he'd entered. He hit the ground hard and continued to breathe heavy. He lay on his back.

Carl crawled out, stood, and looked around.

"My God," Carl said. "Are them chickens?"

Charlie glanced up. Never in his life had he seen anything like it. A half dozen chickens completely plucked of all their feathers stood like statues, their claws in a death grip with the ground. A moment later, two of them moved their legs. With blank eyes, they staggered around the yard as if drunk. One of them actually walked backwards a few steps before timbering over like a fallen tree.

A cow nearby bellowed. It lay on its back, a long board through its side. With a short, violent quiver it quit bellowing and lay still.

Charlie rose and stood beside Carl. The two gangsters stared as they turned slowly in a circle. Nothing was left standing as it had been. Not a house, a bush or even a tree. A nearly crushed train boxcar lay on its side a hundred yards away, several miles from the nearest tracks. Just beyond it was an upside-down building.

"Is that a house or a barn?" Charlie asked.

A horse head appeared in what had been a hay loft window, but was now at ground level. The animal whinnied and squeezed through the small opening as if from a birth canal. When it tried to stand, its two back legs buckled, obviously broken in several places.

"You got your gun?" Carl asked. "I left mine in the building."

Charlie pulled it and handed it to him. He turned the opposite direction as Carl jogged over to the mare and put a single slug into her head.

"Carl, it looks like the whole of Murphysboro is on fire."

Carl turned around. Smoke rose in the distance.

Neither of their automobiles were anywhere in sight.

Carl returned to Charlie's side and handed him back his revolver.

"I see a house standing to the south," Carl said. "Let's go that way first."

Debris covered the road, so they walked across a field. Bricks, boards and pieces of metal were strewn everywhere. A few hundred yards later, the body of a woman with bright red hair, her face and chest bashed nearly flat, lay in front of them.

Charlie found a long board, and they rolled her onto it. They each took an end of the makeshift stretcher and carried her on up to the farmhouse.

An elderly woman casually sat in a porch swing, which seemed no stranger than the other sights just witnessed. Her two-story home appeared undamaged, except for the window missing behind the swing. Debris, though, littered her yard.

"I'm too old to hide from an act of God," the old lady said without introduction. "I watched the whole thing from my bedroom window. About a year ago, I saw a barnstormin' aereoplane pass by here. That storm today was traveling near as fast."

"Do you know who this dead lady is?" Carl asked. He tilted his end of the board so she could see.

"Ain't enough left of her face to recognize her for sure," the lady said. "I'd 'spect she rode the twister from down around Murphysboro or so."

"Murphysboro is on fire," Carl said. "We'd like to get there to see if we can help."

"Ain't no need to interfere with the workin's of God," she said. "You'd just as soon stay here. Go fetch me one of them fat hens that's lost all its feathers and I'll cook us some chicken and dumplin's."

"No, ma'am," Charlie said. "We're going to see if we can help."

"Well, I ain't got nothin' to take you there but an old mule with no saddle. I'd 'spect he'd be better getting across all that trash than a horseless carriage anyway. Stick that corpse in the smokehouse, and make sure someone retrieves it before it draws too many flies. Then fetch me one of them yard birds before you leave. All this talkin's made me hungry."

The mule couldn't be coaxed to much more than an uncomfortable trot, a gait that bothered Carl more than it did Charlie. They stayed south of the majority of tornado damage, but because of all the debris, they seldom knew if they were on the dirt road or off. The next farmhouse they came to had lost a barn and a part of a roof, but after a thorough inspection, proved to be unoccupied.

"These folks is gonna come home to a mess," Charlie said when they were back on the mule and moving again.

"I was thinkin' maybe we could have our boys lend some of these folks a hand for a while," Carl said as they trotted along.

"Maybe so," Charlie said. "My gang's mighty handy with a hammer."

"I heard they's built you quite a fortress back in the woods from highway thirteen. What they call it? The Shady Place?"

"The Shady Rest."

"Sounds like a cemetery. You planning on getting buried there, Charlie?"

"Nope. It's built to be a fortress to ensure we don't see a cemetery none too soon."

The two hushed at the sight of a farm truck zig zagging its way through the debris. It stopped next to them, and a tall, thin man got out, his clothes covered with coal dust.

"You fellas been to that farmhouse up yonder?" The man didn't know what to do with his hands as he spoke. They shook as he rubbed them together, then through his hair, behind his neck, then rubbed his stomach.

"Yes. We were just there but didn't find nobody inside."

"Didn't take nothin', did ya?" His eyes teared up. "That's my house."

"No need to kick a man while he's got his face in the dirt," Carl said. "You got anymore family livin' with you?"

"I hope I still do." The man wiped tears with coal-stained hands, then words streamed from his mouth. "I was shovelin' coal when the storm hit. We could hear it clear down in the mine. When we came up, there was hardly nothin' standin'. My kids were at school. My daughter Maggie said her teacher asked the boys to shut the windows when it started hailing. She saw her brother and the other boys get cut to pieces when glass blew across the room. We found his body a half mile away. My wife and her sister were on their way to DuQuoin to visit their mother. I'm prayin' they made it."

Just then a little red-haired girl came out of the car and ran into her father's arms. Carl looked at Charlie, who turned his head away.

"Sir, can I ask if your wife has red hair?" Carl asked.

The man's eyes provided the answer.

"You might want to stop by your neighbor's house to the north before you go home," Carl said.

"My wife's sister has red hair too," the man said, nodding.

Carl could only nod back.

Charlie reached down and touched the man's shoulder. "You must pray for the light in the darkness."

"I pray the Lord to be shown," the man said. He lifted his daughter, walked back to his truck, and was quickly on his way.

Ten minutes later, Carl guided the mule through what he suspected might have once been the easternmost streets of Murphysboro. Not a complete building stood anywhere. Men rushed about, carrying the dead to a makeshift morgue next to a pile of rubble. The wounded were put in automobiles or horse-drawn carriages to be taken to whatever hospital might still be standing. Carl wasn't sure where that would be.

"It's mostly women and children dead," Charlie said and chewed his lip.

"Most of the men must've been working underground in the coal mine when it hit," Carl said.

"Would you fellas let us use your mule to pull a cart?" a man asked as he approached. "There ain't many animals fit for such purpose."

Charlie slid off the back as Carl swung his leg over the mule's head to dismount.

The man quickly led the animal off.

"They may as well just toss them bodies in a common grave," Charlie grumbled. "Earth is nothin' but a place for bones to rot. We'll all be there soon enough."

"They're probably hoping to plant loved ones in shady meadows with a nice bench nearby for the living."

"Carl," Charlie's voice crackled a little. "I didn't tell you that Betty left me while I was coolin' my heels in that Danville lockup. I fear she might have been in Murphysboro today. She's got relative's here."

"Do you think you could find the street they lived on?"

"I don't know." Charlie looked around at the wreckage. "I've been right here on this street a dozen times, but I don't recognize a thing about it now."

They had only walked a short distance before a man ran up to them, pleading for help removing rubble from some trapped people.

"We're lookin' for a person our self," Charlie said. "She lived about a mile from here."

"Then you might as well look here as well as anywhere else," the man said, his voice shaking. "This house we're looking under was carried here from two mile away."

Charlie and Carl spent the next three days pulling survivors and corpses from under rubble. By then, some of the telephone and telegraph lines were working.

"Betty's father said she wasn't in the path of the storm," Charlie said. He had waited two hours to take his turn on the telephone, but the wait had been worth it.

Carl was also relieved by the news. Charlie had been driving him crazy with worry. Even better, Earl and Bernie showed up a few minutes later and brought six carloads of men and supplies.

"The newspapers are saying one thousand dead, three thousand injured," Earl said as they unloaded boxes.

"How could one tornado stay on the ground across three states?" Bernie asked. "It had to be more than one."

"Doesn't matter," Carl said. With as many dead and injured he'd seen in the past three days, how they died didn't seem important. "I'm goin' home. You boys help out around here as long as they need you."

"We need to organize a fundraiser," Charlie said before Carl could get in the car.

"Those in the rackets don't make the most charitable kinda folks, you know?"

"Now, I'll disagree with you there, Carl." Charlie pointed at the boxes of supplies.

"How we supposed to make folks give up their hard-earned gains, Charlie?"

"Well, the same way you get protection money. You ask 'em nice. Earl asks 'em less nice, and if that don't work, you send Bernie in to ask 'em his way."

***

Thelma Down's face was pointed toward the windshield of the car, but her eyes were on the man who was designated to be her driver. Had it not been for the gun she had spotted beneath his suit jacket, she might not now be sitting with one hand on the doorknob. She was eighty years old and grey, but she'd heard there were men who would still seek satisfaction from any source available.

Bernie Shelton didn't look like a molester. Still, many people did compliment her on her unwrinkled skin, a tribute to her clean living. But today, perhaps her smooth skin was a curse. When her Pastor was divvying up the Christian Ladies Auxiliary with volunteer drivers, Thelma was hoping to get the pleasant-looking Charlie Birger. He looked like a man who would never hurt anyone. This Mr. Shelton seemed as uncomfortable in her presence as was she in his. He drove silently, keeping his eyes on the dirt road ahead.

Their first three stops had resulted in no contributions to the tornado fund. She thought that perhaps it was because Mr. Shelton standing behind her was too menacing, so the following two solicitations, she asked him to remain in the car. These also proved unsuccessful. When Thelma returned to the car after the second attempt, she gave a frustrated sigh.

"These poor people barely have enough to feed themselves," Thelma said.

"Then," Bernie said without looking at her, "let's go to where there *is* money."

Five minutes later, he turned the car down a narrow, grassy lane to a dilapidated building. Smoke rose from a chimney, unusual not only because it was a warm day, but because of the peculiar odor it emitted.

"Just do like you did before." Bernie advised. He removed his specs and set them on the dashboard. "His name is Jones."

Thelma couldn't hide the fear showing on her face. She followed Mr. Shelton to the front door. He knocked hard, then stepped back behind her, took off his hat, and set it on the porch swing. The door opened and a scroungy looking man in bib overalls and a dirty undershirt stood staring at her. He held a large hammer in one hand and grasped a short two-by-four in the other.

"Sorry to bother you, sir." Thelma recited the same words she had repeated several times that morning. "We are collecting for the Methodist Church in an effort to help the victims of the recent tornado."

The man looked from her to the man standing behind her. "Do I know you?" he asked Bernie.

"Possibly," Bernie replied.

"Well, if I don't know you, then get the hell off my property," the man said and slammed the door shut.

Thelma walked to the car.

"I forgot my hat. Why don't you wait in the machine, Mrs. Downs?" Bernie said. He opened the car door and helped her in, then rolled up the window. "I wouldn't want you to get cold, Mrs. Downs."

Thelma settled into the seat. She was watching the V-shaped flight of a flock of geese when she heard the feint sound of screaming mixed in with the honking of the birds. Several moments later, she heard a tapping on her door window. Mr. Shelton, with a smile, and Mr. Jones, with a grimace stood together, looking in. She rolled the window down just a little bit.

"Mrs. Downs," Mr. Jones said through clinched teeth. "I forgot that I had a few dollars stashed away in my cookie jar." He pushed a wad of bills in through the opening in the window.

"God bless you, Mr. Jones," Thelma said. "Oh, my goodness, what happened to your hand, Mr. Jones?"

"I just had a little accident with my hammer," Mr. Jones said, looking at Mr. Shelton.

"Oh, dear. Well, soak it in cold water with baking soda, Mr. Jones."

If Thelma Downs thought it strange that most everyone who turned them down that day had accidents soon after, she didn't say anything to Mr. Shelton.

That evening, they returned to the church where a potluck had been set out for the volunteers who went out soliciting money. After everyone had eaten, the pastor stood at the head table and collected the money that had been brought in.

"Seventy-five dollars," the first church lady said proudly as she gave the pastor her envelope. She glanced at her driver and hurried back to their table to shake his hand on their success.

"Two hundred and nine dollars," the next lady said. "Thanks to my wonderful driver, Mr. Birger."

Thelma waited until all the other ladies had turned in their money, then walked up to the pastor empty-handed. "Oh, Mrs. Downs," the Reverend said, "please don't be embarrassed. Not everyone was expected to be successful today."

"Oh, heavens, no, Pastor. The bags were just too heavy for me to carry." Thelma chuckled, then turned to her driver. "Bernard!"

Bernie walked sheepishly to the head table and set two overstuffed bags in front of the astonished pastor.

"Four thousand, three hundred, and sixty-two dollars," Thelma announced.

Charlie Birger turned from his table and looked to where the other two Shelton brothers sat. "Bernard?" he mouthed.

Big Carl and Earl shrugged and smiled.

18

Maude Young's hate for the Ku Klux Klan became almost unbearable the day she found out that Madge Oberholtzer was dead. It wasn't that she knew Madge all that well, but she did know D.C. Stephenson. It didn't surprise her that he was being held responsible for her death. Maude's nurse read the newspaper aloud to her.

> *Ku Klux Klan Grand Dragon D.C. Stephenson is being charged with the kidnap, forced intoxication, and rape of Marge Oberholtzer. His abuse led to her suicide attempt while she was still in his captivity. It is believed that Stephenson's physical abuse of the woman was also a contributing factor that eventually caused Oberholtzer's death. Therefore, Stephenson is being charged with murder.*
>
> *It is stated that Stephenson had bitten her many times during his attack. The attending doctor*

described a significant bite on her breast. He later testified that the bite wounds that Stephenson inflicted on her were a leading contributor to her death, due to a staph infection that eventually reached her lungs. The doctor also testified that she could have been saved if she had received medical attention sooner. In her dying declaration, Oberholtzer claimed that Stephenson had refused to give her medical attention unless she agreed to marry him first.

Also included in Oberholtzer's dying statement: "Stephenson took hold of the bottom of my dress and pulled it up over my head. I tried to fight, but I was weak and unsteady. Stephenson took hold of my two hands and held them. He chewed me all over my body, bit my neck and face, chewing my tongue, chewed my breasts until they bled, my back, my legs, my ankles, and mutilated me all over my body.

"I took the gun, not to kill Stevenson, but to kill myself in Stephenson's presence. Then I decided to try and get poison and take it in order to save

> *my mother from disgrace. I knew it would take longer for the mercury tablets to kill me."*

Maude wept. So many bad things could have been prevented had her husband lived. *If my Glenn had known what was happening to Miss Oberholtzer, he would have done something about it.*

Then something else caught Maude's nurse's attention.

"Maude, there's also an article on this page about that evangelist I was telling you about. I think we should go hear him."

The article named several ministers Maude knew who claimed that Rev. Harold Williams had literally won hearts and souls in communities all over the country. They testified that what Little Egypt needed was a good dose of spiritualism to save the good citizens who had so recently fallen under the evil influence of Satan.

Maude wanted so desperately to find hope. "Yes, I do want to hear him."

***

Many citizens of Little Egypt felt the horrid tristate tornado was the wrath of God, punishing them for the wickedness they had allowed into their communities. Though not everyone had lost property, few had escaped the loss of friends or loved ones.

Blame and guilt were plentiful. Several hundred had participated in the torture and slayings of the nineteen strikebreakers in Herrin. Even more had been ghoulish spectators to the three day display of the corpses. Thousands were complicit by their subsequent silence that protected the eight men who stood trial for the bloody murders. Then, in the following months, nearly everyone in Little Egypt had contributed to even more sinful behavior either on the side of the bootleggers or the Ku Klux Klan.

Now this outsider had arrived among them with the piety of one of the twelve disciples. The Reverend Harold Williams was a young man with no physical characteristic that made him attractive to women or a threat to men. Children wanted him to play ring-around-the-rosie with them and the elderly wanted him to come over for supper, then sit on the porch and visit. He always began his sermons in a low, calming voice stating facts that were so simply explained no one could find fault in them.

"We say in the Declaration of Independence that all men are created equal. But what, exactly, does that mean? We know it doesn't mean we are all born the same physically, or with the same intelligence or the same abilities. We all understand that these are qualities that will affect *what* we may become as adults. After all, it would be difficult to become a carpenter if you were born with no arms or legs."

Maude had heard these words before in Klanguenese. She thought she knew what was coming next; that God created Protestant White men superior to rule over everyone else.

"But are these factors that should determine how we treat others or how we should be treated by others? Does not a person with no arms or legs have the same rights in a courtroom as everyone else? Aren't there a few places where we should all have equal rights? Doesn't every child have the right to learn to read and write, and to develop job skills that can be useful to everyone in their community? Isn't it important to understand the difference between being equal physically and mentally and having equal rights? Isn't this where we sometimes get ourselves into conflict?

"To hear Paul say, 'There is no longer Jew or Greek, there is no longer slave or free, there is no longer male and female; for all of you are one in Christ Jesus,' is *both a comfort and a challenge*.

"It's wonderful to feel like we're not alone in the world, but it's terrifying to lose our identity. We take such pride in being unique as individuals, and yet we have a natural need to be with others. Perhaps that is why we so often choose to ally ourselves with people who look like us, talk like us, and who have the same interests as us. Sometimes, it just feels like too much trouble to get to know someone who is different. It's easier for us to tell ourselves there must be something wrong with them—that *they* need to change and be like me.

"But people from other countries and other cultures need time to get to know you and your beliefs, just as you need time to get to understand theirs. By sitting down and sharing what you do have in common, you will better be able to grow together as a community."

Maude understood. She and Glenn had begun losing their personal identity the day they joined the Ku Klux Klan. They began to think that anyone not exactly like them must have something wrong with them. The realization caused Maude to raise her head, as though her sight had returned. The complete silence from the thousands in the audience was incredible; as if everyone were holding their breath. In just a few sentences, Rev. Williams had gotten to the very heart of the Ku Klux Klan—as well as to the gangs who opposed them.

"That we are *all* one with Christ Jesus is frightening. If that is so, then how can *I* be special? This demonic drive for too much independence creates isolated individuals who assume 'my' individual or 'my' group identity is *the one and only right way*. Individuals are turned *not* into a community, but into 'legions.' And the great diversity of human experience is thus reduced to a single point of view, and held to a single, *often unattainable*, standard."

The reverend took a long pause.

People shifted in their chairs. Some sobbed.

Warm tears ran down Maude's cheeks. Her throat tightened as she recalled a wooden cross, not burning with Earthly fire, but lighted with the spirit of the trinity.

"True Christianity is difficult, but not unattainable. Jesus sat with prostitutes like Mary Magdalene, murderers like Saul, thieves, Romans, Jews and Greeks, slaves and free, and on and on. Christianity brings together and binds us despite our differences, knowing all the while that we are all *works in progress*. And that is frightening but absolutely necessary if we are to become one with Jesus Christ!"

"Hallelujah, brother." Some in the congregation shouted as the reverend's voice became more powerful. "Praise the Lord!"

"Relationships often feel safer when we're around people who *are* similar to us. People who like us, and whom we like. Yet, the walk with Jesus is constantly asking us to open up that circle and to accept, and *even love, people who aren't like us*. Not by chaining them to us, but by allowing and loving our differences. Every day each of us has an opportunity to learn from those who are *different* from us.

"These are the kinds of relationships we as Christians are called to. We are called to relationships where a marvelous side-by-side living takes place. '*Love one another,'* Jesus commanded. 'Love one another!'"

Reverend Williams was now shouting, pausing often to allow the audience to shout, "Amen" and "Praise the Lord!"

"Jesus didn't go into the wilderness to prove something to God, but to learn for himself who he was. That's true for us as well. That's our wilderness journey whether from the wilderness of sorrow and loss from the recent tornado, or the wilderness of hatred and violence in our communities. Survival in these wildernesses will either make us stronger in our faith or it will destroy us."

"Save us, Reverend."

"Pastor, please don't let us burn!"

"If you have seen this wilderness in your own community," Reverend Williams shouted, "if you want to rejoin the community of our Lord Jesus Christ, I invite you to come forward now. Repent your sins and be forgiven, for ours is the house of the Lord!"

"Yes!"

"Forgive me Lord!"

"I was at the massacre!"

"I killed!"

"I sinned!"

Maude recognized not just footsteps moving toward the Reverend, but crawling. She herself dropped to her knees, sobbing. She fell to the ground and lay on her stomach, her arms and legs flattened to the ground as if she could not get low enough to be deserving of forgiveness. She sensed that Little Egypt was being transformed from a Sodom and Gomorrah to a little piece of Heaven—at least for a little while.

***

The first thing Carl noticed when he returned from a business trip to Florida was the absence of weaponery on the streets. Signs all over town told of churches and tent revivals where someone named Rev. Williams would be speaking for the next several weeks. Not only were there fewer guns, but more smiles and even greetings from citizens who Carl had always assumed despised him.

"Good mornin', Brother Carl."

"Praise the Lord for a glorious day, Brother Shelton."

"Grace to you and peace to your family, Mr. Carl."

"The Lord be with you, Mr. Shelton."

"What the hell is wrong with this town?" Carl shouted when he entered the barbershop. His brothers were already there and pacing the floor like alley cats.

Bernie pulled his revolver and stationed himself in front of the window. "I don't know, but I'll shoot the next son-of-a-bitch who says he'll pray for me."

"It's that new evangelist that's in town," Earl grumbled. "This towns got a bad case of religion. He's got the whole county so het up on bein' saved, business at the roadhouses is down nearly fifty percent."

"Everything is down?" Carl asked in disbelief. "Alcohol, gamblin' and whorin'?"

"Well, not whorin' yet," Earl admitted, "but it might be if that preacher man ain't stopped."

"So, what are you boys doin' about it?" Carl sat in the barber chair, where his face was immediately covered with a hot towel.

"I sent Charlie Briggs to have a visit with Rev. Williams," Earl said.

"You sent Briggsy?" Carl shouted, ripping the hot towel off his face. "Why, he ain't talked to nobody since Jack Skelcher got kilt."

"I didn't tell him to talk," Earl said. "I loaned him a revolver that belongs to John Smith, the Klan leader. That way, we can get rid of two enemies with one bullet."

"Here comes Briggsy now," Bernie said. He shut the curtain and turned toward the door, pistol still in hand.

Charlie Briggs walked into the barbershop, a smile on his face. It was not the smile that Briggs displayed after a killing or a good fistfight. It was a smile of contentment and peace.

"Peace be with you, my brothers." Briggs grasped his hands together and gave a slight bow. He looked directly at Bernie. "I've been praying for you, my friend."

Earl jumped forward and grabbed the gun out of his younger brother's grasp. That action saved Charlie Brigg's life, but not his faith. It took Bernie resorting to his fists to beat the holiness out of the young gangster.

***

After analyzing the situation, Carl decided the religious fervor would soon pass. A man's thirst for distractions to life's hardships in the form of booze, gambling and whoring would eventually prevail. To inspire the return to debauchery, he ordered the prostitutes to take to the streets and flaunt as much skin as possible without getting arrested. At all the roadhouses in Little Egypt, the first taste of spirits was on the house, and the slot machines were doctored to provide more favor to the player.

When Kentuckians and customers from The Valley of East St. Louis discovered the benefits found in southern Illinois, the customary atmosphere of guns and fistfights returned, making at least the Shelton boys feel much more at home.

"The Egan Rats are all up in arms over losing business in St. Louis," Earl told Carl.

"They'll get over it." Big Carl sat at a table counting money from a recent bank heist.

"They would if Art Newman wasn't stirrin' 'em up," Earl added. "He's been sore ever since he kicked us out of the Arlington. If we hadn't took up headquarters across the street and took away all his business, he'd have nothin' to bitch about."

"How 'bout you taggin' his wife, Earl?" Bernie asked.

Earl's face turned red. Bessie was a sore subject with him. He blamed Helen Holbrook for telling Art about the liaison. The brothers believed the extramarital affair had been the excuse for kicking them out of the hotel. Carl had been skimming Art for several months, causing the Newman profits from the rackets to diminish to the point Bessie was taking on additional tricks to keep up her lavish lifestyle.

The brother's conversation was suddenly interrupted by a loud bang from the back of the room. Several men held their ears and backed away from the blue smoke emitting from a vegetable can. Blackie Armes remained seated, laughing. The dark-skinned nineteen-year-old had got his taste of explosives working in the coal mine. Now, he played with black powder as a hobby.

"That Blackie sure likes to blow shit up, don't he?" Bernie said. "Maybe you should have him get rid of Art for you, Earl."

Earl didn't laugh. He was thinking of ways to show both Art and Bessie that you don't mess with a Shelton.

***

The Newmans lay as far apart in the big bed as was possible. The fact they hadn't spoken to each other in several days was nothing unusual. Even when they were getting along, they mostly only spoke when plotting ways to get more money. Art didn't mind. They both knew Bessie was the brains of their operations. He was proud to be a cheat at gambling, a careful and deliberate thief, and, when he needed to be, a back-stabbing killer. There was no shame in these characteristics to a man who had known poverty and had been kicked when he was down.

Bessie put down her copy of the book *Fanny Hill* and turned off the light on her side of the bed. Art knew better than to challenge his wife's schedule. Rolling onto his side, he laid the next day's race-track schedule on his side table and turned out his own lamp.

As if that were the signal, the house rocked from an explosion. The big mirror above the bed crashed right between where the married couple might have been had they not been quarrelling.

Grabbing for the pistol he always kept on his side table, Art rolled onto the floor. Smoke billowed up the stairwell, so he quickly shut the bedroom door.

Bessie automatically stepped into her slippers and threw her robe around her shoulders.

"Out the window!" Art barked at her. He struggled to open the window all the way so they could fit through.

"I'm not going out onto that roof," Bessie squawked.

"Okay, bye." Art went through the opening headfirst. Flames rose from the front of the house, so he moved toward the lattice on the opposite side. He had just turned around and was about to ease himself down the side when Bessie wrapped her arms around his neck.

"Don't leave me, Artie," she implored.

The flames spread quickly toward them. The lattice wouldn't hold them both. Grabbing his wife by the shoulders, he pulled her quickly toward him and dropped her over the side of the building. The bushes would break her fall, but there was always a chance they would also break her neck. When he reached the ground, he found that only her left hand was broken. Then she broke her other hand with a hard right to his jaw.

***

"Blackie, what the hell did you use on that house?" Earl shouted when he found out the results of the Newman house bombing. "I could've done the same with a string of firecrackers."

"I guess there weren't enough air inside the house," Blackie mumbled, his face turning ashen. He had told Earl when he was assigned the task that he had never tried to take a house down before. "The fire department being only a block away didn't help much either."

"Earl, why don't you have one of them Cuckoo boys from St. Louis take care of Art?" Bernie suggested. Being close to Blackie's age, he understood how his older brothers sometimes had unrealistic expectations of less-experienced men.

"Charlie Gordon," Carl said from the piano where he was tapping out a tune he needed to perfect by church time Sunday.

"What about Gordon?" Earl asked.

"Gordon's got a new batch of whiskey arriving this week from Canada," Carl said, never missing a note. "Plus, he's been itching to plug someone ever since he got those new pistols of his. Tell Art that Gordon has to find a buyer for the liquor quick, and that he's willin' to let it go for a song."

"You think Gordon will do it?" Earl didn't sound very confident.

"Tell him we'll cut him in on that load of stolen cars our boys are bringing up from Memphis." Carl shut his eyes and rolled his head as he played. "Play against the greed of both Art Newman and Charlie Gordon, and one of them will go down."

***

Art figured out the second that Charlie Gordon reached for his guns that the Sheltons were trying to get him killed. The dynamiting should have created enough suspicion, but when Earl told him there was a profit to be made on the whiskey purchase, he had lowered his guard, letting his greed get the best of him.

As luck would have it, Gordon had tried to pull both weapons out of his shoulder holsters at the same time. Otherwise, Art would've never been able to outdraw him. For some reason, several gangsters had recently been trying to use a Bill Hickok cross-draw. In theory, it was a glamorous idea, but in practicality, it required the shooter to be able to clear the weapons of each other during the draw—an ability that Charlie Gordon had not seemed to have mastered as well as had Wild Bill.

Art was feeling so proud of having dropped the would-be assassin, he stuck around to brag about it to the law. It also helped that there were several witnesses who saw the entire gunfight and wanted to slap the winner on the back and buy him a round.

It was only when he got to his room in the Arlington the next morning and told Bessie about his exploits that she made him understand the seriousness of having the Shelton boys put out a contract on him.

"We've got to get out of town!" Art shouted, then began crying and breathing heavy.

"Out of town, hell," Bessie squealed as she pulled a suitcase from the closet. "We've got to get out of the state."

***

The dough was coming in so fast; Carl couldn't count it fast enough. With the Newmans selling the Arlington, the Sheltons ran the whole block in the Valley of East St. Louis. Bernie collected protection money from what few joints they didn't own. It was Earl's job to make the payoffs to the police and the city officials. Blackie Armes and his brother Floyd, who they called Jardown, took care of the stills that dotted the Little Egypt countryside. Charlie Birger kept track of the slot machines, although Carl was pretty sure he still cheated on the profits—a problem that would have to be dealt with at an opportune time.

To make matters worse, Charlie seemed to be in some kind of cahoots with the Williamson County State's Attorney Arlie Boswell. Carl wasn't sure what kind of action they had going but he certainly intended to find out.

***

Being an educated man, State's Attorney Arlie Boswell missed the learned atmosphere of a more gentile culture. However, he did recognize that his own skills were lacking when competing with comparable intellects. The rural brains of Little Egypt offered him much greater opportunity for financial gain. He had done well enough with the Ku Klux Klan, but with their imminent demise, he saw the bootlegging bumkins as his next easy game.

The climate of religious fervor was an opportunity to clear his incredibly busy docket of prosecutions. With a sweep of his pen, he struck one-hundred-forty-five cases with the pretext that it would heal the community. There were few objections, since it exonerated penalties of gangsters as well as Klan members. He liked to brag that he stood eye-to-eye with gangsters from both Carl Shelton and Charlie Birger gangs, and told them he would not tolerate their bad behavior in his county. In reality, he and Charlie had several underworld dealings that were lucrative for them both. This graft ranged from car-stealing swindles to blackmail and extortion.

Luckily for Arlie, even as his relationship with the Klan was ending, his deals with Charlie were growing. It also helped that the Harold Williams evangelical ministry was coming to an end. The feeling of goodwill that had encompassed Little Egypt for two months had indeed hurt bootlegging and gambling profits, especially since a fool in Tennessee named John Scopes had tried to say that humans were descended from apes.

Arlie made the mistake of stating that God must have been a great scientist himself, and maybe evolution was simply his way of creating things. That caused quite a ferver as good Klan members beat their chests and threw all sorts of feces in his face. Arlie quickly stated he was misquoted.

"You need to kill John Ford," Arlie told Charlie one day.

"How do you come off tellin' me who I need to kill?" Charlie retorted.

"If he becomes circuit clerk, and it looks like he will," Boswell said, "he's going to start digging into the financial records. He'd have to be an idiot not to see the money you, me and Lory Price are scamming on the stolen car business."

"Then we lie low for a while and either payoff Ford or kill him," Charlie said matter-of-factly. "Crime don't stop just because one man is constitutional against lawlessness."

19

Charlie Birger brought Carl to his newly built Shady Rest Hideaway by way of the barbeque stand and gas station on Route 13. He wanted to show off the high level of security he had in place. No one would be able to get down the narrow dirt lane without getting past the barbeque stand, where there would always be plenty of Birger Gang members as a first line of defense. Carl, though, didn't look impressed as he eyed the wooded area around the big log cabin.

"What you looking at, Carl?" Charlie asked. "This place is a damned fortress."

"Lots of trees," Carl said.

"Sure are. Trees we can hide behind if we're attacked."

"Yes," Carl said, "and trees close enough to your house the enemy can hide behind 'em and shoot at you."

Charlie looked around his property as if seeing it for the first time. Carl continued walking toward the big front porch of the house.

"You thinkin' of attackin' me, Big Carl?"

"No, I just don't want my men trapped back here

if someone else does."

Carl was much more impressed when they entered the log cabin, where nearly a dozen members from both gangs were already enjoying themselves. Helen and Blondie were dressed to kill. While the fashion was for women to wear clothing that tightly bound their bosoms, the two Shady Rest hostesses preferred to show off their twin mounds in peasant skirts and blouses.

Taxidermized animals of all kinds were on display in every room. The walls were covered with deer heads and antlers. A hollowed-out elephant's foot held canes and umbrellas. A stone fireplace was wide enough to accommodate enough leather furniture to seat a large crowd. The remainder of the gangsters stood or sat on high stools around a long bar that curved around one entire side of the room. Almost all the men were dressed in shirt sleeves with revolvers in shoulder harnesses.

"Okay, Charlie, I'm impressed."

"Wait until you see the back."

The two passed through a long hallway with several closed doors. Sensual gasps of pleasure came from within many of them. When they exited the building by way of a back door, they walked through a covered breezeway to a building where the excited shouts of men and women could be heard above angry barks and growls. A dog fight was about to begin—and cocks were being readied for their own fights to the death. The dirt arena in the middle of the room was already a pool of blood mixed with animal parts from previous events. It was surrounded by two rows of wooden benches, with other spectators standing behind them all the way to the walls. Paper currency fanned from each person's hand as they exchanged money in last second bets. Meanwhile, dog trainers struggled to hang onto their snarling animals' collars—a feat all the more difficult because they teased the canine gladiators. They would bring them in close to their competitor's heads, then pull them away just as they were near enough to snap at the other's face.

When the dogs were finally released, they came together in a vicious clash of claws and teeth. Carl focused his eyes just above the animals at a pretty lady's lily-white legs on the far side of the arena. Not being a fan of blood and gore, he had used this tactic on many such occasions. The childlike whine of one of the canines brought an unexpectedly quick end to the competition. Carl averted his eyes again as the lady's legs were covered with a thick flow of crimson squirting from the neck of the defeated animal. The woman gave a delighted, shrill laugh as if she had just won a game of bingo.

"Looks like fun," Carl said to Charlie. He handed his partner a cigar. "Let's go for a walk and talk business."

Carl was on his guard as he led the much shorter

gangster out into the woodsy yard. Here and there, guards were stationed among the trees. When Carl turned to hand Charlie a match for his stogie, a tall, broad-shouldered man stood beside him.

"Carl Shelton, I want you to meet Conrad Ritter," Charlie said as he accepted the box of matches. "Connie is one of my new accountants."

Carl found it somewhat amusing that his partner would have a numbers' man who clearly looked big enough to down a small bull with a single punch. He handed Connie a cigar, and then shook his hand.

***

Helen knew the minute she saw Connie Ritter, she had to have him. Never mind that he worked for Charlie Birger to help keep track of money. She had never seen an accountant who was so big and handsome—he could've been a film star like Jack Pickford. His good looks made his deficiency in the bedroom all the more frustrating.

"What the hell kinda copulation is this?" Helen shouted after thirty seconds into the process. "Why don't they provide every male a book when he's born so he'd know how to play his instrument for a woman when they fornicate?"

"I'm just tryin' to be slow and gentle," Connie answered.

"To hell with that! I don't want an easy lope, you fool. I want a hard trot!" Helen would not be denied her amusement. She probed inside his long johns. "Now, give me fast and hard!"

Connie didn't know how to respond. When Helen slapped him so hard his head swam, he figured she was done with him, but a moment later, he lay on his back with the Shawneetown dame riding him like a bronco in a rodeo. And she didn't stop just because she quickly finished. For the next hour, she hit and bit Connie in places he'd never been hit and bit, cussed him and tossed him around the room into positions on the furniture that he was pretty sure the designers had never anticipated happening. Their breathing was hoarse and raw and became synchronized. Both were covered in sweat, making their skin slide easily against each other.

When she finally told him he could go, Connie, never certain what she would do next, grabbed his clothes and ran outside to the chicken coop to get dressed. The hens were not happy to have their home so abruptly invaded, and they let him know by pecking and flapping at him. Connie figured there was nothing they could do to him that the Shawneetown dame had not just done.

***

Anything could happen when the Shawneetown Dame and the Blond Bombshell got together. Most gangsters invited one or the other to their parties, but never both at the same time. Charlie Birger was different. He enjoyed watching the two beauties trying to outdo each other. If Blondie put a lampshade on her head and danced on top of the bar, Helen took off all her clothes, grabbed two pistols, and shot holes in the ceiling.

When their moods were right, they would share a bed with Charlie, though he might as well not even have been there, since they spent most of their time enjoying each other. Charlie didn't mind that so much until the night Helen suggested they invite Connie Ritter to join them. He went into a wild tantrum and locked both women in the fruit cellar for the night so they wouldn't sneak out to see Connie.

Every time Charlie's mind became clear enough to realize that morphine was causing his mood swings, he became so depressed he had to shoot up to make himself feel better. His life had become a vicious rollercoaster, but he didn't know how to get off. The comfortable feelings he got playing with his daughters lasted about as long as his satisfaction after sex with Helen. Time after time, he left his little girls crying when he abandoned them so he could drive out into the country and shoot up. At least sex with Helen could also be a boxing match, which brought him an additional bit of relief. But his daughters' reactions broke his heart. He needed to get them a new mother.

***

Bernice Davis had loved Charlie Birger since the moment she saw him six years before. It was right after her father and brother drowned in the Mississippi River boating accident. Bernice didn't sleep well in those days. She always woke up just before sunup, which was the time of morning the accident had happened. When the insomnia came, she would take her mind off her loss by walking to the outhouse. She could have used the little pot inside, but her father had crafted that for her and it made her sad. One morning, she had finished her business when she heard someone stirring around on the back porch. Peeking through the little crescent moon that was cut into the door, she spied the most handsome man she had ever seen. He had left a bucketful of coal and a sack of groceries on the porch. She waited until he left, then she went inside to wake her mother.

At least once a week for the following two years, the man came. Almost every time, Bernice saw him in the same manner as the first time. Then one day, she answered a knock on her door.

"Hello, my name is Charlie Birger. Is your mother home?"

Bernice turned red and ran into the kitchen. Breathing hard, she flopped down in a chair. Her mother turned from the kitchen sink as Charlie stepped into the middle of the living room.

"Mrs. Davis, I'm here to ask you if you'd be my housekeeper."

After that day, Bernice always accompanied her mother to Charlie's home to help clean. Her mother cleaned house at many other homes and her daughter helped occasionally in them. But she never missed a cleaning day at the Birger house. Both Charlie and his wife Betty were very kind to her. She loved playing with Little Minnie and helped care for little Charlene after she was born.

Then after Charlie's wife left him and the sadness of the loss was finally lifting, she noticed he was not looking at her the same as he once had. Bernice knew she was ripening into a beautiful woman, but she never imagined someone like Charlie would give her a second thought. Then one day her mother took ill, and Bernice took over her housekeeping chores. The day she was to do the Birger home, she spent twice as long cleaning up. She wore her favorite light blue dress, and rubbed peanut oil on her arms to make them smooth.

When she arrived at Charlie's home and didn't see his car, she thought she'd just been silly. One of his friends who always hung around the house let her in. Bernice knew Charlie was a bootlegger.

Everyone in town knew it, but few people condemned him for it. In fact, she heard more good words about him than she did bad, although when it was bad, it was very bad.

She went about cleaning the house as she and her mother always did, starting downstairs before going up to the bedrooms. In other homes, they did the bedrooms first, but in the Birger home, there was usually someone sleeping until noon. Knowing that, she carried her buckets up as quietly as possible, though it was afternoon by then.

All the doors were open, so she assumed no one was home. When she stepped into the master bedroom, she was so shocked to see a shirtless Charlie standing in his trousers. She dropped the wash bucket. The soapy water ran across the wooden floor to his feet. Certain she had lost her mother's job for her, she lowered her head and sobbed. Then she felt Charlie's bare arms around her, comforting her as if she were a child. *But he must not think of me as a child!* Six years of adoration were pent up inside her. Without any instigation from him, she put her mouth to his. At first, he shied away, but the movement of her body against his aroused him as she hoped it would.

His lovemaking was tender and unselfish—a quality she was grateful for. They stayed together in the bed that entire day and next night. She awoke to the smell of bacon and coffee. Her blue dress was dirty from cleaning the day before, so she put on one of his silk shirts. When she came in the kitchen, Charlie took her in his arms and kissed her.

"I called the courthouse and arranged everything. We get married at noon."

***

Charlie was feeling so good the day after his wedding, he killed Jimmy Stone, set him up in the backseat of his car, stuck a cigar in his mouth, and drove around showing him off to his friends. Since Orb Treadway was driving, Charlie waved at passing cars, including policemen. When they came across friends, Orb would honk the horn and Charlie would yell at them that he was giving Jimmy Stone a ride back to his Egan Rats Gang hideout in St. Louis.

When they were done having fun with the corpse, they dumped his body in a ditch near the Halfway Roadhouse and pinned a note to his lapel:

He stole from his friends. KKK

20

Herrin garage owner John Smith did love his country. With Glenn Young and Caesar Cagle both dead, he was the only one who could revive the Klan in Williamson County. This day's primary election could be that opportunity. Much of Smitty's leadership responsibility had been thrust upon him following the now famous shootout in his garage that had left six men dead. Smitty still had nightmares when he went to bed thinking about how close Bernie Shelton's shotgun blast had come to finishing him that day. He knew he probably wouldn't have such bad dreams if he hadn't told so many of his friends that an indentation in his shoulder was from one of the shotgun pellets. It was an infallible lie, since no one but his dead mother knew the little hole was actually the result of chicken pox when he was six years old. Now the lie had brought him both notoriety from the Klansmen and death threats from the bootlegging gangs. Truth be told, he was also more than just a little worried that being the number one Klansman in town put a bullseye right in the middle of his forehead. The Klan had been good enough to provide security guards for both his garage and his home, which relieved the tension a little.

Now, here he was on Election Day, a town hero feeling awkward to be standing before a roomful of Klan members who would serve as election judges and security officers throughout Herrin. His hand shook as it held the paper with the speech his wife had written for him. Though it was short, memorizing and public speaking was not Smitty's strength, causing him to read the words louder and in a much higher pitch than normal.

"Everything I know about foreign races and cultures tells me that only Whites have contributed to freedom for all. Ancient Greeks used direct democracy. Romans used representative democracy. The British gave rights to even more men through the Magna Charta. The American and French Revolutions pressed for freedoms for all men.

"Besides Whites, I have never heard of any race or culture that has done so much to inspire freedom and liberty. If America allows these foreigners to come here, we need to make sure they will not try to destroy the basic freedoms our founders fought so hard to gain for future generations.

"Do you want people in this country who think a robber should have his hand cut off? Those types of people need to stay in their own country if they aren't going to follow our laws that forbid cruel and unusual punishment. Can you imagine if people like Muslims were allowed in our country? They state clearly in their Koran that all Christians and Jews should be murdered or enslaved. Those types of people need to stay in their own countries if they're not going to follow our laws guaranteeing freedom of religion.

"It is our responsibility today to make certain that those who vote are bona fide Americans who are allegiant to our country's values and no one else's. Let today mark the resurrection of the Ku Klux Klan in Williamson County."

Without another word, Smitty sat in a wicker chair while many of the Klansmen patted his shoulder as they left the building. He wasn't certain if they were congratulating him on his speech or letting him know it wasn't that horrible. When the hall finally cleared, he was the last to leave the building. By then, it was thirty minutes until the polls opened, but there were already several carloads of men slowly patrolling the streets. Klan members standing on running boards on either side of the flivvers would have been unusual enough had they not also been sporting rifles and shotguns. Then there were the cars and trucks filled with Shelton and Birger gang members, who waved their Tommy guns as they passed the Klan vehicles.

When he reached his assigned location to serve as poll watcher, Smitty was surprised to see a line of men and women waiting to vote—all of which, he was pleased to note, were good Protestant supporters of the Klan.

The first hours were uneventful—until just before noon. Two carloads of known Catholics exited their vehicles across the street. Still feeling the embarrassment of his earlier high-pitched speech, Smitty decided to take charge. He nodded to former police chief Ford, who sat nearby. Ford quickly called three other Klansmen in from a back room.

The first person to walk in the door was a feisty Catholic nun named Sister Margarete. She was followed by several burly men whom Smitty remembered had been denied the right to vote earlier that morning.

"John Smith," Sister Margarete said firmly, "are you the one who told these parishioners they can't vote?"

"Why, yes, ma'am." Smitty's voice had gotten high again. He coughed, then struggled to make it more masculine. "We want folks votin' who follow America's laws and our United States Constitution, not the laws of some damned Pope in Italy."

Ford and his Klan followers crossed their arms and nodded.

"Then, young man," Sister Margarete said, folding her arms and standing as tall as her minus five-foot frame allowed, "you go in that voting booth and vote for people who will repeal your fifteenth amendment to the U.S. Constitution that you so love. Until you do that, we are going to vote."

She took a step to get around Smitty. He quickly blocked the little nun. While she glared up into his eyes, a vicious fistfight broke out all around them. Smitty was too mesmerized and embarrassed by Sister Margarete's reprimanding stare to join the scuffle.

"Get outa here, Smitty!" Ford yelled. "You're the one they want to kill."

When other Klansmen entered the building to join the fight, Ford grabbed Smitty by the arm and pulled him to the back door. The two men traveled down alleyways to the Smith garage, where two other Klansmen joined them.

"Keep Smitty here," Ford ordered. "I'm going to the Masonic Lodge to warn my brother Harland to have his men on guard."

Smitty was shaken, so he poured himself a double shot of whiskey. His entire morning had been one embarrassing moment after another. Now he had been stood up to by a midget nun in a penguin outfit spouting off something about a fifteenth amendment. Feeling stupid that his wife had written the speech he had given that morning, he downed another double. He felt even dumber when he realized he wasn't certain what the fifteenth amendment even was. He didn't want anyone to know he had never read the U.S. Constitution. In fact, he wasn't sure anyplace in town even had a copy. Surely the library wouldn't, he thought, though he had never been in it.

"You drink much more of that hooch, and you'll be sick all day," a bodyguard said.

"You get sick your way, and I'll get sick mine." Smitty took a big swallow of the whiskey. "I got cobwebs in my head. I need to flush 'em."

That made him even angrier than having the police chief tell him to go into hiding. Smitty helped himself to one more double, then announced to his bodyguards that he was going back to the polling place. Neither of them protested when he grabbed up his handgun and staggered to the door.

The streets were filled with automobiles full of men going one way or another. Sunlight reflecting off the vehicles made him cover his eyes with the hand in which he held the pistol. He watched the movement of the clouds and became dizzy, and then his vision blurred with floaties.

"Hey, Smitty," came a voice from one of the cars that stopped directly in front of him. "Heard you're pretty tough with old lady nuns."

"Why, you son-of-a-bitch!" Smitty shouted. He staggered back a step. "I'll show you tough."

A loud pop and a flash of light brought a buzzing sound near his face. He swatted with his left hand across his cheek, then stood staring in amazement at the blood on his open palm. Dozens of guns coming to life was so instantaneous, it sounded like a firework display that wouldn't stop. When he looked down the street, hundreds of puffs of smoke came from cars and from men firing as they raced into buildings and alleys. Smitty backed up into his garage, ducked down between two automobiles, and covered his head. For fifteen minutes, gunshots continued to penetrate the building and destroyed every car inside the place.

***

Carl Shelton sat comfortably in his Buick in front of the European Hotel smoking cigars and directing his and Birger's men toward Ku Klux Klan strongholds. Charlie had chosen to remain at Shady Rest for fear he'd be thrown in the hoosegow again. Plus, he had just married Bernice Davis the month before, and he hadn't broken her in yet to his carousing and racketeering activities.

Bernie, though, was having the time of his life riding around with Blackie Armes, who was tormented by the fact that he'd only grazed John Smith's cheek with what should have been a clean kill.

"That son-of-a-bitch Smitty was bobbin' around so much I nearly missed his head clean," Blackie lamented.

Blackie's youth and inexperience made teasing him hard to resist. That morning while the other gangsters were busy checking their weapons, Blackie combed his hair and sprayed himself with cologne. When the others made fun of him, he turned to them and said, "If I'm going to die today, I want to smell good." That sense of humor was why Bernie liked the young hoodlum. Still, he decided this was a teachable moment.

"You sure is green. Couldn't you see he was snozzled?" Bernie laughed. "If you'd taken his lack of sobriety into account, you'd have tried for a body shot. Remember the gunfighter's code—aim big, hit big."

"I don't need no shootin' lesson." Blackie blushed. "I'm a head shot man. You just wait until next time."

The next time came more quickly than Blackie had imagined. He and Bernie arrived back at the hotel, drunk with excitement, as were most of the others who had been involved in the gunfight. Carl's presence seemed to quell all merriment. The mood of the dozen men gathered around him became grim and stayed grim.

"There are several Klansmen vetoin' voters at the Masonic Lodge," Carl announced. "Get in and get out quick." He pointed to a veteran gangster he trusted for being smart. "Harold Weaver, you do the talkin'. See if you can use friendly persuasion to make the voting impartial."

Excited for more action, the gang jumped back into their vehicles and motored to the Lodge. They left the cars running while they exited, spread out, and began moving carefully up the lawn toward the building.

Inside, former police chief Ford had just warned Klansman guards Mack and Ben Sizemore there might be trouble. Ben was a hot head who lacked skills at fisticuffs and tried to make up for it with his gun.

"You seen any of our Shelton or Birger foes?" Ford asked as the three men stepped out of the building onto the front lawn.

"I hope we do," Ben said. "Your brother Harland is stationed across the street with a rifle in case the gangsters attack."

Three cars roared up and skidded to a stop down the street. Ben reached for his gun.

"Hold that hog leg, mister," Ford warned him. Being a former police chief, he still had an urge to deescalate confrontations. "We deal with them peaceably first."

He and the Sizemore brothers walked out on the lawn to meet two approaching men. Several others from the cars were seeking cover behind trees and bushes. Blackie Armes and Harold Weaver were the two who approached. Blackie was as reckless as Ben, but Harold was as reasonable a gangster as any.

"Here's one of the sons-of-a-bitch we're going to kill," Blackie said.

Harold halted the young man with a raised hand. "Ford," he said, "it's our understandin' that these Klan boys have been denyin' folks of their votin' rights."

"We are actually here to make sure that don't happen," Ford said calmly.

"Why are you so slow to get around to it?" Blackie asked.

"Why you talkin' such bosh?" Ben snarled.

"What we do is beyond your concern," Ford told Blackie. Still, he held up his forefinger and thumb to show he didn't want a fight, then slowly extracted his service revolver from its holster.

Harold reached equally slow and took it from him. "We'll leave you to do your job, Ford," Harold said. "But if you don't, we'll be back." He turned and walked back toward the cars.

Blackie's shoulders drooped as he followed along. He had a sense of incompletion. The venture seemed a futile expedition that accomplished nothing. The Klan would be right back to their escapades as soon as the gangs departed.

A gunshot rang out from behind them. With a bullet in his back, Harold lurched forward and fell face down onto the ground.

Blackie pulled his gun, spun, and fired at John Ford's head. His bullet was on its way before he saw that Ben Sizemore was the back shooter standing with a smoking gun.

Blackie swore aloud when he saw that for the second time that day his head shot had only nicked his target, this time in the neck. It did, however, cause Ford to spin to the ground. This impulse saved his life, since the gangsters watching the scene from cover opened up, blasting both Sizemore brothers off their feet. Hearing the well-placed shots buzzing past his head, Blackie turned and raced back toward the getaway cars, leaving the dead body of his friend Harold Weaver lying in the grass.

Meanwhile, John Ford's brother Harland lay spread-eagled far enough away he was afraid an errant bullet at Blackie or Harold might hit one of the Klansmen. Just as Ben shot Harold Weaver in the back, an automobile sped down the street toward Harland. He rolled to his side.

Orb Treadway drove a turtle-backed Buick Coupe. Harland pulled the trigger as fast as he could get the gun cocked. Struck in the face by one of the bullets Orb's hands flew off the steering wheel and over his head. The Buick's tires screeched as the vehicle spun sideways and came to a stop alongside the curb.

When his rifle jammed, Harland sat up so he could clear it. He felt a hard thump to his chest. When he tried to draw a breath, no air seemed able to enter his mouth. Rolling onto his back, he looked down at the white shirt he wore. It was speckled red, like he had gotten caught in a rain of blood. The wind whistled through the trees around him, and he knew he was about to die. With no air filling his lungs, it was only a matter of seconds.

The realization caused his fighting spirit to rise. Bringing the rifle up, he thought if he could just get his gun cocked, he might get off one more shot before he expired. He managed to clear the jam and cock the weapon, but forgot to remove his finger from the trigger. The blast split right through a small branch on the cottonwood above him. White flakes floating slowly to the ground landed on his face. They tickled like the butterfly kisses his young daughter had so often given him with her eyelashes. It was a pleasant thought to die by.

***

After so many violent skirmishes, Bernie preferred whiskey to women. He and Blackie set outside the Herrin hospital passing a flask as they counted wounded being brought in. The death toll was even with three Klansmen dead and three racketeers.

"There is no excuse for artillery that fails during an engagement," Bernie told Blackie, who felt somewhat vexed to have watched Harland Ford die because his weapon failed him.

"Did you see how he went down fightin'?" Blackie said admiringly. "You know, if he hadn't died, he'd have been one man I'd be proud to buy a drink."

"You're a strange duck, Blackie." Bernie chuckled. "You put a bullet in a man's chest, then say you wish he'd lived so you could buy him a drink."

"I was just saying, Bernie." Blackie frowned. "Why, I thought you'd compliment me for my hip shot to Harland's chest."

"Oh, okay, good shot, kid." Bernie couldn't help adding, "But John Ford counts as another missed head shot, too."

***

Charlie was well-barbered by the time he left the tonsorial parlor the next day. Even his nose and ear hairs had been plucked. He was not as accustomed to dirt as was Carl. In his estimation, an unwashed leader diminished his efficiency to command. Therefore, when he arrived at Carl's farm and found the Shelton gang leader underneath a truck, he was not impressed.

"I discovered a new way to smuggle moonshine inside the gas tank," Carl said. He wiped his greasy hands on his expensive silk shirt.

"Well, I don't wanna be near if the hooch and the gas get close to a flame."

Carl laughed. "Me neither."

"Any word on how Treadway and Briggs got touched off yesterday?" Charlie asked.

"I know that Briggsy's revolver wasn't fired," Carl said.

"Did it jam?"

"Not Briggsy's gun." Carl was somewhat insulted. He was meticulous about checking his arsenal and spared no expense for his men's weaponry. Economy in such matters led to lives lost, and dependable men were rare these days. Charlie, on the other hand, preferred to get his arsenal by stealing it, an unpredictable method at best.

"Connie Ritter told me the state militia showed up with twenty men to guard Smitty's garage," Charlie said for lack of conversation.

"Hell, with all the bullet holes, there ain't hardly nothin' left of that garage," Carl said. "Ol' Smitty packed up last night and headed for Florida. He said he ain't got the stomach to start another Klan raid, even if they put a saloon next door to him."

"Sounds like the end of the white sheets." The conversation was getting around to what Charlie wanted to talk about.

"So, what's next?" Carl asked. He looked his rival gang boss straight in the eyes.

"Well, come to mention it, I'd like to ask if you'd give me a hand bringin' some of my relatives over from Russia."

"How we supposed to help with that?"

"I've made arrangements to bring them to the Bahamas, but I reckon my name ain't good enough to get them into the United States."

"So, you want me to bring them in, along with the rum?"

"That's the general idea."

"I'll think about it," Carl said. He slid back under the truck and began tinkering again.

Charlie didn't like the way the Shelton gang boss delivered his answer.

21

Charlie's men had been suffering with the shitting sickness for several days. He blamed it on the summer heat, but his thugs feared the Sheltons were poisoning the spring. Tensions between the gangs had been mounting since the election day gunfight. The problems mostly involved mistrust concerning the opportunities that arose from the many roadhouses springing up throughout Little Egypt.

The diarrheal ailment passed, but then a daffy young man who liked to hang out at Shady Rest was found nearly beat to death in his parked automobile. He never recovered enough to say who had done the beating. All he could say was, "What the hell was that?" He repeated the bewildered comment every few minutes for the remainder of his life, which wasn't more than a few days.

It was indeed a hot summer, and tempers were quick to flair. Every night there was a fight somewhere. When a waiter at the Jefferson Hotel was nearly clubbed to death over a mistake in an order, Blackie Armes was suspected along with Shelton gang members Ray and Harry Walker. The two were brothers and personal bodyguards for Carl. During the Herrin massacre, their father had been a police chief and Harry one of his deputies. Maybe that was why when UMWA leader Otis Clark was murdered, Harry had been one of the suspects. Since he joined the Ku Klux Klan soon after that, many suspected him of being a Shelton spy sent to keep an eye on Glenn Young. This suspicion was confirmed when it was proven that Harry was withholding liquor confiscated during the Klan raids and selling it back to the Sheltons. Similar to Carl, Harry was the brains and brother Ray was the Bernie-like muscle—a fact proven out when the elder Walker brother convinced a thug named Ed Rocassi to shoot it out with Boyd "Oklahoma Curly" Hartin.

Being short, very thin, and quick afoot, no one in the Shelton gang had ever imagined that Oklahoma Curly would ever perish from his inability to dodge bullets. The result of his demise came instead from the simple mistake of not counting his six shots. The customers present at the roadhouse neither knew nor cared for the reason the two began firing away at each other. At the first shot, they exited the building through doors and windows. When the gunfight became a matter of hide and seek behind tables and chairs, Rocassi became economical with his ammunition. Oklahoma Curly, on the other hand, must not have remembered that he was firing a six shooter instead of his Colt M1911, which fired seven shots. After just a few seconds, Rocassi boldly stepped into the open, smiled at the dumfounded Oklahoma Curly clicking his weapon on empty chambers, then unloaded three bullets into his opponent's chest.

Harry Walker provided Rocassi with money for his defense and the grand jury eventually determine the killing had been self-defense. Harry never told anyone why he had wanted Oklahoma Curly dead.

***

The day Art Newman sauntered into Shady Rest might have been a further sign that a gang war was brewing between the Birger and the Shelton gangs.

"You got a mighty determined walk for a dead man," Charlie said when Art put a walking stick in the elephant foot umbrella stand.

"Carl Shelton lied about me to bootleggers all the way from here to Tennessee," Art said. "I want to get them brothers back for slandering me. I imagine you're the fella to help me do it."

"So, what you planning to do to the Shelton brothers?"

"I was thinkin' torture and dismemberment would be a good start."

"Okay, Art. Well, I was thinkin' we might slice the soles off your feet to make it easier for you to go crawlin' back to them."

"Then you wouldn't be no better off, would you?" Art said through clenched teeth while lighting a cigarette. "Of course, since I know where all the Shelton stills and hideaways are, you might prefer for my boots to stay on."

To the annoyance of several in the room, Charlie not shooting him was a signal that Art enjoyed his protection.

Charlie poured the little gangster a spot of rum.

***

When Joe Chesnas and two of his youthful friends robbed an elderly Harrisburg mail carrier named William Unsell, they were unaware of both written and unwritten law. First, no one had ever told them that robbing a postal worker was a federal offense. They assumed they were going to make a few dollars found in the envelopes. They were also hoping the letters might contain some bits of gossip that they could be the first to share around the community. Second, no one had ever told them that Charlie Birger had an unwritten rule that made crime off limits in Harrisburg.

The storm clouds hovering to the north the day after the robbery were foreboding to Joe. He had never trusted anyone, especially women, which might explain his brusque treatment of them. The fact that he had told a gal he'd been courting about the robbery weighed on his mind. So too was the fact that he and his fellow thieves had not taken the precaution of wearing masks.

Bill Unsell had known each of them since they were toddlers, but intimidation had always gotten them through previous mischief. So they saw no reason that a tottery old man couldn't be bullied into silence. Indeed, the postman had seemed scared enough when Joe made the threat. Still, Joe was getting so worried that Unsell might talk, he was beginning to feel sickly.

The rain hit the windshield, and Joe's girl seemed to be getting anxious. Having the windows up on the hot summer day made the humidity inside the car almost unbearable. The dirt road was bumpy, making his head ache and his stomach all the queasier. Finally arriving at the little field he had used on previous excursions with girls, he parked the car and leaned over closer to her.

"I'm partial to a strappin' fella like you," she said shyly. "I'd approve a kiss, I'd imagine."

When their lips touched, the salty wetness from his sweat flavored the kiss.

"Oooh," she said, wiping the kiss off her mouth.

"That's okay," Joe said. "What I want is in here, anyway." He grabbed the top of her blouse and pulled it down.

"No, Joe, stop! I'm a preacher's daughter."

"Listen, preacher's daughter, let me tell you about the here-after then." Joe pushed her down on the front seat and lay on top of her. "If you're not here after what I'm here after, you're gonna be here after I'm gone."

Five minutes later, the wind howled and the rain blew sideways. The young girl was left sitting in a large puddle of mud crying while he drove his flivver back toward town. His anger was an anger he was unable to put down. It seemed everything he attempted lately had resulted in failure.

That night he tossed all night in his bed, thinking about all the bad decisions he had already made in his short life. Now, if the old postal worker talked, Joe's bad choices might result in prison time. He buried his head beneath his pillow. But the ghost continued to howl, reiterating his lifetime of regrets.

The next night, William Unsell died.

***

Sheriff Small arrested Joe the following day. The young, would-be gangster couldn't figure out how anyone could have known it was he who sent the postman to his maker. Since Small didn't say what he was arresting him for, Joe decided to keep quiet. Therefore, when he was put in a cell with Charlie Birger himself, he was ecstatic.

"Mr. Birger, what are you doin' here?"

"Just payin' my yearly respects to Sheriff Small." Charlie lay on a cot, smoking. "What they got you in here for, Joey?"

"I don't know for sure. Probably for being the best lookin' kid in town." He snickered at his own wit.

"I heard they were bringin' you in for your own safety," Charlie said without looking at him.

"You heard whaaaat?"

"Yeah, they said you kilt Bill Unsell last evenin'." Charlie now stared at him as if really seeing him for the first time. "I didn't know you was a gunfighter, Joey."

To have been paid a compliment by the likes of Charlie Birger made the young man's chest swell. "Well, I ain't kilt near as many as you did by my age, Charlie, but I'd 'spect I got time to catch up."

"I sure hope so." Charlie looked away again as if he had doubt.

"Why'd you say they brought me here for my own protection?"

"Haven't you heard?" The crime boss handed Joe a cigarette. "They's getting up a lynch mob. Seems ol' Bill was a mighty popular fella."

Joe loosened his tie. "Lynch mob?"

Charlie set up. "Don't be frettin', Joey. I've been in your situation quite a number of times."

"What'd you do, Charlie?"

"Oh, I confess right up every time. Seems all the law wants is someone to pin the crime on so they can look good in the public eye. They usually keep me in lock-up for a few weeks or months, then send me home early for good behavior. How'd you kill him anyway, Joey?"

Joe wasn't prepared to relive that moment. "Talkin' 'bout it just don't sit right with me."

"I'll tell you what, Joey. You tell me how you did it, and if they try to hang you, I'll have my gang break you out."

Joey thought about his options. There must be truth in what Charlie said, but he hadn't planned on reliving the killing before he could reinvent it to make himself look better. He really didn't want anyone to know the assassination had nearly been botched. The moment was clearly imprinted on his memory. He entered the house by tearing through a window screen, then stumbled loudly across two chairs. To make matters worse, the window he had chosen was in Unsell's bedroom.

"Don't shoot me! Don't shoot me!" Unsell pled. He sat up in his bed while fumbling for his spectacles and the handgun on his vanity.

"Okay. I won't," Joe said, then promptly put two bullets into the old man.

"I didn't shoot you," William Unsell lamented. "Why'd you shoot me?"

"I thought you would shoot me!" Joe shouted.

"No, I said I wouldn't. Now you've done for me, Joey." The old man struggled to say before he pitched forward on his bed. His head on his knees reminded the young murderer of a closed jack knife.

Joe told the story as best he could. His was the dreamy talk of a dissatisfied criminal. A few moments later, a deputy came and unlocked the cell.

"Sheriff wants to see you, Charlie."

In leaving, the crime boss nodded a friendly goodbye to Joe, who flushed with gratitude. The youngster felt a certain sadness seeing the famous gangster leave. He hoped Charlie didn't think him incompetent for the sloppy killing. He immediately resolved that if he got out of this predicament, he would never again preform a holdup without wearing a mask.

A few moments later, Charlie and the deputy arrived at the sheriff's office. When the gangster entered the room, John Small and the state's attorney stood and gave him a disconcerting look. Charlie sat down in the chair and put his feet up on Small's desk. The sheriff handed him a whiskey, and the state's attorney gave him a cigar. After Charlie was comfortable and ready, he related to the two men everything the young murderer had told him.

A month later, Joe Chesnas was hanged.

22

Just about the only time the Shady Rest got quiet was when the Blond Bombshell sang. That was out of respect for her fine voice—but also for fear that she and Helen would make everyone's life miserable the rest of the evening. A good night would mean plenty of wild and crazy dancing and maybe some fisticuffs. Then there would be the usual dog and cock fights, followed by some sharpshooting contests out on the lawn.

Charlie liked to spoil his special guests with uncut liquor and girls. On this night, those VIPs were the Shelton boys and a few of their lieutenants. Of course, it also gave him the opportunity to point out some of the muscle in his gang.

"That fella with the gold teeth is Steve George, my groundskeeper," Charlie told the brothers. "He spent four years in Missouri State Pen for the murder of his wife and her lover. He killed them during a Labor Day picnic."

"Why would they send a fella to prison just for killin' an unfaithful wife and her scumbag boyfriend?" Bernie asked.

"Well, sir, I don't know fer sure." Charlie shook his head. "Maybe they took into account that he's also a drug addict and a petty thief. But I'll tell ya what, I believe I could get Steve George to kill anybody for maybe a cigar—or at least a five-dollar bill."

"I heard he weren't like that when he was younger," Blondie said. "They say he only got mean after he learnt to use a gun."

"He sure don't appear to be no killer," Helen said. "Did you notice how polite he was at the dinner table?"

"Being correct with a knife and fork don't make a person a gentleman," Bernie said.

Connie Ritter walked toward them and whispered something to Charlie, who then followed him out the back door.

Bernie took the opportunity to aim a spit of chaw toward a spittoon that was sculptured in the shape of a naked woman. His spittle fell short—just the right amount to provide a modest covering for the ladies frontside.

"That's as fancy a cuspidor as I ever seen," Bernie said to hide the embarrassment of his poor aim.

A man staggered onto the dance floor.

Bernie grinned. "Now there's a ring-tailed drunk."

"He sure got a snoot full, all right," Helen whispered to Carl. "That fella with three sheets to the wind is John Howard. We call him Howie. He just got fired as Charlie's slot machine accountant. You may want to visit with him, if you get a chance. He's mad at the boss."

Finding men with enough schooling to keep track of money was tough enough, but finding ones who were honest was an even greater challenge. The one thing Helen admired about Carl Shelton was his ability to do his own accounting. Many a time she would be having a conversation while the elder Shelton sat counting and sorting bills.

"That's the payroll there." Carl would point at several stacks, each individually banded. "Here's protection money for law enforcement. Here's the cut for the owners of the roadhouses, and here's the rest to be divided between us."

Charlie, on the other hand, was on his fourth accountant in the past year. Connie Ritter was doing okay with the payroll and miscellaneous numbers. The problem was with the slot machine money. Max Pulliam had wanted paid too much, so he was replaced with John "Howie" Howard, who worked only for five weeks. For no real good reason other than lack of trust, Charlie fired him and put a former coal miner named Ward "Casey" Jones in his place. Thieving among thieves was expected, but hardly tolerated.

Howie's blind staggers at the party was a direct result of that termination. He was miffed to lose the cushy job of counting money, especially the money that found its way into his own pockets. To make matters worse, Charlie had called him lazy when he fired him, a degradation that riled Howie to no end. "You're as lazy as a fat sow in summertime," Charlie had said.

Howie didn't consider himself lazy, but he *was* against unnecessary movement. That trait had more than likely been the reason Harrisburg Police Officer Hardrock Gowan had been able to shoot him that past winter. On that day, Gowan had just walked past Howie's car when he glanced inside and saw him sitting in it smoking, a pistol on the car seat beside him. That was reason enough for the hot-headed police officer to draw his .44 caliber service revolver. In his normal nonchalant manner, Howie reached for the pistol next to him. Gowan considered that a personal affront, and let loose of a single shot that happened to imbed itself in the gangster's gold pocket watch. Since the watch was hanging just below his sternum, the force of the impact knocked the wind out of him, making arrest a simple matter.

Now in his inebriated state, the formality of the party vexed Howie. Charlie expected all guests—from gangsters to their molls—even coal miners—be in proper attire. Having been too drunk to dress himself properly, Howie felt as sloppy as he looked. Besides, when it was hot and there was a breeze, keeping his shirttail out kept his stomach cool.

"You're Carl Shelton, ain't ya?" Howie asked when a tall gangster walked up to him.

"Oh, I think you've got me mistaken with someone else," Carl said casually.

Howie lurched, gagging.

Carl caught the back of his head and directed it toward a flower vase. When the vase overran and the vomiting became dry heaves, Carl took the drunk by the arms and led him out the front door.

"You sure is makin' short work of good hooch," Carl said when they reached a row of parked automobiles.

"This ain't no box social." Howie stumbled a little, then put the back of his hand to his forehead. "This heat feebles me."

"I heard ol' Charlie done you wrong on that slot machine bookkeepin' deal," Carl said matter-of-factly.

"You sure you ain't a Shelton?"

"Not unless my mama lied to me."

"That's good," Howie stammered. "'Cause I wouldn't stool on anybody, even for store-bought whiskey."

"Here." Carl produced a flask. "Have a snoot from the hair of the dog that bit you."

Howie accepted, rinsing and spitting with the first mouthful, then swallowing hard on the next. "Damn, that's good stuff."

"So, why did ol' Charlie fire you?" Carl asked.

"Oh, 'cause I wasn't shortin' the Shelton boys enough," Howie said. His eyes rolled back in his head. “Charlie was holdin’ back forty percent and telling the Sheltons it was the cost of protection durin’ transport from Florida.” Howie’s entire body turned stiff as a poker.

Carl recognized the symptom. He stood back while John Howard timbered like a giant oak, face down on the ground.

The information on Charlie’s deceit, while not surprising, *was* disappointing. Using his fingers, he started counting the number of men and guns he had at the party versus the number the Birger loyalists had.

***

“I believe I’ll bet on that gamey lookin’ rooster,” Helen Holbrook said.

“I will too,” Charlie said. He didn’t care much for the way Carl had been staring at him since he’d taken a seat in the bleacher across the arena. Jealousy was a trait he hadn’t experienced much in his life.

“I don’t believe the way Carl is admirin’ you,” Charlie said. “I aim to disabuse him of that notion once and for all.”

“Oh, piddle, Charlie, he knows I’m your girl. Just settle down and watch the fight.”

The rooster Charlie and Helen bet on might have won a foot race, but not a cockfight. The bird ran around the outside of the pen until it wore itself out, then was pounced upon and almost clawed to death before its trainer grabbed it up. If the young cocksman was thinking he might be able to use the animal in a future bout, his plan was quickly destroyed when Charlie plucked it out of his hands, twisted its neck completely off and threw the head into a corner.

The applause from Helen, Blondie, and the ladies of the evening was followed by cheers from the men—and even a laugh and a thumbs up from Carl. That seemed to appease Charlie's rage for a moment. He raised a bloody hand, smiled and then wiped it off with a handkerchief.

The dog fights were next. Charlie quickly recouped some of the money he had lost on the cowardly cock. He still didn't like it, though, that every time a fight began, Carl seemed to stare across the arena at Helen. That didn't last long, though, because the oldest Shelton stood up after a few fights, tipped his hat to Charlie, and left the arena.

Later, when one of Charlie's favorite bulldogs was brought out, there appeared to be no challengers until Earl volunteered one of his own animals.

"How much he weigh?" the referee asked.

"Sixty-two pounds," Earl answered.

In the interest of the Shelton-Birger consolidation, Charlie figured he shouldn't insult his business partner by demanding a weigh-in. He nodded to the judge, and Earl's cur was brought out of the holding pen. Long, snarling fangs were contained by a thick leather muzzle. The mongrel's red eyes and drooling nose brought gasps from the spectators.

The room erupted with the shouting of odds, followed by men passing money to holders. Earl's dog seemed to relish in the excitement and violently shook his head—an action that only increased the odds in his favor.

When Helen and Blondie gave five to one in favor of Earl's canine, Charlie's eyes became a mirrored image of the muzzled bulldog. He laid down all the money he had gained that evening on his prized animal.

A few moments later Earl's champion was unmuzzled, and the trainers began the teasing process. No incentive was necessary, though. Before the referee could officially start the match, the heavily-favored dog broke free of his handler, took his opponent by the throat, and thrashed him from side to side like a terrier shaking a rat. It took two men to pry the victor's teeth away from the bloody loser.

"Check that animal's weight!" Charlie's shout brought an instant silence to the room.

"You questionin' my honesty?" Earl shouted back. He and all the Shelton thugs stood as one. The Birger men did the same. The two gangs glared at one another.

The crowd waited anxiously for the dog to calm down enough to be placed on the scales. Finally, the shaking referee raised his head. In a weak and broken voice, he announced, "Seventy-three pounds!"

The sound of handguns drawn from shoulder holsters was as much in unison as the cocking of each weapon. A brief pause followed, as if both sides had silently agreed to allow the screaming women to exit the room. Meanwhile, the two gangs selected their targets, and each man looked around as if weighing options. An itch in someone's trigger finger set every man in motion. Weapons fired even as the men dove for the nearest cover behind barrels, hay bales, or thin wooden coops housing the cocks.

"Boots, can you get out through that hole there?" the referee shouted over the gunfire to one of the young dog trainers. The two were huddled together next to the cages, where dogs went wild from the constant barrage of gunshots.

"I don't know!" the boy called Boots shouted back. "That there's a doggie door."

"Well, I'm going out through there. I can't get out no other way." The referee dove for the hole and squeezed headfirst through the opening. The britches at his rear-end hooked on a nail, but a bullet through one cheek of his ass seemed to propel him to freedom. The young boy followed.

When they reached the referee's car, he leaned in his seat on his good buttock, started the vehicle, and drove as fast as the flivver would motor down the lane, past the barbeque stand, and on toward Herrin.

"By golly," he said when they were in the clear, "that ain't no place for a preacher's son, is it?"

***

"Them Shelton boys ought to never to have messed with Harrisburg," Charlie told Art and Connie the afternoon after the gunfight. "I wouldn't let Joe Chesnas get away with murder in my town, and I sure as hell ain't gonna have them brothers heistin' jewelry. If it's a gang war they want, then it's a gang war they'll get."

In reality, the jewelry heist had been little more than a sting to get back what was owed them. But Art also had a grudge against the Sheltons, and planned on using their indiscretions against them. Though several from both sides had been wounded in the previous night's fiasco, no one had died.

"I heard it was Harry Walker who put Ed Rocassi up to killing Oklahoma Curly," Art said. He wanted to ingratiate himself to Charlie. Getting revenge on one of Carl's main bodyguards seemed a good way to accomplish that.

"I'm going to try talking to Carl one more time. If that doesn't work..." Charlie took a wad of bills from his breast pocket and set it in front of Art. "This is for Harry Walker's head."

23

“Last time you and I scheduled a talk, you came alone,” Charlie said when Carl entered Shaw’s Garden Roadhouse along with his brothers. The only other person in the tavern area was the very nervous owner, Bob Shaw. He stood behind the bar cleaning glasses that were already so clean they sparkled.

“Yes, and as I recall, last time you had just engaged a whole room full of varmints.” Carl sat in the chair backwards as before, only this time he didn’t set his revolver on the table. “Unlike today, when you keep your rats in the backroom.”

“Seems we’ve lost trust in each other.”

“Sad to say, it’s true. Now, what you propose we do about that?”

Charlie considered the odds of trying to end the feud right then and there. He had snuck Rado Millich and Steve George into the backroom the night before. How Carl knew, he wasn’t sure. The fact that he had only brought his brothers indicated he thought he would have the upper hand in a shootout. He was probably right. Though Steve

George was a cold-blooded killer, he was more of a knife man than a gunfighter.

"I told you before, I'm a businessman," Carl continued when Charlie failed to answer his question. "There is no reason we can't just live and let live."

Charlie's dark eyeballs jerked in their sockets like Mexican jumping beans.

Carl felt the confusion—the irrational logic occurring in his rival's brain. He had also noticed the gauntness of the man's face, the hollowness in his cheeks, and the dark circles under his eyes. Charlie would have the strength of insanity, but the stamina of a man who had spent too many days and nights lying in bed with a needle in his arm.

"I ain't goin' to fight you outside where your thugs can shoot me in the back," Charlie said, removing his shoulder harness and setting it on the table.

"If two fellas like you and me fight in this place, it's likely to get tore up pretty good." Carl followed suit with his own weapon.

"I can practical guarantee it," Charlie said.

Bernie handed the owner a wad of bills. "This should cover the damages."

Shaw laid the money out on the counter and divided it by the denominations.

Charlie went over to the backroom door and opened it. Rado and Steve walked out and stood on the far side of the room across from the younger Shelton brothers.

Carl tried to stretch his muscles without appearing to be a prize fighter waiting for the match to start.

Charlie just crouched, waiting to spring—which he did seconds later when Carl took his eyes off him. His blow barely made Carl's head move, but a right-handed counterpunch sent Charlie flying backwards into a table that crushed under his weight. Bob Shaw moved two bills off the stack in front of him.

Carl waited patiently for the smaller man to get up. Charlie charged with a head butt, which Carl caught under his right arm, but that sent them both crashing into the player piano. Shaw extracted several of the larger denominations from the pile. Charlie was already breathing hard. Trying to get free of Carl's grip around his head was exhausting, so he bit the man's forearm. Carl pushed him away and delivered another hard blow, this time a left to the jaw.

When Shaw started to reach for the money, Bernie set his revolver on the counter and the bartender withdrew his hand.

Charlie was clearly defeated, but still game for one more assault. He feinted with a left and delivered a hard right to his opponent's mouth. Deciding the fight had gone on long enough, Carl grabbed the gangster by his neck and the seat of his pants and threw him through the glass window and on to the hood of a parked car. Watching Bernie from the corner of his eye, Shaw began extracting bills until the gangster retrieved what was left.

The Sheltons waited for Rado and Steve to collect their boss, put him in a car, and drive away.

"You think that will be the end of it?" Bob Shaw asked.

"No, sir, I don't," Carl said. "I think it's just the beginning."

***

"How many words you got inside that hat?" Everett Smith asked Harry Walker a few nights later. He raised the pistol he'd been hiding under the table. Everett didn't like fancy talking dudes like the slick Harry.

The two men had been arguing over one of the girls who was for sale—a fourteen-year-old virgin who had been drugged and was being offered for a hefty price. The two competed at draw poker for hours to gain enough of the other's money to make the purchase. Lucky for the young girl, the competition was currently a stalemate.

"Looks like she's a heap more costly than either one of us can afford," Harry said, looking at the weapon.

"You came the long way around," Everett said, putting the revolver back in his shoulder holster, "but you finally got to what's right."

"Would you have really kilt me?" Harry asked.

"You don't call, you don't see the other fella's hand, do you?"

"I still don't like you," Harry told Everett. "but I don't want to kill you no more."

Everett seemed satisfied with that. He turned and walked out the front door.

Harry finished his drink.

"I'll be havin' me some more of that rotgut before I leave."

"I'm all out, Harry. How 'bout some gin?"

"That bathtub gin ain't green yet." Harry turned toward the doorway. "Disappointing intoxication. Disappointing evening. Good night, boys." No sooner than Harry was out the door, those inside heard him yell, "I got no quarrel with you, Art!"

Two pistol shots were almost simultaneous. After a few moments, the patrons in the roadhouse filtered out the front door. Two bodies lay a few yards from each other. Art Newman stood over Harry Walker, a thirty-eight aimed at his head.

Harry shivered violently. The back of his white shirt turned scarlet. "Well," he gasped, "I'm about to die anyway. You might as well go ahead and finish me. It might help advance your career as an assassin."

Art obliged the gangster by providing him a lethal bullet. He then sauntered over to where a group of men stood over Everett Smith, who lay on his side, breathing shallowly.

"Make sure I'm buried next to my brother," Everett whispered. "Would you, Art?"

"Of course, I will, Everett. I'd come to your wake too, but they might arrest me for your murder."

"Well, that's good to know," Everett said. "I thought it was Harry done me in. I was kinda growin' fond of him." With that his eyes shut and his head drooped to the side.

***

The first inclination the Sheltons had that Art Newman was back in Little Egypt came when a shaken Ray Walker entered the Farmer's Clubhouse.

"Carl, I promised you that before I killed anyone, I'd let you know," Ray said. "Well, sir, I'm fixin' to kill Art Newman."

"I'd have no objection to that, Ray," Carl said. "If you know where he is, I might even go along, just to watch him die."

"Hop in my car, then, but you may not live long enough to enjoy the moment. He's hidin' under a rock at the Shady Rest."

"That's news to me. Why you want to kill him?"

"He killed my brother last night."

"Harry? Dead?"

"And Everett Smith."

Carl shook his head. "Well, I guess the gang war is started."

***

"No one was at the roadhouse by the time we arrived," State's Attorney Arlie Boswell told Carl and Ray Walker. "The bartender said he called us after he heard the shots, but said he'd been too busy to remember who'd been there last night."

Carl didn't like or trust Boswell, but this was a situation where if he could use the law to get rid of Art Newman, he might be able to stop the gang war—or at least get the public on the Sheltons' side.

Charlie's mental state was shaky at best. If Carl could just keep his own men under control, he believed his rival would self-destruct.

"I've got it on good authority," Boswell went on, "Art Newman is going straight."

"Yes, and if my grandma had wheels," Carl said, "she'd have been a wagon."

When they left the law office, Ray was determined to kill Art Newman.

"Not yet, Ray," Carl said. "Please trust me on this. Art will get his, but we have to work this so the entire Birger gang goes down with him."

Ray Walker had always followed his older brother's advice, and Harry had told him many times to trust Carl's judgment. Ray handed the boss his weapon. "Okay," he said, "but you'd better hold this for me until I quit seein' red."

***

Early in the crap game, John Howard spotted Sod Gaddis stealing cash off the table. Since it wasn't his money being stolen, Howie decided to keep quiet. A few hours before dawn, though, Sod tried to slip a late bet onto the table, and Howie decided enough was enough. Since he was six inches taller than the cheat, he chose to embarrass him by slapping his face like the little baby he was.

Bright red finger marks decorated Sod's cheek as he raced out of the roadhouse. When he rushed back into the room a few minutes later brandishing a shotgun, Howie leapt to safety behind the row of players on the wall side of the table. Hands went up from men and women who couldn't avoid being in the path if a blast was let loose.

"Sod, don't shoot!" the stickman from the craps game shouted. "There are dodgers out on you! You'll never get away with murder!"

The argument worked. Sod released the hammers on the weapon and backed out through the doorway.

"Pour me a short one, would you, barkeep?" Howie said with a sigh now that he felt safe. The only thing the bartender gave him was the same angry stare as he was getting from everyone else in the room.

With head and shoulders down, Howie moved slowly through the silent crowd to the doorway. Tipping his hat, he opened the door and stepped out to leave. A shotgun blast raised him off his feet and flung him onto his back in front of the crap table.

Everyone continued to stand silently for a moment, listening to Howie's gasping breaths.

"I'll give five-to-one odds he don't live until mornin'," one of the gamblers finally said.

Another leaned down and checked Howie's pulse. "I'll take that bet."

An hour later the bet was paid off.

24

The sun set orange the night Charlie and his gang headed out to kill Carl Shelton. Since the weather had turned cool, they wore their suit jackets. The revolvers hidden beneath were most likely unnecessary, since everyone was armed with either a Tommy gun or a shotgun.

Charlie loved his Thompson Model 21 machine gun so much, he carried it everywhere—even sleeping with it next to him. He planned to be buried with it, but tonight he wanted to use it to get the Shelton brothers buried first. Lyle "Shag" Worsham had set the stage for the massacre. He told Charlie all three Sheltons would be at Bernie's roadhouse, along with Ray Walker, Blackie Armes, Wild Bill Holland, and Max Pulliam. Charlie wanted Max killed almost as much as he did the Sheltons. Max had been his slot machine bookkeeper until he got greedy and demanded to be paid more. Now he was hanging out with Bernie and spending less time at Shady Rest.

"Max'll be in an ivory-colored sport-model Oakland roadster with a blue stripe around the body," Shag told the sixteen gangsters before they piled into four cars for the trip to the ambush.

"No backseat for him to hide in," Steve George said gleefully as they sped away.

Shag knew how to burn candles at both ends. After ingratiating himself to Charlie by informing him of the Sheltons' whereabouts, he beat it to Bernie's roadhouse to tell Carl the Birger gang was coming. He was pretty proud of himself for his own cleverness. He'd been collecting money and favors from both gangs to feed his heroin, gambling and whoring habits.

"They had sixteen gunmen when they left, but were going to stop by and pick up Art Newman and a few others." Shag accepted the handful of bills from Carl and beat it out the back door.

"We're gonna stay and fight ain't we, Big Carl?" Bernie asked.

"You know something, younger brother," Carl said. "I always thought you was a bit smarter than Earl. But seven of us against maybe twenty? Come on, Bernie."

"We better get goin', then." Wild Bill told Max and his wife. They hurried out the back door, followed by the others. The Sheltons, Ray, and Blackie climbed in a Lincoln Sedan and drove toward Johnson City.

"Go towards Herrin," Max advised Wild Bill. "If Charlie's boys stop them, we don't want to get caught up in it."

Bill Holland was called Wild Bill because he was anything except wild. Max was mildly irritated the twenty-one-year-old seemed to want to prove he deserved that nickname. Remaining calm, he piloted the getaway car as if he were out for a Sunday drive.

"Step on it, Holland!" Max shouted.

Mildred sat between her husband and Wild Bill, biting her fingernails.

Wild Bill gave the big engine gas, and they quickly ate up several miles.

Max relaxed when they were almost to Herrin. Then, as they came around a curve near the town cemetery, a car heading toward them blocked their lane. Two cars behind it also stopped. Wild Bill braked hard to a full stop, then shifted into reverse and backed up.

A fourth car sped around the other cars and squealed to a stop on their driver's side. Charlie and Casey Jones leapt from the vehicle and opened up with machine gunfire. Wild Bill's body was immediately riddled with bullets. His foot dropped off the accelerator. The roadster rolled to a stop.

Max felt angry stings on his left side and right shoulder. He kicked the passenger door open, and while rolling onto the pavement, took another bullet to his back. Immediately following him was Mildred, who clutched at her right thigh.

"Damn this gun!" Casey Jones shouted as he moved around to their side of the car, struggling to clear a jam. When he saw that Max had finally been able to bring his own weapon from beneath his jacket, he backed quickly away and jumped into the sedan.

The three shots Max fired at the Sedan was encouragement enough for the Birger gang to make their exit, but not before Rado walked calmly over to behind the Oakland and blasted the back of Wild Bill's head.

When the cars were gone, Max and Mildred crawled over into the ditch and applied pressure to their wounds. Wild Bill was clearly dead, and Max would be too if he didn't get to a doctor.

"A car is coming from Grover's Place," Mildred said.

"Try to stop it," Max told her. "But don't look too desperate. They might get scared and drive on."

Limping, Mildred retreated as far from the bullet-riddled Oakland as she could. When the headlights got close, she waved and tried to look in need but not in despair. The car stopped and the driver rolled down the window on his side. "Car break down?" he asked.

"Tumbleweed," the man in the passenger seat said to the driver, "that vehicle is shot to pieces."

"Oh, please don't leave us!" Mildred pleaded. "My husband is badly hurt and needs to get to the hospital."

"Who shot him?"

"The Birger gang!" Mildred hoped that since they were close to Herrin, they would get sympathy.

"Well, in that case, get in," the driver said. "We go to church with the Shelton boys."

At the hospital, Dr. Smith took care of their bullet wounds as if that's all he did—which, in Herrin, was about the truth. The deputy sheriff on night duty was George Wright, another who was not a stranger to such maladies.

"George," Max said. "I heard they just brought the roadster in with Wild Bill's body. Would you check and see if he still has the fifty dollars in his pocket that he won in the poker game tonight?"

"No money," George said when he returned twenty minutes later. "Guess someone rolled him."

"What did he look like, George?"

"He was sitting there." The officer shook his head. "His eyeballs were out on his cheeks. He'd been shot in the back of the head. I suppose with a shotgun with slugs. I walked around on that side and opened the door. A thumb fell out on the running board. It was off him. I'd say he took about twenty machine gun bullets and at least one shotgun blast."

"Doc said Mildred had some pellets in her right arm, but a bullet went right through the fleshy part of her thigh."

"Well, sir, if I was you, I'd hightail it outa here as quick as you're up and able. Ol' Charlie ain't gonna be too happy when he finds out you're still alive."

***

Nightmares destroyed Charlie's sleep for the next two nights. He kept seeing Max Pulliam testifying in court and the judge saying, "Hanged by the neck until dead." Finally, he chanced a phone call to the Herrin Hospital.

"Could you tell me if you have had anyone brought into your hospital who has been wounded or possibly even pronounced dead?"

"Why, yes," the receptionist answered, "we currently have a Mr. and Mrs. Patrick Pulliam under our care, and a deceased gentleman named William Holland has been sent to the county morgue."

"That's good," Charlie said on the other end and hung up.

"Sir," the nurse said when she tracked down Dr. Black a few minutes later, "I just had the strangest phone call."

When undertaker Ed Nolan and his son Joe arrived at the hospital an hour later, they assumed they would be transporting a corpse to Benton. The combination coach Ed brought served as both an ambulance and a hearse. He was a little confused when a heavily damaged Max Pulliam was wheelchaired to the back of the vehicle and quickly loaded.

"We want this to look like a funeral," a man carrying a Tommy gun said, "so don't drive over thirty miles an hour. We'll have two cars behind you."

Ed recognized him as Strawberry Wells, a local gangster and friend of the Pulliams'. He was called Strawberry because of the strawberry shaped birthmark on the left side of his face. Max's mother and father came out of the hospital arguing.

"That boys been telling us for a year that he's a travelin' salesmen," Fred Pulliam shouted at his wife, Nora.

"Well, he is, Daddy," Nora said, climbing into the back of the ambulance with her son. "So what if he sells slot machines and alcohol instead of groceries. He's still our son, and I ain't gonna let that nasty Charlie Birger hurt my baby boy."

Carrying his machine gun, Strawberry also got into the back of the ambulance and shut the door from the inside. Fred got into his car and pulled up behind the ambulance. Mildred and her father followed in the next car.

The procession was just north of West Frankfort when Fred realized he had forgotten his son's x-rays. He quickly turned around and hurried back to get them. A mile later, a sedan full of men pulled around the car driven by Mildred's father. When Charlie Birger waved his Tommy gun at them, the father ignored his daughter's pleas to help her husband and turned at the next crossing.

"We're in for it!" Strawberry shouted when he saw Charlie waving the ambulance over.

Ed Nolan immediately did as instructed, skidding the vehicle to a stop in the wet morning grass. He and his son leapt from the car and ran into the woods. Seeing half a dozen heavily armed men getting out of the car, Strawberry opened the back door and threw his gun out.

"My hands are raised!" he shouted as he exited the ambulance.

The sight of Charlie Birger crawling into the back of his ambulance carrying a machine gun made Ed Nolan nervous.

"That vehicle ain't insured for machine gun damage," he shouted from behind a tree.

"Oh, well." Art laughed as he followed Charlie. "We wouldn't want you to go getting holes in your hearse."

Meanwhile, Charlie had his hands full trying to pull Nora off her son. She was strong and stubborn, so when he couldn't make her break her grip, he used the butt of his machine gun to get a few good licks in on Max's head. He managed to knock the man unconscious before Nora got her arm over her son's head to protect him. "Well, Max," Charlie said when he recognized he had to make a choice, "we don't intend to kill no woman to get to you. You'd better get out of this area and never come back."

A moment later, the Birger gang members were back in their sedan and driving away.

When Max regained consciousness in a hospital a few hours later, his wife and parents stood over him. His mother's arm was in a sling.

"Why didn't Charlie kill me?" he asked.

"I wouldn't let them," Nora cried, holding her bandaged arm up for him to see. "I took as much of the beatin' for you as I could, son."

"Oh, Lordy, why did you do that?" Max shouted. He rested his forearm over his eyes. "Get outa here, woman! My ego could stand being kilt by Charlie Birger, but I'll never be able to live down my mother saving my life." He took Mildred's hand. "I guess we'll have to go rob banks in Springfield, honey."

***

When the Shelton brothers entered the barbershop for their morning shaves and manicures the next day, a dozen newspapermen followed them in. They stood wall-to-wall, trying to get the scoop on the violence that occurred almost nightly.

"So," Carl said as a pretty manicurist did his fingernails, "Birger says I have hot cars and that I'm a bootlegger, does he? Well, let me tell you, I'll run a list of the registry numbers of my cars in the newspapers any day, and that's more than he'll dare do."

"I'll admit I'm a bootlegger," Earl told a newspaperman, "but he is, too, and the people in Williamson County have known that about both of us for a long time."

"I can prove enough on Birger," Bernie bragged to the group of reporters watching him get shaved, "to make him Uncle Sam's border for a long, long time, and I'm going to do it."

"William Holland was a dear little chap," Earl lamented. "A young miner who supported his widowed mother and sister."

"Our so-called gang consists of friends," Carl said. "All natives of Williamson County, with a common cause in our fight against the Ku Klux Klan. We are not robbers or gunmen, but we never run away from trouble. We don't know whether any of our friends are in the fight against Birger, but if they are, they will take care of themselves. We're out of it."

"He's got himself all hemmed in with armor and machine guns," Bernie added, "and whenever you see a man hiding behind a fortress, he's afraid to come out in the open. He's talking about wantin' to meet us on the highway. If we didn't know he was only blowin', we might get excited and go up there to see what it's all about, but we know Birger, and we aren't taking his loud talk seriously."

***

"I know who's been double dealin' you and Carl," Art said to Charlie that night at the Shady Rest. "Shag Worsham. His short cardin' got him kicked out o' many a casino, and now he's playin' one gang against the other."

"We gonna be down another gang member, boss?" Harvey Dungey stirred the flames in the big fireplace.

"Chalk it up to profit and loss, I reckon," Charlie said. He reclined on the leather sofa, smoking and watching his smoke rings rise toward the ceiling. "Harvey, I want you to take care of this one."

***

"Could we sit and jaw a spell?" Harvey asked Shag as they stood at the long bar of the Shady Rest.

"Go to work and sit down." Shag sat on a stool and Harvey took a seat in one next to him.

Charlie and his boys suddenly quit talking and gathered nearby. With a forefinger and thumb, Shag twisted his thick eyebrows, a habit he had when he was nervous. His nickname came from those shaggy eyebrows and the long eyelashes he thought the ladies adored.

"Some men talk too much, and some not at all," Harvey said. "I imagine you're the one who's been talkin' to Carl Shelton."

"That's mighty thoughty of you." Shag produced a cigarette and lit up. "What's your proof?"

"Come with me, and I'll show you." Harvey rose, took his hat from the stand, and headed for the door.

Charlie nodded at Shag, prompting the gangster to also rise from the stool and follow.

"Right pretty evenin', ain't it?" Shag told the bartender as he left. "I'll be back directly."

Harvey opened the front passenger door of the Hudson coach and nodded for Shag to enter. Harvey then sat directly behind Shag while Joe Booher drove. As if that weren't bad enough, Charlie followed in a Lincoln, accompanied by Art Newman, Connie Ritter, Rado Millich, and, worse of all, Steve George, who frightened Shag the most.

When the cars passed through Marion, Shag thought of jumping out and trying to make a break for it into a building. Joe drove fast, though, and he didn't trust that Charlie wouldn't run him down if he stumbled. His opportunity only lasted a moment. The car sped up, heading west out of town, then abruptly turned south onto a lonely road with tall timber on both sides. Joe stopped the car. The headlights shown ominously against the trees.

"This ain't no snipe hunt, is it?" Shag asked, "'Cause I know that gag."

From the back seat, Harvey put a revolver in Shag's ear. "Why don't you go look for a snipe anyway?"

Charlie's car was equipped with a spotlight on the passenger's side. One of his men turned it on and aimed the bright light at the door Shag would exit.

Sweat poured from the doomed man's face. It was about twenty yards to the protection of the nearest tree. Even if he made it, though, he would have to keep moving— or the big Thompson machine guns would flank him and cut him down.

"Now, Shag!" Harvey said, cocking his pistol. "If you make it to the hill, we'll let you go."

Shag pushed the car door open and ran. The first two shots that hit him felt like bee stings on his back, but then the sound and impact of Thompson machine gun bullets dropped him to the ground like a deer in mid-leap. He lay on his side and looked at the headlights—and at the silhouette of the men's legs as they walked toward him. He'd never noticed before that one of them was bow-legged. His brain was still alert enough to know he was paralyzed from the neck down. That was why he felt no pain.

"Throw him into the brush," said a voice that sounded like Connie Ritter.

Tall grass passed beneath him, but only for a moment. Then nothing. The right side of his face hit the dirt. The men moved away, getting into the cars and slamming the doors. The cars backed up, then their engines faded into the distance as they drove away.

Night sounds. Crickets, cicadas, owls, the distant howling of a dog. Maybe Shag wasn't going to die after all. Maybe none of the bullets had hit a lethal area of his body. But why couldn't he move even his mouth? He couldn't even make a sound. He sniffled, just to see if he could. His nose moved, but the sound seemed muted. Maybe he had been temporarily deafened by the roar of the guns. An insect crawled across his face. He relished in the touch of the little animal's feet and tried to distinguish each tiny step. He had no idea how long he'd lay there before a car arrived. A car door slammed. Footsteps.

"He's right over here!" a voice yelled from nearby.

"Charlie's goin' crazy, you know," a different man said. "It's that damned morphine. Makes him paranoid."

"Well, just do what he says. Wrap this blanket around Shag so he don't bleed so much in the trunk of my car."

Shag was carried face-down toward the car. He didn't feel anything as he was tossed into the back and the trunk shut. The car doors slammed again, and then the car backed up before finally roaring down the paved road.

"Steve thinks Charlie's losin' it," Connie Ritter said, his voice so clear it was as if he lay next to Shag in the trunk.

"Charlie's right in what he said," Art Newman said. "You fellas usin' a Tommy made it too obvious that it was a gang killin'."

"Yeah, well, Charlie didn't need to scream at us like that."

"He's the boss, Steve," Connie said. "You don't like it, you can join the Sheltons. I'm sure Carl'd be glad to have a killer like you workin' for him."

Shag bit his lip. Connie had better shut his mouth. Steve George might cut his throat just to see red. A moment later, the car left the hard road and pulled into a driveway. It stopped. The next thing Shag knew, he was being carried again. His arms and legs were wrapped in the blanket, but his head dangled backwards so he saw the front of someone's legs as they carried him. This time he was thrown onto his back on a hard floor. He almost lost consciousness. When he smelled gasoline and felt a splash on his face, he wished he weren't awake.

"Wait!" Connie Ritter said. "Did you see Shag's face move?"

"Does it matter?" Art said.

"Guess not," Connie said. "This whole place will be ashes by mornin'."

The gasoline exploded with a loud pop. Shag watched in horror as the blanket around him burst into flames. He couldn't shut his eyes. The top of his head grew hot as his hair also caught fire. Then his pride-and-joy brows and lashes burnt right before his traumatized eyes. *Can hell be any worse than this?*

25

Connie Ritter had grown accustomed to Helen and Blondie's wild ways and even enjoyed the lazy days in bed with the two beauties. When one of the boys popped a stranger passing through Little Egypt, he decided to make the corpse a gift to them. He had come up with the amusing idea from Steve Stone's demise—and subsequent cigar-smoking road trip with Charlie.

Helen and Blondie had the time of their lives with the dead body, which they kept on top of Helen's large, flat party roof. Each day, the ladies would bathe and dress him as if he were a store-bought doll. Then they posed him on chairs, stuck a cigar in his mouth, and put a drink in his hand. When guests arrived, they loved to place bets on how long it would take them to recognize the well-dressed man sitting with his legs suavely crossed was a stiff. Since the corpse was a small man, Helen liked to drag him out on the dance floor and trip the lights fantastic with him while Blondie sang:

They call her Flamin' Mamie, she's the hottest thing in town
When it comes to loving she's a human oven, she can really mow 'um down.
Every time she shimmies, every time she shake
Mamie do more damage, than the San Francisco quake.
She could love a man till he falls dead
There's Connie, Art and Fred.
She told Charlie, Carl and Jack.,
She would love them all, till she breaks their backs.
Mamie loved her way to hell; she loved the devil and she loved him well.
Little devil running up and down the hall
Saying do something daddy, she's gonna love us all.

The handsome corpse was nicknamed Smoky. He was the life of the parties for several nights—until one morning the girls came out on the roof to prepare him for the festivities and found his face eaten away by wildlife. The next day, they held a funeral for Smoky with the bullet hole in his forehead. Over one hundred people came to the wooded area near a hog lot that Connie owned. Helen and Blondie cried all day.

***

Blond Bessie Newman's hate for the Sheltons reached its peak the day their gang members shot her in the leg. She had never liked Carl's aloofness, and though Bernie was sometimes a riot at party time, he was scary when crossed. Earl was the only one she could half-way tolerate. She had even lay with him on occasion, but he was usually more inclined to turn a buck than pay for a jaunt in the sack.

The attempted assassination occurred as Art and Bessie were traveling west on Route 13 Highway near Harrisburg. Roads in the country always scared Bessie—not because of their haunting appearance at night, but because of all the critters that ran out in front of their car. The little animals that only left blood on their front fender weren't the problem. It was deer that scared Bessie—especially the ones with antlers. The wife of a local farmer had recently been bludgeoned to death when a six-point buck tried to hitchhike a ride by leaping through their front windshield. The farmer was so upset, he refused to eat the sausage that the deer meat was ground into—though he did sell it to help pay his wife's funeral costs.

When a big truck came around the curve toward the Newman car, Art didn't think much of it—until he noticed that it was a gas tanker with gun ports and a rifle sticking out of each. It was less than fifty yards away when the tanker slowed, and so did Art. He recognized Connie Ritter in the driver's seat. Because of the deep ditches on either side there was no room on the little country road to turn around and run. The tanker would easily ram his car if he tried. It was inching slowly toward him when Bessie finally saw the danger. She screamed and grabbed for her husband's arm. He pushed her away, his brain searching for a solution. The weapons sticking out the gun ports would have limited mobility. With nowhere to go but forward he impulsively floored the accelerator and ducked sideways as low as he could get in the seat. Bullets shattered the windshield and struck like hail against the side of the car. The Newman vehicle almost flipped over when he piloted it along the embankment of the ditch. Somehow it stayed upright—though its passenger side rubbed hard along the culvert until it broke free.

When Art estimated he was clear of the tanker, he sat up—only to be instantly driven back down by bullets hitting the back of his car.

Bessie's screaming as she dove for the back seat didn't help his ability to blindly navigate the vehicle.

"Shut up that caterwaulin'!" he yelled as the machine gun mounted to the backend of the tanker stopped. He sat up in the seat and grabbed the steering wheel just in time to prevent them from going off the road and hitting a tree. He glanced over his shoulder. The truck struggled to turn around on a side road. He could outrun the heavy tanker.

"I gave them Shelton boys their start in the rackets," Art complained. "As soon as they make it big, they shoot up my car."

"Not to mention your wife," Bessie said. "Why'd you keep goin' when you saw them guns?"

Art glanced back over the seat. It was just like his wife to not appreciate the scrap he had just got them out of. She lay on her side, holding her bloody dress against a wound beneath her buttocks.

"Don't be blamin' me for that, woman. If you'd have lost weight when I told you, you'd have moved faster."

***

That night, the Shelton gang shouted at one another. The one thing Earl hadn't counted on was that everyone firing at the same time from inside the tanker would leave the gunmen deaf for several hours.

"Cut the top half off that tanker so it's a trough!" Carl shouted so Earl could hear him. "Then you won't have the heat or the echo, but you'll have the protection."

Later that day, Carl met Helen at a hotel in East St. Louis. When they had finished their pleasure, he sat in the chair by the window sipping tea and thinking. The tank had been Earl's idea. He had supported it mainly because it would make Charlie's skin crawl. The idea was ludicrous, of course. It was too big and slow to be effective, but to a paranoid drug addict, it would seem a greater threat than it was. The Birger gang was sure to make a counter move, most likely on an easy target.

"Helen," Carl said to the nude woman standing before a large mirror combing her hair. "Where do you think Charlie will hit?"

Helen stopped brushing. "I think he will hit a roadhouse he thinks you'll be at."

"Tell Connie Ritter that Earl and I'll be at The Hill for the next two nights. Tell him I'm making a big business deal with some members of the Cuckoo gang, and the roadhouse will be closed to the public."

Carl got on the telephone to Bernie. "I want a half dozen stolen cars parked in front of the Hill Roadhouse each night, and all the lights left on in the place. Put a closed sign up. Remove anything of value, but leave enough to make it look legit. Yeah, I think it's gonna get torched."

***

"We knew something was up," Steve George said the next day at Shady Rest. "The Shelton gang drove that tanker right down Main Street with rifles stickin' out the gun ports. I heard that slimy mayor of West City, Joe Adams, is hidin' the tank for them in one of his warehouses."

"Good thing we ain't next to an ocean," Connie said. "Them Sheltons would be attackin' us with U-boats."

"The Sheltons move from one place to another so much, even they probably don't know where they's sleepin' tonight," Charlie said. "I'm startin' to think Shady Rest is a liability. Havin' all us gathered in one place may not be such a good idea after all."

"Maybe we need to fortify," Connie suggested.

The gang boss paced. He wasn't sure he didn't want to go into a rage. He'd done it before. Sometimes a good tizzy fit made him feel better. Still, Connie's idea was one Charlie had thought of before—back when he'd first gotten the idea for Shady Rest. It had seemed a good plan then, so why not now?

But he knew why he had doubts. Carl Shelton had scoffed at the hideaway when he'd first seen it. "Trees close enough to your house the enemy can hide behind 'em and shoot at you," he'd said.

"High Pockets," Charlie yelled to McQuay, "you and Casey Jones take a truck into town and load up on canned goods, flashlights, water barrels—anything you can think of to have in the basement in case we're under siege."

"Boss," Rado said, "I'll rig floodlights outside house—like ones used in coal mines."

"Good idea." Charlie turned to Steve George. "You find out where we can steal more ammunition and weaponry. I want to be fully prepared if they try an attack."

"The coal mine has a full armory," Steve stated as if he'd always wanted to rob it. "I'll get right on it."

"Connie." Charlie put his hand on his lieutenant's shoulder. "I want you to take my car and bulletproof it. Mount a tri-pod machine gun on it. Have it ready by tomorrow night."

"Yes, sir." Connie raced out the door.

"We ain't gonna let them get away with what they did to Bess and me, are we?" Art asked Charlie.

"Hell, no!" the Boss shouted. "Tomorrow night, we'll take down the roadhouse Connie was talkin' about!"

***

The next night when Charlie's fully-armored car arrived in front of the Hill Roadhouse, twenty men came out of the timber. As the machine gun that was mounted to the car fired at the building, so also did the foot soldiers. The barrage lasted five minutes before the Birger gang rushed inside.

When Charlie saw the house was empty, he was so mad, he personally emptied three gats into the walls and ceiling.

An hour later, carrying their Tommy guns, Charlie and his entire gang strutted into the Jefferson Hotel in Herrin during dinner time. Women screamed and men gasped when the boss held his Tommy gun high above his head. "If anybody wants to know who did the shooting down at the Hill Roadhouse today," he shouted, "tell them that Charlie Birger did it. Go look it over and see what these babies can do."

Later that evening, his gang drove four cars into West City. Busting down the door to Joe Adams' house, they stuck their guns in the mayor's enormous face.

"You old son-of-a-bitch, you give me that armored truck," Charlie shouted, "or I'll drill you so full of holes, people won't recognize your corpse."

"The Sheltons will kill me if I do," Joe said, wringing his hands.

"It's almost midnight now," Charlie said, looking at his pocket watch, "and if you deliver that truck to Shady Rest before five a.m. day after tomorrow, you'll save yourself a lot of trouble with undertakers and caskets—if you know what I mean."

Charlie fumed all the next morning, counting down the hours and looking outside every few minutes to see if the truck had arrived. "If that truck ain't delivered to me before five o'clock tomorrow morning, he told Harvey Dungey during lunch, "we're going to kill that double-bellied son-of-a-bitch, and the God-damned Franklin County law isn't big enough to stop us!"

***

When Carl got word of what Charlie had done at the Jefferson Hotel and at Joe Adams' house, he smiled. He could sense his rival gangster's frustration.

"Bernie," he said as he and his brothers were having a drink that afternoon, "hire some of the boys from the Cuckoo gang to protect Joe's home. Earl, you see to it that a couple of Charlie's boys get a bad tip on a horse race. You know how much Charlie hates to lose."

"High Pockets McQuay and Casey Jones are Charlie's most gullible thugs," Earl said. "Those two chumps would believe anything."

"Them boys fancy themselves lady's men, don't they?" Carl asked. "I'll have Helen and Blondie invite them to a little private party. That will get ol' Boss Birger's blood up."

A week later, High Pockets McQuay's body was found in a bullet-riddled car between Herrin and Johnson City. The next night, the corpse of Casey Jones was wrapped in a blanket and thrown from a bridge near the town of Equality. It was discovered by a young Black boy who spotted a hand sticking out of the water in the creek.

"Charlie's gone kill crazy," Bernie told Carl and Earl when they got the news. "Keep up the pressure, and he'll murder his entire gang for us."

"Them Birger boys sure do catch death like most folks catch a cold." Earl agreed.

"Let's stoke the fire a little more," Carl suggested. "Bernie, that County Line Roadhouse of Charlie's seems an easy target for arson, don't it?"

Bernie smiled. "Blackie Armes has been itchin' for something like this. He's been playin' with firebombs."

***

The night after the County Line Roadhouse burned, it was Charlie's turn to ask Williamson County State's Attorney Arlie Boswell to do something about the Shelton Gang. When Boswell snubbed him. Charlie went into a rage that quickly emptied Shady Rest. When he finally calmed, he saw that only Steve George remained in the hideaway. Without hesitation he handed the killer a C-note.

"Take a rifle from the armory and kill that son-of-a-bitch, Boswell." Charlie shouted. Grabbing a bottle of rum off the liquor shelf he went into his bedroom.

***

The next day Charlie made certain he was visible in downtown Harrisburg all day long. He took his daughters shopping, to lunch, and then to the park to listen to a church choir sing. Many eyes were on them everywhere they went. It was a secret to no one that when Charlie Birger spent that much time in public view, someone would most likely get shot.

"Wrong man for weapon like that, boss," Rado Millich complained that night after the assassination attempt failed. "Steve no sniper. He knife man. Ural Gowan, me, gunfighters."

Rado was right. Steve had nearly missed Boswell. In fact, he'd barely nicked his target's leg as the attorney walked from the courthouse. Rado and Ural had finished off High Pockets and Casey clean and proper. Their only mistake was killing Casey at the Shady Rest, then leaving his body outside until they could sober up enough to dispose of him. Ural was a slender boy who looked more like a farmhand than a killer, but he was smart enough to not miss an easy target.

"I felt like I had to give Steve somebody to kill, or he might have started in on us," Charlie answered. "That man gets bloody at least once a month."

"Like werewolf, Montenegro," Rado said. He and Charlie, both descended from Eastern Europe, had often discussed the effects of the full moon on the legendary monster—as well as on some killers.

A breathless Art Newman rushed in the front entrance. "Boss, Earl Shelton is in a hospital in East St. Louis."

"Nothing minor, I hope."

"Yes, but we could make it major." Art could barely contain his excitement.

"How we get men past Shelton guards?" Rado asked.

"Why do they have to be men?" Art said with a limp wave of his hand.

That evening, Art and Freddie Wooten had the time of their lives letting Blond Bessie doll them up. Being fairly thin, both men fit nicely into the ensemble she picked out for them. Rado watched but refused to take part. Bessie thought his reluctance a good thing, since his facial features were hardly suitable for a male, much less a female.

For her husband, Bessie picked out clothes befitting a middle-aged woman that wouldn't draw attention to his less-than-feminine face. Freddie, on the other hand, was insistent he be both attractive and classy, so he chose a Hudson seal fur coat, a black turban, a silk dress, and stockings. Amazingly, he fit perfectly into Bessie's size six shoes. He tried to add a fur scarf to his outfit, but when he went for his gun, it became tangled in the fabric.

Rado was embarrassed to be associated with the two, but Charlie had told him he only had to be the getaway driver. So, with Bessie in the front seat and the two drag queens in the back, they started off for the hospital. Unfortunately, Rado's worst fears came true. In the hospital parking lot, St.

Louis detectives intercepted them. After the officers had a good time teasing Rado for his choice of girlfriends, they let it slip they'd been tipped off.

And no doubt it was Carl Shelton who had set them up. Earl Shelton wasn't even in the hospital. To make matters worse, the presence of weapons violated Rado's parole.

Art was so mad, he immediately turned the tables on the brothers. Knowing Carl had most of the East St. Louis police on his payroll, he insisted on speaking to the state's attorney, whom he hoped was honest. "I can prove the Shelton brothers pulled the 1925 Collinsville mail robbery," Art told the state's attorney when they were alone. It was his lucky day. Within an hour, he was whisked off to Springfield to testify before a grand jury.

Unfortunately, it was not a lucky day for Rado. Before the evening was out, he was told that in addition to the parole violation, he was being charged with the murder of Casey Jones.

***

Meanwhile, the Sheltons were planning their next move in the chess game called gang war. Blackie had done such a good job on the County Line Roadhouse, Carl thought he was ready to try bombing again.

"How would you go about blowin' the shit outa Charlie's barbeque stand?" Carl asked him one day as he counted money.

"Wow!" Blackie slammed the palm of his hand onto the table and thought fast. "It would have to be a drive-by bombing. His security men usually change about two in the mornin'. The dumb thing is, the fellas who are supposed to take their shift are usually partyin' in Shady Rest and forget. The guards goin' off duty get antsy and finally go get them. That leaves the place unguarded for about ten minutes."

"Who you want to drive?" Carl asked.

"Bernie and me do pretty good together."

"Go tell him to sober up. You're goin' out tonight."

***

Telling Bernie to sober up and getting him to do it were two different things. Blackie had his hands full brewing coffee and putting together the bomb. Bernie slept on the couch with a newspaper over his face until he was awakened with a hard shake.

"Can you drive?" Blackie asked. He was close to asking someone else, if he could find anyone else who would still be sober at one-thirty in the morning.

"Of course, I can drive," Bernie said, sitting up. "I've been practicing driving drunk for years."

The trip to the barbeque stands in front of the entrance to Shady Rest was uneventful. Bernie seemed in control, although very quiet. Blackie had him do a drive by once at a few minutes before two. As he had predicted, several Birger men stood on the porch smoking and waiting for their replacements. It was when Blackie had Bernie park behind some bushes a half mile away the problem started. The youngest Shelton's eyes grew heavy and his head began to nod. When Blackie shouted, "Let's go," Bernie double-clutched, killing the engine. He got it started again, but swerved several times trying to bring the car up to its maximum speed of sixty miles per hour.

Blackie had a ten second fuse on the bomb, and had practiced that day leaning half his body out the window so he could get a good throwing motion. He lit the fuse at the right time for the release, but, for some reason, Bernie thought he had one more shift to get to fifth gear. His struggling with the grinding clutch slowed the car just enough that Blackie had to throw the bomb early.

Blackie knew the second he released the package, he had missed. It fell just short of the front porch. The explosion, though, was greater than he anticipated, causing Bernie to completely lose his grip on the steering wheel.

Blackie reached over and grabbed it just in time to prevent the car from skidding off the hard road.

When Bernie took the wheel again, Blackie hurried to looked back. The front porch was completely gone. Every window in the house was broken, but otherwise, the target seemed undamaged.

He settled back in the seat and glared at his driver. With both hands on the wheel, Bernie was sound asleep as they cruised down the highway at fifty miles an hour. Disgusted, Blackie pulled the gangster's foot off the accelerator, took the steering wheel and guided the machine to a stop. Without a foot on the clutch, the automobile sputtered and died. He got out of the car, walked around to the driver's side, opened the door, and shoved Bernie down on the floorboard, where he promptly puked a stinky, gray mess.

After driving back to their roadhouse, Blackie parked the car and went inside to give his report, leaving the tough Shelton brother to wake up the next morning with his face in his own vomit.

***

Carl wasn't upset in the least when told the bombing had only been moderately successful. He knew the effect it would have on Charlie's mind, and that was all that mattered.

"Birger's trying to get you and your brothers framed for the Collinsville job," Helen told him as they lay in bed that evening.

"He can't frame us for something we *did* do." Carl laughed.

"Well, you know what I mean." Helen didn't find it amusing. "He'll get Art and Harvey Dungey and others to lie to prove you did it."

"We'll cross that bridge when we get to it."

A knock on the door startled Helen, but not enough to inspire her to get dressed. Carl, though, got up, threw his trousers on, and wrapped a suspender over one shoulder.

"What you want?" Helen asked through the closed door.

"Joe Adams," A voice said. "I have someone here I want Carl to meet."

Carl nodded to Helen. She unlocked and opened the door. Joe Adams' immense frame filled the doorway. He didn't appear as shocked to see a completely naked woman standing before him as were the two tall men peering over his shoulder.

"Carl, I want you to meet Elmer Kane and Henry Mundale," Joe said. "Their airplane landed in Benton for some repairs. They're barnstormers."

26

Sitting in the parlor of Gus Adams' home that night would have been a completely comfortable and normal experience for the two pilots—if it hadn't been for Blackie Armes and Ray Walker building bombs on the dining room table. Joe and his brother Gus occasionally passed through the room, sometimes accompanied by Carl or one of his brothers. They gave nervous glances at the bomb makers, asked a few polite questions concerning if they needed anything, and inquired if the device would be ready in time. Then they went across the yard to Joe's house.

Gus's chubby little wife, though, acted like nothing out of the ordinary was happening. She was delighted to have pilots in her home. Scampering in and out of the room, she seemed oblivious to the two men handling nitroglycerin and strapping dynamite into bundles using copper wire. Since Mr. Shelton had instructed her that no one in the room was to be served alcohol, she baked them one of her famous pineapple upside-down cakes and kept them supplied with fresh brewed coffee.

Then, when she learned they would be staying the night, she prepared the children's old room, even finding a wooden airplane her Jimmy had made before he died in the 1918 flu epidemic. She cried as she hung it from the ceiling above the bed. *My goodness, how excited little Jimmy would've been if he'd been here to meet the pilots.*

The pilots left before sunrise the next morning, along with Blackie and Ray, who told Mrs. Adams they were taking them to the airport. Heartbroken to lose her guests, she handed them a little sack of sandwiches and kissed them all goodbye on the cheek.

An hour later, Mrs. Adams sat on the bed in Jimmy's room, staring at the walls filled with pictures he had drawn. One of them was of Eddie Rickenbacker flying his famous Hat-in-the-Ring airplane in a dogfight with the German ace of aces, Manfred von Richthofen, known as the Red Baron.

Several automobiles roared down the street in front of the house. Mrs. Adams ran to the window. Over two dozen well-dressed men jumped out of the cars, all carrying machine guns. Finding cover behind trees and outhouses, they surrounded her brother-in-law's home. One of the men stood behind a sedan and spoke into a speakerphone, "We are federal agents.

We know you Sheltons are in there. Come out with your hands up."

Carl and Bernie strolled out of the house like they were greeting the preacher for dinner. "How are you boys?" Carl asked as two officers stepped forward to search him.

"Carl Shelton and Bernard Shelton, you are under arrest for the January 27, 1925, robbery of the Collinsville payroll truck."

"Why, sure officer," Carl said with a smile. "I remember that date well. We were buryin' our good friend Ora Thomas that day. Ain't that right, Bernie?"

"Sure is, Carl."

The feds loaded the brothers in a paddy wagon, and the caravan of vehicles sped away. *Oh dear,* Mrs. Adams thought as she returned to her spot on the edge of the bed, *I'm so glad little Jimmy didn't see that.* In her mind, he was still little Jimmy, not the adult he would've been by now had he lived.

She looked at other drawings on the wall. Oh, how her little Jimmy had loved to draw. Several of them were of cowboys, another of his passions. Pictures of rodeo riders on bucking broncs, throwing lassoes and shooting rifles and six shooters. Several wooden guns were in an old gunrack Jimmy had found at the garbage dump. He had a Winchester, and even a little toy machine gun. Taking the machine gun down, she held it on her lap and began imitating the sound of the gun firing as her little Jimmy had once done. “Rat-a-tat-tat. Rat-a-tat-tat.”

Cars revved their engines as if they were preparing to race past the house. Again, she rushed to the window. Three big sedans slowly drove by, Tommy guns sticking out each of the curtained windows. Flashes erupted from the weapons as they all fired at once at her in-law’s house. Bullets penetrated the siding and broke glass. Someone screamed from inside the house.

Mrs. Adams did the only thing she could. She raised little Jimmy’s machine gun and aimed it out his window. “Rat-a-tat-tat,” she shouted as the drive-by shooters sped away. “Rat-a-tat-tat.”

***

Meanwhile, Blackie and Ray Walker argued.

“Carl told me I’m the one who gets to go up in the airplane!” Ray shouted at Blackie.

“Oh, yeah?” Blackie shouted back. “Well, they’re my bombs made with my nitroglycerin, and if I don’t get to go, I’m goin’ to take my bombs and go home.”

Closer to the two-seater Curtis airplane, the two pilots were having a different and much quieter argument.

“I’m not goin’ up there with those nuts carryin’ them bombs,” Elmer Kane whispered.

"Oh, yeah?" Henry Mundell hissed back. "You were the one who said 'Let's land at the Benton airport because the people there are so friendly.'"

Earl drove a car—much faster than necessary—to the end of the grass runway. When he stopped and got out, he walked purposely toward the four men.

"The feds arrested Carl and Bernie this morning for the Collinsville robbery," Earl said. "I'll turn myself in later, but right now we need to get this project underway. Ray, you ready to go up?"

Blackie turned away, shook his head, and pulled out a cigarette.

Earl walked over to Elmer and held out a piece of paper. "Here's a rough map of the area." He pointed at a big X on the paper. "This is your target."

Henry turned away, his head bobbing as he laughed and pulled out a cigarette.

Elmer considered scuttling the plane at the end of the runway. But he knew just enough about nitroglycerin to know a sudden impact might send him and his airplane up in smoke. It was hard to believe, but that was actually the least of his worries. Ray needed to light a fuse while in the front cockpit seat, then toss the explosive hard enough and far enough away that it wouldn't blow back into where Elmer was flying the plane in the seat behind him. Worse, they had to make two or maybe three passes over the target to get rid of all three bombs. That meant time for anyone on the ground to take careful aim at them with weapons that could send bullets flying for nearly a mile.

The one thing he had going for him was Ray was dropping the bombs, not the other gangster. Blackie had told the pilots they would need to fly low to the ground and slow to almost a stall so he could effectively make the toss. Ray, on the other hand, seemed more like a schoolboy just excited to be part of the adventure.

As they neared their destination, Elmer decided they needed to make one high pass just so he could get his bearings as to exactly where, within the thick timber, the house was. The problem, of course, was no matter how high he went, the sound of a flying machine excited folks who had rarely, if ever, seen an airplane pass overhead. As he predicted, several men emerged from the house and pointed skyward.

Elmer tapped Ray on the shoulder and shouted that he was going to fly directly along the highway.

"When I get over the barbeque stand, you need to light the fuse and throw. I'll dip the right wing to give you a better view."

Ray gave him a thumbs up, then tilted his head down to sort out the bombs—as well as the cigar he would use to light them.

When Elmer brought the plane back around, he flew as low as he dared. He didn't expect his first pass to bring any gunfire. He was only half right. When the men on the ground saw a package being airmailed, at least one of them had his finger close enough to the trigger to get a few shots off before the Jenny disappeared past the tree line. No explosion.

"Get lower!" came the ominous words from Ray—words Elmer had been dreading.

"You'd better get rid of both bombs this time around," Elmer shouted back, "'cause I guarantee they'll shoot us out of the sky if we try a third pass."

Ray gave another thumbs up. Elmer took as sharp a turn as he could. He didn't want to give the Birger gang any more time than necessary to set up their armory. He was right, too. The Shady Rest was barely in sight than a heavy barrage began. It was the longest twenty seconds of Elmer Kane's life.

***

An hour later, Charlie was about to come unglued. Using his boot, he sifted through the rubbish that had once been his cock and dog fighting building. The arena was gone—as well as one of the bulldogs and an eagle the boys kept in a cage as a pet. Other than the glass broken out of all the windows, the sturdy log cabin that was the Shady Rest was undamaged.

Kicking a pile of scrap heap, Charlie thought about the easiest Shelton targets available to him. He looked at Connie Ritter. "I want Joe Adams' house leveled tomorrow night."

***

As he was departing the airplane, Ray handed Elmer Kane a thousand dollars cash. The pilot took the money without even getting out of the cockpit. He immediately got back in the air and flew to a small airfield near DuQuoin, where Henry Mundale waited for him in the automobile that Carl Shelton had promised would be part of the deal.

"I'll drive," was all Elmer said to his partner. Henry slid over, but kept glancing at his friend from the corner of his eye.

After only a few miles, they were stopped by a police officer.

"Did you know the vehicle you are driving was stolen from Herrin two weeks ago?"

Feeling as if he were in quicksand, Elmer sank down in the seat. He reached up with both hands and pulled his hat down over his eyes.

***

The one deficiency within the Birger gang was a competent bomb maker. Most of the boys had a little coal mining experience, but much of that work had been done with black powder. Nitro and dynamite were the preferred combination for homicide. Luckily, two of the three bombs dropped from the airplane had not detonated. The first one had fallen apart mid-air. The second was fully intact. A few of the boys volunteered to use the second one as a guide and put together what would hopefully be a lethal blast.

As had Blackie Armes, though, their throw fell short and only minimally damaged one side of Mayor Adams' house.

Charlie sat the entire next day shooting morphine in his darkened bedroom in Harrisburg. During his lucid moments, he weighed the reliability of each member of his gang. None had his full confidence. His obsession with having Joe Adams killed filled his every thought. Part of the reason was to save face. People knew he had guaranteed Joe's death for not turning over the Sheltons' tank as he had demanded. To not make good on the promise made him look weak. Adams was also virtually unprotected since the Shelton brothers' arrest. The Sheltons were being freed on sixty-thousand-dollars' bail, but they would almost certainly be hiding somewhere in East St. Louis. Their trial for the Collinsville job was to begin in two months, so Charlie expected them to lie low until it was over. And if he, Art and Harvey Dungey were allowed to testify, the Sheltons would spend hard time in Leavenworth.

Pacing the bedroom while thinking about the people he loathed, Charlie felt bloody. He wanted to do something, anything, to relieve some of the pent-up hatred. The telephone sat on the dresser. Impulsively, he picked it up.

"Get me Joe Adams' house in West City," he said to the operator, then added, "and you better hang up your end of the line when they answer, or you'll regret it."

"Hello," a woman's voice answered a moment later.

"Mrs. Adams?"

"Yes?"

"Do you have life insurance on Joe?"

"No, not very much."

"Well, you'd better get a lot more, because we're going to kill him, and you'll need it."

Sweating, Charlie slammed the phone receiver back on the hook. Now he had to have Adams killed. The problem would be finding someone he could count on. Someone who wanted to get in his good graces. Someone who could walk right up to Joe Adams without suspicion.

The doorbell rang, and he knew the answer. He'd been expecting the delivery of morphine.

27

The main reason Harry Thomasson had joined the gang was so the kids at school would know he was now the bully, not the bullied. He and his brother Elmo were only gofers, but no one needed to know that. Therefore, when he made the delivery to Charlie's house, and the boss asked that he and Elmo meet him the next day at Shady Rest, Harry was ecstatic.

"We've got a job for you boys," Charlie said the next day, "and it's got to be done tomorrow night."

"You fellas ever kilt a man?" Art asked.

"No," Harry said, "I never hated anyone enough to kill them."

"You are the boys to kill Joe Adams," Art said. "He don't know you, and the law won't suspect you. I want you to do this. Go to West City and leave your car about a block from Joe Adams' house. Then go up to the front door and knock. If Carl Shelton, Joe Adams or Ray Walker come to the door, shoot, and don't ask questions. If anybody else comes to the door, ask for Joe. If they say he's not there, stick around in the neighborhood and watch the house."

"I'll give you boys fifty dollars for every bullet you put into those son-of-a-bitches," Charlie added.

Harry and Elmo's eyes lit up. "Yes, sir," Harry said, while Elmo nodded with a bit too much enthusiasm.

"Take them bullets to the basement," Connie Ritter said, "and dose them with poison. I'll show you how to hide the gun in your sleeve so you can bring it out quick when you need it."

"Okay," Harry said. "There's just one little problem. Elmo and me don't know how to drive."

***

On November 12, Ray Hyland, known as Izzy the Jew chauffeured the two youth in their first assassination attempt.

"Why are you lettin' us out so far from the house?" Harry asked when Izzy parked the stolen car two blocks away.

"You want folks to know what kinda vehicle we're using?" Izzy the Jew asked. "You boys are twice as fast as any of Adams' bodyguards. Put bushes and trees to your backs when you make your getaway. I'll have the doors open and the car running."

Harry and Elmo slammed the vehicles doors when they left.

Someone in a nearby house looked out a window, so as soon as the brothers were out of sight, Izzy drove the flivver around the block. When he arrived back on the same street and passed the Adams' house, the two boys stood on the porch, talking to Mrs. Adams through the open door.

"Is Mayor Adams home, ma'am?" Harry asked. "We have a note of introduction here from Mr. Carl Shelton, if you'd kindly give it to your husband, please."

Mrs. Adams was so taken with the two boys' politeness and clean-cut looks, she immediately accepted the note.

"You boys wait right here," she said. She found her husband sitting in the bedroom reading the newspaper. She handed him the note. "There are two nice-looking boys at the front door."

Joe read the note. *Friend Joe. If you can use these boys, please do it. They are broke and need work. I know their father. C.S.*

Feeling a little gruff for having his quiet evening disturbed, the mayor put down his paper, lifted his immense frame from his favorite chair, and waddled on arthritic legs to the door.

Meanwhile, Harry's heart beat so fast, it shut off his brain. A flash of darkness came over him. When it cleared, a fat man in bib overhauls stood before them. His brother fired a shot. Harry added two bullets of his own to the gasping man's chest, then turned and raced across the yard. Someone shouted at the boys as they ran, and there might have been a gunshot. The car was right where Izzy the Jew had promised it would be. They had no sooner dove in through the open car doors than the tires squealed. The sudden acceleration caused the doors to slam shut. Harry and Elmo lay on the floorboard breathing hard and sweating profusely. The darkness of the night hid their tears.

***

"I don't know who killed Adams," Charlie told John Rodgers, the *St. Louis Post-Dispatch* reporter, "but I'm certainly glad he was killed. Everyone comes to me to ask who did this and that. What am I—a detective force for southern Illinois? What the hell does anyone care who killed Adams?"

When word got to Charlie three days later that he was the primary suspect for the murder of Joe Adams, his ability to think rationally further fell apart. While his young daughters danced around the big Christmas tree in the living room, Charlie sat in his dark bedroom contemplating which of his compatriots had ratted on him. There were so many possibilities, he couldn't even keep track of them in his mind. He tried writing down the people he didn't trust, but it filled so much of the paper he ripped it to shreds. *Maybe if I write down who I do trust.* He set staring at the blank page for over an hour. Then he tore that one up also.

***

"When a man takes to drugs," Helen told Carl and Blondie, "there's just not a darn thing you can do about it, nothing at all."

"Charlie finished that whiskey bottle last night without nary a breath," Blondie added. "That can't be good when you're already high on morphine."

"You got every right to be unsettled," Carl said. "He's got all his faculties, I'd imagine."

"Well, his worm still works," Helen said, "if that's what you mean."

"No, I mean does his memory seem sharp? Can he stay focused on one thing until it's done?"

"Come to think of it," Helen said, "he ain't been a very efficient outlaw lately. It seems a lot of his boys been getting shot up."

"He don't show no inclination to listen to nobody neither," Blondie added. "Sometimes you ask him a question, he don't seem to know how to answer, then he gets irritable."

"Oh, for heaven's sakes." Helen shook her head. "Who would he listen to? Them convicts ain't none smart enough to provide sound advice."

All night, Carl weighed the ladies' observations in his head. The next day, he told Earl, "It ain't gonna look too good for ol' Charlie, I'd imagine, if he keeps goin' on them drugs."

***

Every day that passed brought fuzzier and darker thoughts for Charlie. He took to solitude like it was a new mistress. During the daytime, the curtains in his room were shut. He sat for hours dwelling on his failures, placing blame on others when he could.

Then, on another day, he might wake up and feel he were on top of the world—indestructible and too smart to be defeated by anyone. On those days, he ventured out, still as charming, witty, and in command as he'd always been. But even on those good days, a moment came when he counted the seconds until he could get back to his room where a shot of morphine took all the painful thoughts and memories away. At least for a while.

His newest obsession concerned those who knew the events surrounding the murder of Joe Adams. He cursed himself for hiring boys as young as the Thomasson brothers to do the shooting. Kids that age liked to brag. He'd already overheard Harry boasting to Elmo that he'd put two bullets in the mayor to his brother's one. Then there was Steve George, who'd been fine until he married Lena, a woman who liked to get her husband jealous enough to fight for her. She also liked to stir things up, even complaining that Charlie should have given the Adams assassination job to Steve.

The more he thought about it, the more he believed having so many outlaws congregating at Shady Rest was a liability. Now he understood why Carl Shelton stayed footloose. Charlie longed for the old days.

28

State Police Officer Lory Price had recovered nineteen stolen cars in 1926, and received substantial rewards for each. It was a sweet deal. Charlie stole the cars, State's Attorney Arlie Boswell found out how much reward was on each, then Charlie's boys would leave them on some back road and tell Lory. Even after splitting the reward three ways with Arlie and Charlie, he was still doing pretty well for himself. He and his wife Ethel also enjoyed the parties at Shady Rest. Ethel's beauty rivaled both Helen and Blondie's. Unfortunately, it also stirred the loins of many gangsters. Since he was one of the first state troopers in the area to get a motorcycle to use during good weather, Lory enjoyed entertaining the gangsters at Shady Rest with his wheelies and other tricks.

January 8 was a frigid evening, so Lory used his regular cruiser to take Ethel to a picture show. Afterwards, he dropped off his wife at home and told her he was going to make a few rounds. What he meant, of course, was that he was going to enjoy a few rounds with his buddies at the Shady Rest.

"What's going on here tonight, Steve?" Lory asked when he entered the hideaway. Many of the prized wall pieces were missing.

"Charlie says spring cleanin'," Steve George slurred, a nearly empty bottle of rye in his hand. "We spent the whole day moving most of the weapons and ammo outa the cellar. I'm about sloushed, occiffer." The gangster put his arm around Lory's shoulder. "Hey, buddy ol' boy, you wanna meet my ol' lady?"

"Sure." Lory took the drunk's elbow and guided him across the room to the fireplace, where Elmo Thomasson was passed out on the wood floor. On the couch above him was a woman wearing only a slip.

"Lena, Lena!" Steve shouted. "This is our occiffer patsy, Lory...what's your last name?"

"Price," Lory said.

"Yeah, Occiffer Rice, of the Royal Mounties." Steve's eyes rolled back in his head. He was unconscious before his body landed across the bare legs of his wife.

"Hi! Are you a cop, Mr. Rice?" Lena said, drool foaming at the corner of her mouth. Her eyes were almost closed and her head bobbled on her neck.

"Yes, ma'am."

"Well, let's you and me go a few rounds before the old man wakes up."

Two seconds later, Lory ran out the door. Lena scared him even more than her murderous husband. In her drug induced state, the foam on her mouth caused her to look more like a rabid dog than a woman. No sooner than he got on the hard road, he passed Art Newman's car heading for Shady Rest. He recognized Charlie slouched down in the front seat. Not being tired, Lory stopped at a nearby all-night café where some of his friends ate an early breakfast. As they enjoyed crackling and eggs, the state trooper thought about something Steve had said. *Moving weapons and ammo out of the cellar?* Charlie had just spent weeks fortifying Shady Rest for an attack. *Why would he be emptying the building of everything of value?*

The sound of an explosion and the trembling of the cafeteria were almost simultaneous. From his vantage point by the window, he saw a wall of flames rise up above the distant trees in the direction of the Shady Rest. He and the other customers raced out into the parking lot in time to see the fire turn into black smoke, followed by a second explosion—this one louder but with fewer flames. The second detonation was set off when the fire reached whatever was left in Charlie's armory.

"Those damned Sheltons have done it." Someone nearby said. It only took the state trooper a few seconds to add the facts and another few seconds to realize that federal officials would ask him some tough questions—questions that would not only make him uncomfortable, but also a certain underworld crime figure named Charlie Birger.

***

Though he, Art, Connie, and Freddie Wooten had set the fire to burn down the Shady Rest, Charlie was almost able to make himself believe that someone else had done it. This delusion made it easier to go into a hysterical rant in front of investigating law enforcement. He was so convincing, even Art Newman would rub his hand through his hair and wonder for a moment if the memory of pouring gasoline around the building had only been a dream. Privately, Charlie seemed happy that the four burnt to death in the fire were Steve and Lena George, Elmo Thomasson, and Bert Owens, who had only recently joined the gang but already knew too much.

"If Harry Thomasson had been killed along with his brother," Charlie told Art and Connie, "it would have made the roast complete."

Because of his own diabolical interests, Arlie Boswell was becoming as paranoid as Charlie. "We've got to kill Lory Price!" he said to the Birger gang boss. "He's loose with his tongue and likely to slip up if they keep asking him questions."

When Charlie learned Lory was being interrogated, he didn't have to dwell on the problem long before he made another impulsive decision. The following night, the Birger gang sat in two cars down the block from the Price home, waiting for the last of his visitors to leave. After his bedroom lights went out, they felt obligated to give Lory a few extra minutes in case he wanted to have sex with his wife one last time. The seven men then exited their vehicles and approached the house. Riley Simmons carried several short ropes. Freddie Wooten stopped alongside the house and cut the telephone line.

Since there was no dog, they found getting into the house a simple affair. It was Art's idea for them to sneak up to the bedroom and stand around the bed looking down at the sleeping young couple. Then Freddie Wooten had to laugh. Ethel lay on her back. She opened her eyes and mouth at the same time. Connie was ready with a rolled-up cloth that he immediately gagged her with. Lory's physical strength was legendary among the mobsters, so Ernest Blue and Leslie Simpson leapt onto his back, while Riley Simmons tied his hands and feet and gagged him.

"Put Lory in the backseat of Art's car," Charlie ordered. "I want to show him what happened to my cabin on account of him. You other boys take Ethel and follow in the Buick."

When they were safely on the road, Connie removed the gag.

"Are you going to hurt me, Charlie?" Price asked.

"No," Birger promised. "I just want to talk things over with you."

The smell of charred wood around the bombed building was made worse by the day's on and off rain. When they were parked, Freddie dragged Lory from the car and forced him onto his knees in the grass. The second car pulled up and shone its headlights on the state policeman. Still tied and gagged in the back seat of the Buick, Ethel Price watched the scene before her.

"What did you tell the coroner's jury about the bombing?"

"I swear, Charlie" Lory said. "I just told them that I stopped by there the night of the bombing, and Steve took me in to meet his wife. There was a young fella drunk or maybe asleep on the floor. Then I left. After the explosion, I went back and found it like it is now."

"Liar!" Charlie shouted. He pumped three bullets into the cop's stomach.

A stifled cry came from Ethel, then she fainted onto the car seat.

Lory gasped and coughed, then rolled onto his side.

"I've got a notion, Price," Charlie said, "to knock you off and throw you in one of these mines."

"Art," Lory gasped. He looked at those who had once been his friends. "Can you help me?"

"I'd like to see somebody try to help you now." Charlie looked at the three men standing by the Buick. "Take that woman out and do away with her!"

"Charlie, please don't hurt Ethel." The pain in

Price's stomach caused him to pull his knees up to his chest.

"Shut up!" Charlie sneered. "We're gonna just stand here and see how long it takes you to die."

The three gangsters got back in the Buick and drove toward the hard road.

"I ain't gonna kill a pretty gal like Ethel without getting a good taste of her first," Ernest Blue said as he drove.

"I agree, but you ain't getting her first," Leslie Simpson said from the backseat. He groped up Ethel's skirt just as she regained consciousness. "You're getting her second."

"Make that third, son." Riley Simmons ejected a long puff of cigar smoke. "Age before beauty, boys."

Stopping at an abandoned coal mine near Carterville, Riley dragged Ethel out of the car and into the remnants of the company office building.

Ernest's turn twenty minutes later took much less time than that of his colleagues, and ended with a gunshot. When he emerged, he waved his still smoking thirty-eight. "Since I had to go last and did the dirty deed, you fellas get to dispose of the carcass."

"Fair enough," Riley said. He had enjoyed his time with Ethel. As tribute to her, he crossed himself before he and Leslie tossed her body in a hole at the mine entrance and covered it with rubbish. When they were finished, the mine yard was clear of debris.

"Hell," Leslie said. "We oughta send the coal company a bill for cleaning this place up for them."

They returned to the remains of Shady Rest to find the policeman was still clinging to life.

"Don't worry about the woman," Ernest said as the three approached. "I killed her."

"What did you do with her?" Art asked.

"We buried her in a mine entrance hole," Riley said.

"All right," Charlie said. "We'll put him with her."

"We can't," Leslie said, guilt in his voice. "We filled it up with tin and timber."

"I know another old mine near DuQuoin," Charlie said, angry that he had to come up with Plan B. "Throw this man in Newman's car."

"I'll be damned if you do," Art protested. "Put him in that Buick."

Charlie was tired of being corrected. With a murderous glare he raised his gat. "Everybody will go through this with me, or I'll wipe you all out!"

Art cussed under his breath as he drove. The backseat was cloth, and Lory still had enough blood oozing from him to leave a significant mess. Especially since Charlie had decided to sit on him. After ten minutes of listening to Lory's gasps for breath, the boss told Art to pull the car over. He got out, squatted in the ditch and vomited.

"That's too much for me," Charlie said when he took Connie's place in the front seat. "I can kill a man, but I can't sit on him. I don't know what in the hell's the matter with me. It isn't my nerves.

Every time I kill a man, it makes me sick afterwards. I guess it's my stomach."

"Connie, I'm an innocent man," Lory said now that he'd had a moment to catch a full breath.

"Shut up, you bastard!" Connie shouted as he took the boss's place on top of the dying man. "Or I'll turn this machine gun on you."

"Connie, you'll live to regret this," Lory said in a weakening whisper.

The mine yard in DuQuoin was another disappointment. A night watchman in a raincoat walked through a light rain from one building to another. Art drove on past it until they came to a collapsed schoolhouse that had been abandoned after the tri-state tornado.

"Throw him in there and burn it!" Charlie shouted. He yearned for his morphine.

When the boys came back to the car and sheepishly said the building was too wet to get a fire going, the boss lost it. "What the hell is going on today? Do I have to do everything myself? Drive into that field up ahead."

They parked near a vast wooded area. Art jumped out, grabbed Lory, and dragged him into the trees.

Lory laid a bloody hand on Art's shoulder. "Art, I thought you were my friend."

"By God, I am, Lory," Art said, "but I can't help this."

Charlie raised his machine gun and emptied it into the state policeman.

29

Art and Bessie Newman were surrounded by seven detectives as they walked from their hotel to the Quincy Federal Building. The trial of the Shelton brothers for the 1925 Collinsville holdup had brought national attention, and the city was packed with news reporters and spectators.

"Being on the river, Quincy's a lot easier for us to protect you and Charlie, should Sheltons' friends try to get to you," the lead detective told the Newman's as they walked.

"You don't know the Sheltons like I do," Bessie said as she hurried to keep up with the tall men.

"They'll never get to you," the detective said just moments before a half dozen bullets kicked up the boardwalk around them. Pedestrians screamed and ran for cover in the buildings. The firing only lasted a second, but by then Newman's entourage was in the nearby federal building. When Art came into the courtroom a few minutes later, he smirked at the three Shelton brothers sitting at the defendant's table as if to say, *Ha! You missed me!* Carl and Earl didn't look at him, but Bernie's eyes shot darts full of hate.

"Carl Shelton asked me if I wanted in on a good thing," Art Newman told the jury after the preliminary questions. "I said sure, but when he told me it was a mail robbery, I backed out. I didn't hear nothin' more until the mornin' of January twenty-seventh, when Carl telephoned me in East St. Louis, askin' me to drive him and his brothers to Herrin for Ora Thomas' funeral. I told him I was tired and that he would get in trouble goin' there. 'Well,' Carl said, 'we pulled that Collinsville job this mornin' and we must have an alibi, and it's up to you to give it.' So, I did it. Late that night, I dropped in at Sheltons' saloon. There in the backroom was Carl and Charlie Briggs with bundles of money on the card table before them. 'See you later, Art.' Carl says to me, so I beat it outa there."

The next to take the stand was Harvey Dungey, the man who'd exposed Shag Worsham for being a snitch and then arranged his demise. Harvey dreamed of being a famous artist. The problem was he considered tracing to be art. When Charlie had the entire gang gather for photographs in front of Shady Rest, Harvey found a way to place the pictures under two panes of glass to magnify them. Some of the boys paid him well to have their likenesses made into drawings. He knew that most artists didn't become famous until after their deaths, but when Charlie told him to lie at the Sheltons' trial, he was afraid it was a little too early in his artistic career to make his demise relevant. Still, he needed the money, and Charlie made his perjury profitable—as well as ensuring him his testimony was the only way he would stay alive.

"I was driving from East St. Louis to Collinsville at six-thirty in the morning on January 27, 1925, when I saw Carl Shelton standing by a Buick with Bernie in the driver's seat."

A disruption in the courtroom interrupted Harvey's testimony. Charlie Birger made his entrance to be the next witness. Camera bulbs flashed. Reporters scrambled to get into better positions. The crime boss made eye contact, waved, and smiled at the jury as if they were old friends. He shook hands with John Rogers and a few other reporters he knew personally. Then he outdid Art by giving an even fancier smirk at the Shelton brothers. He replaced Harvey on the witness stand. After he'd taken the oath, the district attorney asked him to state his name.

After establishing his acquaintance with the defendants, the state's attorney got quickly to the point. "Did you have any conversation with the defendants about the Collinsville robbery?"

"It was in January 1925, at Nineteenth and Market Streets, in East St. Louis. Carl said he'd been thinking about hauling whiskey up from Florida. He had a payroll job in Collinsville, he told me, and when he got through with that, he was going to start hauling whiskey."

"And the next time?" the D.A. asked.

"That was at my house, five or six days after Ora Thomas's funeral. Carl, Earl, Bernie and Charlie Briggs were in my dining room splitting money, each getting three-thousand-six-hundred dollars. When I looked in, Carl said, 'This is some of Uncle Sam's money, but we won't need you for an alibi because we were at Ora Thomas's funeral.' I asked Carl how much he got, and he said about twenty-one thousand dollars. He told me he drove the car up to Collinsville, and Bernie and Earl went up with him. His brothers held up the truck, and Earl fell down getting back into the getaway car. That was about all they ever said about the job."

It took the jury five hours to determine the Shelton brothers guilty. The judge gave them each twenty-five years in the federal pen.

***

The fact that the body of Lory Price was discovered the same day the Shelton brothers were sentenced to Leavenworth Prison seemed to be foreboding to Charlie. When he should have been celebrating his enemies going to prison, he found himself back in his Harrisburg bedroom, attempting to shoot complete and total apathy into his veins.

The drug couldn't prevent the state cop from entering his dreams. The ghost of Lory Price's badly decomposed corpse stood over his bed, an arm and hand gnawed clean down to the bone by wild animals, the index finger pointing at him.

He jumped awake with a start. The horrible vision was still in front of him. The smell of rotting flesh filled his nostrils. When it finally faded, he kept looking back at the spot where it had been. He closed his eyes and reopened them to make certain it didn't reappear. Losing his high, he grabbed up the syringe, then applied a tourniquet to his arm so he could find a vein. For no reason he could imagine, he thought about Helen Holbrook for the first time in weeks. After their last fight, which had ended with him severely beating her, she had gone to St. Petersburg, Florida. She had reassured him it was just to get away from the Illinois winter and not because her nose was now bent at an unusual angle.

Helen knows everything, Charlie realized. And she was mad at him.

***

Harvey Dungey's creative juices were flowing. He drew sketches of every criminal enterprise the Birger gang had been involved in. Of course, he had to keep Charlie and his lieutenants from seeing them, since the drawings could implicate the gang in so many crimes. His favorite renditions were of the election day shootout and the Thomasson murder of Joe Adams. Some others he embellished, such as a firefight between Sheldon and Birger tankers. In reality, Charlie only had an armored car with a mounted machine gun, but since newspapers were reporting it as a tanker, he used his artistic license to give the public what they wanted.

Frustration set in when Harvey realized his fine artwork would never be seen as long as Charlie lived. The law seemed to take theft and parole violations more seriously than they did murder. Every murder that had occurred in Little Egypt since the Herrin Massacre in '22 had been proclaimed done by "person or persons unknown." Besides Joe Chesnas' execution a year ago, the only person he could think of who might be charged with murder and get the death penalty was Rado Millich, and that was probably only because he was a foreigner. The law seemed to be under the impression that as long as it was only gangsters killing gangsters, it was okay.

Then the thought struck Harvey. How much would his drawings be worth if he were the one to kill the famous Charlie Birger?

***

Charlie was feeling much better. The Sheltons were in prison, Helen was being taken care of, Harry Thomasson was in a reformatory for petty theft, and Art and Bessie Newman were in hiding in California in case the remnants of the Shelton Gang tried to exact revenge. Charlie rolled over and faced Bernice. Now all he had to do was teach his young wife how to be a more rambunctious lover. He thought about having Blondie join them one night, but Bernice still seemed a little green for such an advanced lesson. Although he would have preferred sex, she made love to him. But he fell asleep anyway, without even a needle in his arm or with the help of a bottle of corn liquor.

Charlie dozed comfortably on his back, one arm around his wife and the other around his Thompson machine gun.

The smell of gasoline caused him to jerk his arm out from under Bernice, grab his Tommy gun and rush naked down the stairwell. "Get the children out of the house!" he shouted over his shoulder to his wife.

The shadows of three men in his living room brought the familiar lust for blood back into Charlie's head. He grabbed a handgun from a table in the hallway, and with that blazing in one hand and his gat doing the same in the other, fired blindly around the room, smashing lamps, ripping through furniture, and putting holes in every wall. The windows crashed as the intruders dove through them to escape the onslaught of bullets. Still firing as he rushed toward the windows, Charlie finally ran out of bullets. As the smoke cleared, he recognized only one of the invaders as they jumped into a parked car. The racketeer artist, Harvey Dungey.

***

The Shelton brothers were provided one privilege when they got to Leavenworth Prison. They were allowed to work side by side in the rock quarry, cutting stones for the new prison addition. It was during a break one day that Carl got the news.

"Helen Holbrook was killed down in St. Petersburg, Florida," a Chicago hoodlum named Frank Nash told him.

The news caught Carl by surprise.

"Poisoned, they say," Frank went on. "Coroner called it suicide, but everyone knows better. They questioned your boy Arthur McDonald about it. He told them he'd never met Helen. Can you imagine them believin' that? What gangster didn't know Helen? Anyway, they say Arthur married your sister Hazel a few days later. I guess there's somethin' in the law that married folks don't hafta testify against each other."

Carl would be a suspect if the law thought her death could be anything other than a suicide. That didn't bother him in the least. Helen had told him she was going to Florida to get away from Charlie.

At chow that evening, Bernie delivered another stunner. "They arrested Charlie for the murder of Joe Adams," Bernie said. "You wanna hear the kicker, though? He only agreed to turn hisself in if he could have his gat in the cell with him. He said he was afraid the Shelton gang would try to kill him."

***

Harry Thomasson never imagined his sexual preference would get him in such hot water. He and Elmo had spent the majority of their youth in a strict boy's orphanage. When they reached puberty, the lack of female companionship led them into some unusual and often invasive sexual situations with the other boys. After release from the orphanage and they were introduced to girls, they discovered their thirst had changed but their preferred sexual position did not. This often made many of their female companions uncomfortable, including Jackie Williams, the proprietor of a cat house in Herrin.

Jackie and her friend Pearl Phelps enjoyed the boys' money—as well as the many fellow gangsters they brought to the establishment. What they did not enjoy was the brothers' interjection of bodily parts into areas of the whores' anatomy that were not suited for long term use. The money being good, though, they tolerated the behavior—until the day the law decided to investigate their den of iniquity. Since the Thomasson boys had virtually moved into the bordello, the cops found several items that had been stolen in two separate robberies. Both the brothers and the women were arrested. Jackie and Pearl felt abused in more ways than one, so they quickly turned state's evidence on Harry and Elmo. Before he could be sent up-river though, Elmo died in the hellish flames at the Shady Rest.

Harry, not wanting to return to ten years of being another man's lady-friend, sat in jail brooding and reflecting on his shattered life. The more he dwelt, the angrier he got—specifically, at Charlie Birger, whom he was becoming convinced had destroyed Shady Rest himself to get rid of Elmo and the others.

When State's Attorney Roy Martin came to visit Harry in Pontiac Reformatory, he had the newspaper man John Rogers with him.

"Hello, Harry," Rogers said, extending his hand. "You remember me? I met you at Shady Rest."

"Yes, sir." Harry's first thought was that Charlie had sent the reporter to help him. That hope was quickly dashed.

"Harry, I feel bad for you. I tried to get Charlie to send money for your defense, but he said he didn't want anything to do with you."

The three men then sat quietly and smoked. Harry's mind raced through a half-dozen scenarios, each one more devastating to his future than the last.

"Harry," Rogers finally said. "We know that you and Elmo killed Joe Adams and are taking the fall for Charlie."

Again, the men sat quietly, letting Harry think. He thumped his fist on his thigh. The thumping became more and more violent, but he did it until his leg hurt so bad, he finally stopped. "I have something I want to tell you," Harry said.

***

The next day Harry Thomasson walked into the courtroom dressed in extremely large prison clothes. State's Attorney Martin had personally chosen the size of the suit to make the prisoner feel small and insignificant. Harry had to keep one hand on the front of his trousers to prevent them from dropping to the floor.

"This is Harry Thomasson," Martin told the judge, "who is one of several Birger gangsters under indictment for the murder of Joe Adams. He wishes to plead guilty!"

The courtroom erupted. The judge banged his gavel. "Why are you insistent on pleading guilty?" he asked when the room became quiet again.

"Because Charlie Birger, Art Newman, Connie Ritter and Freddie Wooten blew up Shady Rest cabin and killed my brother!"

Again, the room turned into chaos.

"On the morning of the Adams' murder," Harry testified, "I went to Shady Rest, where my brother Elmo had stayed the night before. Birger, Newman, Ritter and Ray Hyland were there. They gave Elmo a thirty-eight and me a forty-five."

For the next thirty minutes, Harry told a detailed account of the most horrible night of his life. When he finished, the judge sat back in his seat for several minutes, then called Martin to his bench for a few moments of whispered counsel. When the state's attorney returned to the table and sat next to Harry, the judge leaned forward and wrote something on a piece of paper. The room was silent.

"I shall sentence you to life in prison," the judge said, then banged his gavel. "Court adjourned."

In seconds, the courtroom was cleared as reporters rushed to find telephones and deliver the news to their headquarters. As Harry was being escorted from the courtroom, Gus Adams stood in the hallway. The young murderer offered him his hand. Gus's mouth dropped, but he took the handshake.

"I'm sorry I killed Joe," Harry said, tears cascading along his cheeks. "I never knew him, and he never did me wrong. I had to do it. I'm sorry for you. My own brother was killed too."

***

The night before Harry testified, Charlie Birger sat alone in his Benton jail cell, caressing his Thompson machine gun and counting the minutes until he could return to the solitude of his Harrisburg bedroom. Franklin County Sheriff Jeff Pritchard had promised Charlie, when he arrested him, that he could keep his gat in the cell with him. They placed him alone in a corner jail cell to keep the other inmates away from him. Pritchard even stuck around awhile and played a few hands of poker with him.

The next morning, Charlie was still sitting on the edge of the cot, holding his machine gun, when Sheriff Pritchard walked in and unlocked the cell door.

"They're waiting for you downstairs, Charlie," Pritchard said. "This shouldn't take long."

Charlie followed the sheriff down the narrow wooden stairs. When they arrived in the foyer, Pritchard unbuckled his holster and set it on the counter.

"The judge don't allow no weapons in the courtroom," he said.

Charlie hesitated.

"Trust me, Charlie, they'll be here when we get out—and it should only take a few minutes. We just gotta let the judge know you're cooperating, then you can go on home."

Charlie gave the sheriff a long hard look, then laid his weapon on the counter alongside the holstered service revolver. Inside the small room was the judge, the state's attorney, and three deputies.

"Mr. Birger," the state's attorney said, "before we get started, I wanted to tell you the Shelton brothers are being released from Leavenworth Prison."

"What?" Charlie's foreboding returned. His eyes darted around the room.

"Harvey Dungey admitted he perjured himself at the Quincy trial because you and Art Newman threatened to kill him if he didn't testify."

"That lying son-of-a-bitch! The Sheltons must've paid him to say that."

"Further," the state's attorney said with a smile, "Charles Birger, you are hereby charged with the murder of Joseph Adams that occurred on December 12, 1926."

Charlie's head jerked immediately toward Jeff Pritchard. "You hoodwinked me!"

The three deputies stepped forward and handcuffed the prisoner's hands behind his back. Charlie's demeanor changed from angry to friendly with the loud click of the shackles. "Well, Jeff, I reckon you won't have to pay me back for that poker game you lost last night."

30

The train ride from Kansas City to Los Angeles could be boring for a person not interested in the landscape, but to two men with dozens of stories under their hat, it was a short ride.

"Art Newman's alias in Los Angeles is John Rogers, private eye," Sheriff Jeff Pritchard said.

"You're kidding! Well, I guess I should be flattered," the real John Rogers said.

"That's what the telegraph says. Anyway, we should be able to pick him up tomorrow and start back the next day."

"You think the Shelton boys will throw a wingding for him?"

"Actually, they might, if you can get Art to implicate the Birger gang like you did Harry Thomasson and Harvey Dungey. By the way, how did you get Harvey talking?"

"I always start with fear," John said. "I got him thinking he might be in trouble because folks were saying he tried to murder Charlie in his home. Then I encouraged bravado by saying he seemed a more accomplished criminal than anyone in the

Birger gang. Harvey said if he ever saw Charlie, he'd kill him. Next, I put him in check by saying that just a few weeks ago, he'd acted like a strong supporter of Birger. 'Yeah,' he said, 'and that was all phony. Birger and Art Newman put pistols on me and made me do it. I testified that I saw the Sheltons in Collinsville on the morning of the mail robbery, and I hadn't been in Collinsville in four years. Then that son-of-a-bitch Charlie wouldn't even pay me when it was all over.'" John raised three fingers and said, "Checkmate."

"You should've been a cop." Pritchard laughed.

"Not me. I don't want to get shot at."

***

"You take me back to Illinois, and the Sheltons will bump me off," Art told the sheriff and newspaper reporter as the three took their seats on the train two days later.

"They're going to charge you with Lory Price's murder," John Rogers said matter-of-factly. "Since Harvey Dungey confessed, they know it was your car that hauled Lory's body."

John went silent, giving Art time to contemplate.

"Charlie threatened to kill me when I said they couldn't put Lory in my car." Art's eyes reflected fear. "Charlie shot him both at Shady Rest and later, after we took him to the timber. Nobody else."

"Well," John said, handing the prisoner a cigarette. "I guess you're a smart fella. You know if you come clean, they'll give you life. You'll be out after a while for good behavior and such. Plus, I'd imagine the Sheltons would appreciate you taking the heat off them for the bombing of Shady Rest and the Price murders."

John let him nibble on that idea for a few minutes. "By the way," he finally said, "whatever happened to Ethel Price? You know, they might charge you with that, too."

"Oh, hell, no. I had nothing to do with her. Riley Simmons, Ernest Blue and Leslie Simpson did that on Charlie's orders. I had nothing to do with that."

"So, she is dead." John's heart beat fast anticipating just the right moment to ask the most important question. He waited, watching Art's face. Then he struck. "Where is her body, Art?"

***

When Charlie heard the body of Ethel Price had been found because Art Newman had squealed, he went into a fit, tearing up the newspaper, his mattress, clothes, anything he could get his hands on. The paper told the horrendous story in Art Newman's own words, chilling the public. Seemingly overnight, the name Charlie Birger went from being a Robin Hood to a Jack the Ripper.

The prisoners in the cell next to him laughed and jeered. “Woman killer!” they chanted at him.

Jeff Pritchard came to Charlie’s rescue. He had many of the cellmates transferred and brought in ones who were less hostile to the famous crime boss. But then, a month later, the murder trial of Ward “Casey” Jones ended. Ural Gowan was given a life sentence. The judge ordained that on October 21, 1927, Rado Millich would be hanged by the neck until dead. The legend of Charlie Birger was forever tarnished. But worse still, his own sense of invincibility was gone. For the first time in his life, Charlie saw death as relief.

“You need to get at least one woman on the jury.” Charlie told his attorneys during jury selection. “If you give me one woman, I can charm her into finding me innocent.”

“We tried, Charlie. The judge feels that the gruesomeness of the murders is just too much for a sensitive female to bear.”

“I don’t want Art Newman being tried at the same time as me,” Charlie said.

“Can’t do that either. We tried.”

Charlie put his elbows on the table and dropped his head into the palms of his hands. “Shit, damn, hell!” He rubbed his eyes and muttered, “Nothin’ is workin’ for me anymore.”

By the time the trial started, Charlie had exhausted every form of emotion. On the occasional day the jailhouse was quiet, he brooded. Somedays he felt ecstatic and would laugh and joke with his fellow inmates that Sheriff Pritchard had hand-selected. Other times, he flew into rages, even punching and kicking the square bars of the cell. But on days Charlie was to appear in court, he was always able to regain his composure. He would clean up, shave, and was allowed to dress in his finest suits. His beautiful wife, Bernice, was allowed to sit next to him and hold his hand. Still, it was sometimes hard for him to keep his composure, especially with Art Newman sitting with his own lawyers at a table near him.

"Well," Art said loudly just before the first day of jury selection, "I do know that Birger was connected to a bank robbery a few months before he was arrested."

"Why, that guy's crazy!" Charlie exploded. "I didn't even know him then. Look at him sittin' there. Anybody can tell he's crazy. You dirty, woman-killin' son-of-a-bitch, you oughta be ashamed to ask for a trial. You oughta ask the people to just hang you."

"That's enough of that!" Art shouted back.

"If Newman gets off, I want to hang," Charlie shouted, standing. He only calmed when Bernice took his hand and guided him back to his chair.

Joe Adam's wife was one of the first witnesses for the prosecution. She delivered her version of the story in a stoic, emotionless manner.

"The two young men knocked on the door. They asked me if Joe Adams lived there. I said he did. They asked if he was home. I said yes, but he was resting. I asked them if I would do. They said they wanted to see Joe personally. They said they had a letter from Carl Shelton. I went back and got Joe. I walked beside him to the door."

"What did they do then?" the state's attorney asked.

"They shot him."

The next witness, Clarence Rone, had been sick for several days. Part of the reason for the illness was because he'd been locked up in the hot Williamson County jail for a burglary offense. He avoided looking at the defendants as he took the witness stand.

"The night before Adams was murdered," Clarence said in a weak, low voice, "I saw Charlie Birger, Art Newman, Connie Ritter and Ray Hyland take Elmo and Harry Thomasson into a closed room. When they came out, I heard Connie Ritter tell the brothers, 'Take the bullets to the basement and dose them with poison.' The next night at Shady Rest, Charlie Birger said to the Thomasson brothers, 'That was fine work you boys did. I won't have to worry about that fat son-of-a-bitch anymore.'"

The next one on the stand was Harry Thomasson, the star witness for the prosecution. He stared at the wooden floor as he was sworn in and asked the preliminary questions. When requested, he related the story of how he and Elmo had been recruited to kill Adams, how Connie Ritter had showed them how to poison the bullets, and how Ray Hyland drove them to perform the murder. Then Harry's jaw clenched when he described the shooting and how Charlie had complimented the brothers the next day. He stared directly at Charlie. "Charlie Birger was the one who bombed his own Shady Rest and killed my brother Elmo!"

"Damn!" Art muttered.

Charlie yawned.

"Objection, your honor!" Charlie's defense attorney shouted. "That is pure speculation on the part of the witness."

"Sustained," the judge said. "The jury will disregard that last statement of the witness."

The jury deliberated for twenty-four hours.

Life sentences were handed out to Art Newman and Ray Hyland.

"Mr. Birger," the judge said, "before I pronounce sentence, I am pleading to you, for the sake of your children and in atonement for the evil you have done, please help the authorities clear up the many crimes as yet unsolved."

"I never aspired to be a gang chief, judge," Charlie said in a low voice, "and I never wanted to kill nobody. I blame Art Newman's perjuries for my plight. Other than sayin' that, I ain't no squealer."

"Then it behooves me to announce to you, Charles Birger, that on October 15, 1927, between the hours of ten a.m. and two p.m., in front of the Franklin County jailhouse, you are to be hanged by the neck until dead. May God have mercy on your soul."

31

The fear of dying was usually a short, dark thought. Most of the time, Charlie felt invincible. Either he would outsmart the law or his gang would break him out. He believed that if he carried that thought up the thirteen steps to the scaffold, his legs wouldn't shake.

Most of his time sitting in the jail was nice. After being sentenced, he was moved to a private, enclosed cell away from others. It had many amenities not provided other inmates, including an extra bed where his wife could lie when she came to visit. Morphine was better than hooch, although a good supply of that was available to him also. The biggest problem was when the effects of the drug wore off and the dark thoughts began.

"Some see Gehinnom as a place of torture and punishment, fire and brimstone," admitted Rabbi J.R. Mazur, who visited him every day. "Others imagine it less harshly, as a place where one reviews the actions of their life and repents for past misdeeds. If you repent, then one day you will reach heaven. If not, then hell is just one long eternal damnation of hopelessness. You have your brain, but no body."

"I'll just think of happy things," Charlie said optimistically. "Like my girls."

"That is not the evil that you will be required to account for. You will only remember your worst experiences, the sins you committed on your children."

That scared Charlie more than the possibility of dangling from the gallows if his neck didn't snap clean. He remembered the times he had misbehaved in front of Little Minnie and made her cry. Like the time he beat a woman at a store because he overheard her calling him a gangster. Little Minnie cried a lot that night and wouldn't let her father tuck her into bed. The next morning, she asked, "Do you kill people, Daddy?"

Charlie didn't want to relive such a horrible moment over and over again for eternity. When that thought came, a shot of morphine was the only thing that would do the trick. His ambiguous drug-related behavior was most likely responsible for the denial of his petition to be a witness at the Kincaid bank robbery trial that was taking place in the mid-state town of Taylorville. To have one more shot at framing the Shelton brothers would definitely have made his walk to the gallows more satisfying.

His lawyers were able to prolong his agony by getting him a stay of execution with an opportunity for a sanity hearing and a new execution date set for April 19, 1928. This also allowed him to live longer than Rado Millich, who was hanged on October 21, 1927, in Benton. The same man who had officiated over Rado's hanging was building the gallows for Charlie's. Phil Hanna was called the *Humane Hangman* because he was so sympathetic to the condemned. He told Charlie he had seen a botched hanging when he was a boy. The criminal had hung from the rope kicking and gasping for several minutes before finally dying. Phil decided after that to use his skills to create more efficient gallows. He also refused to get paid for his services and required the local lawmen to actually spring the trap.

"Is it true Rado's hanging didn't go so well?" Charlie asked.

"I won't lie to you, Charlie." Phil told him. "Rado fainted just before the trap door opened, so he didn't fall straight down. I fear he had a moment of discomfort."

"I'll be sure to stand up straight for you," Charlie assured him. "So Sheriff Pritchard will pull the lever for my proceedings?"

"Yes, sir," Phil said. "It is most always the local sheriff's responsibility. One exception was in the case of Joe Chesnas'. For some reason, they allowed a good friend of the man Joe killed to pull the lever."

"Well, long as it's Pritchard and not Art Newman, I'll be satisfied."

Charlie did get a little distraction when it was announced that Harvey Dungey had escaped the Marion jail. Charlie laughed at Harvey's stupidity when he learned he was recaptured a few days later at a friend's house. At least now Harvey would have more time to master his artistry.

If being exposed as the cold-blooded killer of Lory and Ethel Price wasn't enough to destroy Charlie's reputation as a suave, debonair, Robin Hood-type gangster, the sanity hearing certainly did the trick. Even Jeff Pritchard was embarrassed for the unwashed and unshaved bootlegger when he entered the courtroom in shackles, muttering to himself, drooling baking soda from his mouth and lashing out like a bulldog at anyone close to him.

To Charlie, the hearing didn't seem to last much longer than the jury's deliberation, which was only twelve minutes. "We the jury have determined Charles Birger to be legally sane," the foreman said when they entered the courtroom.

That next morning, the jailers went upstairs to check on the prisoners, and found Charlie hanging by the neck from a ripped-up blanket. When they cut him down, the gangster offered an insane-sounding laugh that would have been better used at the sanity hearing.

"I never failed even once in my life when I did-in my enemies, but now I can't stop my own heart to save my life."

"I don't think that's the right expression to use in this case, Charlie," a deputy said.

"Ha, ha! You're right, Harry. Now I can't even talk like a sane man. Where was that when I needed it?"

"Have you tried holding a pillow over your face, Charlie?" Harry asked. He liked Charlie and hated to see him befuddled by such a simple task.

"No, but a few days ago I took enough arsenic to kill three men, but I guess I didn't take enough."

Sunlight peeked through the windows. For the third day, the sounds of hammering echoed through the cell. The scaffold was going up just outside the jailhouse.

A few hours later Charlie got cleaned up to meet Bernice and his daughters for a final photo together. Sheriff Pritchard rationalized it as the condemned man's last request, so he granted it, although he had a dozen deputies in and around the room. After that, Charlie was in a good mood and agreed to meet with newspaper men as long as John Rogers was not among them. He had finally recognized that the ace reporter for the *St. Louis Post-Dispatch* was a major part of the reason for his troubles.

"Any special requests for the hangin', Charlie?"

"Yes, I want a black hood, not a white one," Charlie answered after a moment's thought. "I wouldn't want anyone associatin' me with the Ku Klux Klan!"

"How about your funeral?" another reporter said, laughing at his own gruesome wit.

"I want to be buried in a Catholic cemetery," Charlie replied without hesitation, "'cause that's the last place the devil will look for a Jew."

"Can we get a picture of you, Charlie?" a cameraman asked.

The boss had already taken off his jacket and shirt. "In my undershirt?" he asked with a laugh.

"Why not?" a reporter said. "You'll look more relaxed."

Charlie obliged by standing in front of the blank wall and putting his hands—the missing finger visible on his left hand—on his hips. His hair was disheveled, as it had often been after a rut with Helen Holbrook. He imagined her ghost might be grinning at him. He grinned back, and the cameraman pushed the shutter.

As a spit in John Rogers' face, Charlie allowed another *Post-Dispatch* reporter named Roy Alexander to sit with him during his last night on earth. He had always heard that when a person is about to die, their life flashes before their eyes. Charlie sat silently on his cot across from Roy for better than thirty minutes waiting for the flash to start. The delay made him optimistic that maybe the grim reaper was not coming after all.

"I heard you were in the cavalry out West," Roy said.

The first flash came.

"For a while, 'til I got busted up when a horse rolled over on me. That toughened me up, I'd 'spect. But it was bronc bustin' after that in South Dakota and Montana that were my happy years. Rustled a few cows now and again if we ran across one without a brand. But when I heard the coal mines were running good here in Illinois, I decided to take my chances and come back to St. Louis where I had some family."

Charlie grew quiet again. *What if I'd a-stayed out West?*

"What about women?" Roy asked in a weak, raspy voice.

Charlie's eyes shone dark for several seconds. His mind raced through names. Funny that in this moment, he couldn't remember what sex was like with any of them. In fact, it was as if his recollections of women like Helen, Blondie and dozens of others had never happened. Strange, the only good female he could remember was his first wife Edna, the statuesque blonde who had loved him when he had nothing. She would sit silently beside him, running her hands through his hair as he worked on their bank account and struggled to make ends meet. He often awoke in the middle of the night to find her arm around him—and he didn't need alcohol or morphine to get himself back to sleep.

"I cheated on the best woman I ever knew for only one reason. Because I could," Charlie said. "She divorced me, but you know what? Edna is the only woman in my life in this town right now. She came with her husband to visit me these past days. Can you imagine what a fine man he must be to let his wife do that?"

Charlie got quiet again. *What if I'd stayed true to Edna?*

"What about the men you've killed?" Roy asked quietly, biting a hangnail.

Charlie's eyes gave that same dark stare. "Yes, I've killed men, but never a good one. And that's all I have to say about that."

***

Morning came quicker than his life memories. Along with the sunlight was the barber he'd requested to shave him. When the hand of the man with the blade trembled, Charlie gently removed the razor from him and gave him an understanding smile. The man with only a few hours to live finished shaving himself, then dressed. Rabbi Jacob Mazur arrived as he put on his tie. When he was finished, he gave a satisfied glance in the mirror, turned toward the Rabbi, and placed his kippah over his head. He and the Rabbi had been practicing the Vidui prayer of confession for weeks. Even with that, Charlie's Hebrew was rustier than his singing voice. Still, he said the prayer in a sing-song fashion of his own invention.

"My God and God of my ancestors, let my prayer come before you. Do not ignore my plea. Forgive me for all the wrong I have done in my lifetime. My wicked deeds and sins embarrass me. Please accept my pain and suffering as atonement and forgive my wrongdoings, for against You alone have I sinned—"

Charlie put his hand over his eyes for the recitation of the Shema.

"Hear O' Israel, the Lord is our God, the Lord is One. Blessed is the name of His glorious kingdom for ever and ever. You shall love the Lord your God with all your heart and with all your soul and with all your might... ."When he finished Charlie removed the kippah and handed it to the Rabbi. Squaring his shoulders, he walked confidently out of the cell.

"Goodbye, boys. Be good." Charlie waved to the jailbirds, their faces grimmer and more ashen than his. Looking dapper in his blue serge suit, he strutted down the jailhouse steps as if he were simply coming down for breakfast. He shook the hand of each deputy escorting him. When he stepped outside the building, men, women and children were gathered for as far as he could see. Trees were filled—the most daring as high as the thinnest topmost branches. The roofs of every building had standing room only. Every window was filled, including the jail house where his fellow inmates watched. It might have been a circus parade coming down Main Street had it not been that on top of almost every roof were also policemen with mounted machine guns. Seemingly hundreds of uniformed men mixed in with the crowd.

"Looks like the Western front here," Charlie joked. A few of those who heard him chuckled. The rest of the crowd grew strangely silent.

Several men supported their women, who seemed close to fainting.

"Howdy-doo-dee," Charlie said when he recognized a small group from Harrisburg. Were they thinking about the sacks of groceries he'd left on their front porches? He thought about asking them, but was afraid his voice might crack if he tried to say too much. Instead, he just smiled and walked somewhat quickly, Rabbi Mazur at his left elbow quietly chanting prayers from the Torah. Though shackled, Charlie was able to shake hands with a few people who reached out to him. A large wicker basket beneath the gallows awaited to catch his body when he was cut down. So too was a black coffin he would lie in for eternity. He thought about what his girls would think when they saw their daddy stretched out in it. When he reached the bottom step to the gallows, he wanted to hesitate, but feared he might falter if he did. Instead, he stepped boldly, silently counting each time he raised his legs. All the way to the top. On his thirteenth step, he almost laughed. The hangman Phil Hanna had told him he also used thirteen coils in his noose. *I reckon it's my unlucky number, after all.*

Charlie stepped onto the trap door and performed a military left face toward the crowd. He smiled, pointed and waved. Phil tried to hide the noose behind his back as a courtesy to the condemned. Feeling appreciative for the man's professionalism, Charlie extended his shackled hands and Phil leaned forward to return the heartfelt handshake.

"Please forgive me for what I am about to do," Phil said for the sixty-first time in his un-illustrious career.

"You're a great old boy," Charlie told him.

"Any last words, Charlie?" Phil asked.

"I have nothing against anybody. I have forgiven everybody, all because of this wonderful Jewish rabbi. I have nothing to say. Let her go."

The last human he made eye contact with was Sheriff Jeff Pritchard who stood with his hand on the leaver to the trapped door. Charlie's was a withering death stare—half sneer, half grin. Phil Hanna raised the black hood with the long draping cape behind it, then hesitated for just a moment when Charlie raised his head and looked up at the blue, clear sky. Still smiling, the legendary gangster said one final sentence in a soft voice that carried only to those in the crowd who were nearest.

"It is a beautiful world!"

END

CHRONOLGY OF EVENTS

1920

November 7 - Glenn Young kills bootlegger Luke Vukovic

1922

June 21-22 - Herrin Massacre

1923

May 20 - KKK reveal themselves at church services.

November 14-15 - Charlie kills Cecil Knighton in gunfight.

November 18 - Charlie Birger wounded but kills Whitey Doering in gunfight.

November 20 - Carl visits Charlie in hospital to merge gangs.

December 22 - 1st KKK raid of bootlegging joints.

1924

January 5 - 2nd KKK raids.

January 7 - 3rd KKK raids.

January 19 - Herrin Massacre trial ends in acquittal of all those charged.

January 30 - KKK raid marches 125 prisoners through Benton.

February 8 - Caesar Cagle murdered and KKK attack hospital.

March 4 - Danville bootlegging trial for Charlie Birger and Ora Thomas.

March 26 - Charlie gets one year and Ora 4 months in Danville for bootlegging.

May 23 - Shelton brothers ambush, wound Glenn Young and wife.

May 24 - Jack Skelcher killed & Charlie Briggs wounded by KKK.

August 30 - Smith garage shootout between Sheltons and KKK leaves six dead.

September 27 - Sheltons' failed attempt to rob the Kincaid Bank.

1925

January 25 - Glenn Young-Ora Thomas cigar store gunfight.

February 6 - Charlie enters Harrisburg jail; gets out early for helping with fire.

March 18 - 2-mile-wide tri-state tornado kills 695 people

April 14 - Madge Oberholzer dies after D.C. Stephenson's kidnapping and abuse.

May 24 - Harold Williams evangelical ministering begins.

May ?? - Art Newman house bombed.

June 27 - State's Attorney Boswell strikes 145 cases of both KKK and gangs.
June ?? - Art Newman kills Charlie Gordon
November 30 - Charlie and Orb Treadway kill Jimmy Stone.

1926

April 13 - Election Day: Shelton/Birger gangs vs. KKK gunfight leaves 6 men dead.
July 12 - Oklahoma Curly Hartin killed in gunfight
August 16 - Sod Gaddis kills John Howard, Charlie's former accountant.
August 22 - Art Newman kills Harry Walker, Carl's bodyguard.
September 12 - Wild Bill Holland killed & Max Pulliam and wife wounded by Birger.
September 14 - Max Pulliam in ambulance attacked by Charlie and gang.
September 17 - Lyle "Shag" Worsham murdered by Charlie and gang.
September 18 - Connie and Helen's roof top corpse.
October 4 - Art and Bessie Newman ambushed by Shelton tank.
October 14 - Birger gang machine guns an empty Shelton roadhouse.
October 16 - Birger gang steals machine guns from coal company.
October 26 - Casey Jones & High Pockets McQuay murdered by their own Birger gang.
October 28 - Shelton gang burn Birger's County Line Roadhouse.
November 10 - Blackie Armes bombs Charlie's barbeque stand.
November 12 - Sheltons arrested for Collinsville robbery and drive by shooting at Adams' house and Sheltons' airplane bombing of Shady Rest.
November 19 - Joe Adams' house bombed by Birger gang.
December 12 - Joe Adams murdered by Thomasson brothers on Charlie's orders.

1927

January 9 - Shady Rest destroyed, killing four people.
January 19 - Lory and Ethel Price murdered by Birger Gang
January 31 - Trial of Sheltons for Collinsville robbery begins.
February 7 - Sheltons enter Leavenworth and Helen Holbrook dies.

March 22 - Harvey Dungey and 3 men try to burn Charlie's house to kill him.
April 29 - Charlie spends night in jail with machine gun.
April 30 - Harry Thomasson confesses to reporter John Rogers.
May 4 - Sheltons released from Leavenworth when Dungey admits perjury.
May 22 - Art Newman arrested and confesses to John Rogers.
June 13 - Body of Ethel Price found in abandoned coal mine.
June 17 - Joe Chesnas hanged after confessing to Charlie.
July 6 - Trial begins for Charlie Birger, Art Newman and Ray Hyland.
July 7 - Ural Gowan gets life; Rado Millich to hang for Casey Jones' murder.
July 24 - Art and Ray get life, Charlie sentenced to hang for Adams' murder.
August 29 - Kincaid Bank robbery trial of Sheltons begins.
October 21 - Rado Millich hanged in Marion.
November 9-12 - Harvey Dungey escapes Marion Prison for 4 days before caught.

1928

April 16 - Charlie's sanity hearing
April 19 - Charlie Birger hanged at 9:48 a.m. at the jail yard in Benton.

ABOUT THE AUTHOR

After retiring from a career as an educator, Kevin Corley turned to his love of writing as a way to retell the stories he had shared with history students in his classroom. He recognized that the coal mining communities of Illinois were center-stage in the development of unions in the first half of the 20th century. From the Virden and Pana massacres of 1898-99 to the migration of miners after the Cherry mine disaster of 1909, Christian County became the rallying place for unionization.

Teaching history to many of the descendants of the coal mine wars, Corley developed a bond with the working man, a bond that was strengthened in 1986 when he was selected to research, through oral history interviews, the men and women who lived through these powerful and often terrifying events. His research was used by Carl Oblinger to write his book, *Divided Kingdom*, which was published in 1991.

13 Steps for Charlie Birger is Corley's fourth published novel and the first outside of the coal-mining story.

Corley retired to his hometown in Shelbyville, Illinois, in 2017.

Franklin County Historic Jail Museum

Styled in "Georgian Revival" and listed on the National Register as a rare surviving design of renowned architect Joseph W. Royer, the 1905 Franklin County Jail would most likely not have been preserved, if not for it's historical significance as the site where the notorious gangster Charlie Birger dropped into history in 1928 as the last public hanging in Illinois.

In addition to having a spectacular collection of related weapons and artifacts relating to the Southern Illinois gang era, the museum explores the rich historical inventory of Franklin County Illinois. Displays feature Benton's Civil War Major General John A. Logan, Benton's historic 1963 "before he was fab" visit by Beatle George Harrison, as well as tributes to Benton natives actor John Malkovich and NBA basketball star Doug Collins. The museum is located at 209 West Main Street Benton, Illinois with hours Tuesday-Saturday 10:00am until 3:00pm. Call 618 435 5777 or visit our website at Historicjail.com

Other books by Kevin Corley:

SUNDOWN TOWN

Based on actual events from 1898-99 Pana, Illinois. Big Henry Stevens leads hundreds of African-American coal miners and their families from Alabama to Illinois. When they arrive, they find instead of good pay for honest work, they are strikebreakers crossing picket lines. Meanwhile, the fledgling United Mine Workers of America is prepared to do whatever is necessary to stop the unsuspecting Blacks.

SIXTEEN TONS

The incredible, violent story of central Illinois coal mining from 1898-1933 *Sixteen Tons* carries the reader down into the dark, dirty and dangerous coal mines of the early 1900s, as Italian immigrant Antonio Vacca and his sons encounter cave-ins and the deadly black damp deep below the earth's surface.

THROW OUT THE WATER

The exciting and highly anticipated sequel to Sixteen Tons. Throw Out the Water continues the saga of the Vacca, Eng, Harrison and Hiler families as they choose sides in the bloody Christian County Coal Mine War that that took place in Illinois from 1933 to 1937.

Made in the USA
Monee, IL
23 December 2023

48249793R00231